D1556934

By LISA HENRY

Anhaga

Published by DREAMSPINNER PRESS
www.dreamspinnerpress.com

Anhaga

LISA HENRY

Published by
DREAMSPINNER PRESS

5032 Capital Circle SW, Suite 2, PMB# 279, Tallahassee, FL 32305-7886 USA
www.dreamspinnerpress.com

Anhaga
© 2019 Lisa Henry

Cover Art
© 2019 Tiferet Design
http://www.tiferetdesign.com/
Cover content is for illustrative purposes only and any person depicted on the cover is a model.

Trade Paperback ISBN: 978-1-64405-465-9
Digital ISBN: 978-1-64405-464-2
Library of Congress Control Number: 2019932251
Trade Paperback published July 2019
v. 1.0

Printed in the United States of America
∞
This paper meets the requirements of
ANSI/NISO Z39.48-1992 (Permanence of Paper).

To Kate, who read my terrible fantasy novel when I was thirteen.
I hope this one is better.

CHAPTER 1

THE DAWN limped in like some boot-scraping bastard, slow and lame, and dragging the sunlight behind it like a crippled limb. Min groaned and rolled over to put his back to the window.

"You're lying on my hair," someone told him.

Min peeled his eyes open. "Ah," he said.

He had a vague recollection of this woman. Vague enough that he remembered sharing a smile and more than one drink with her last night. And sadly vague enough that he doubted he had acquitted himself well. The woman's arched eyebrows told him as much.

He shifted slightly and let the woman tug her red tresses back to herself.

"Aiode," she told him, holding out a pale, freckled hand. She kept her other arm clasped across her chest, keeping the blanket from slipping down and revealing what Min was sure was a lovely bosom. "Aiode Nettle. Since I'm sure you don't remember."

The surname surprised him a little. Min wasn't in the habit of bedding the Gifted, even though with the name Aiode had chosen she probably ranked no higher than a hedgewitch. Clearly he'd made an exception because Aiode, even with her tangled bed-hair and lines on her face from the pillow, was beautiful.

"Aramin Decourcey," he said, shaking her hand.

"That's quite a mouthful," she said.

"I'm more than a mouthful, sweeting."

"So you promised last night," Aiode told him. She raised her eyebrows again. "Sadly, you did not measure up."

Min was too hungover to be truly offended. He rolled back over and squinted at the shaft of light stabbing through the sagging shutters and then, figuring the day was already ruined, sat up and swung his legs over the side of the bed. His soles met the gritty floor.

The garret room was cheap, its only recommendation. That, and the view over the back alley behind the Footbridge Tavern. Min did most of his work out of the tavern. His work wasn't exactly reputable, and Min liked to know if it tried to follow him home like a tick-ridden stray. The view of the alley afforded him at least a little forewarning.

Min blinked around the room.

Pants. Pants pants pants.

He wasn't much of a gentleman, not in any sense of the word, but pants were probably in order. He spotted his breeches in a rumpled heap over by the damned window and levered himself off the bed to go and fetch them. He picked them up, shook them out, and stepped into them. When he turned back to face Aiode, she had the look of a woman who had very much enjoyed the view but wasn't going to puff up his pride by mentioning it.

Please. Min knew his ass was a thing of beauty.

He smirked at Aiode, then bent down to pick up his shirt. He tugged it over his head. "Well, I'd invite you to stay and break your fast with me, but…." He gestured around the room. "As you can see, I have neither a kitchen nor food."

"Even if you had both, I'm sure I would decline," Aiode said, casting a critical gaze at the grimy floor, the spider's web hanging in a corner of the water-stained ceiling, and the collection of empty bottles that littered the floor. "I'm expected back at the shrine in any case."

The closest shrine Min knew of was the Shrine of the Sacred Spring. Aiode was definitely a hedgewitch, then. Of all the Gifted, hedgewitches were the least objectionable. Their powers were generally benign and grounded in nature. They helped to ensure good harvests and rains, and although most were based in the city, they regularly traveled the countryside to offer their service to the kingdom's farmers. Hedgewitches were generally looked down upon by the rest of the Gifted, which Min felt was a point in their favor. The *single* point in their favor.

"Well then," Min said.

"Well," Aiode echoed, narrowing her eyes slightly.

Min feigned interest in a book Harry had left lying around. Harry and his damn books. The boy was too curious for his own good. Besides, books were expensive. Although Harry had undoubtedly stolen the one Min picked up and leafed through. Min had taught him well.

Behind him, Min heard the rustle of fabric. He was tempted to turn around and at least give himself a good look at what he'd missed out on last night, but Aiode gave the impression of a woman well versed in testicle kicking, and Min didn't want to provoke her. Also, she was Gifted. True, a hedgewitch probably couldn't do much but try to curse him with a few warts here and there, but there was no point in risking it. Not the warts, of course, but exposure.

Min had a gift of his own as it happened, and he preferred to keep it secret.

"I shall see myself out," Aiode announced.

Min set Harry's book on the rickety table and turned around again. Aiode was wearing a plain green kirtle over a white smock. How disappointingly modest.

"I'll walk with you to the street," Min offered. "Some of my neighbors, alas, are not at all gentlemanly."

Aiode raised her eyebrows. "Do you think me incapable of protecting myself?"

Min flashed her a smile. "Not at all. In fact, I was relying on you to protect me."

Aiode laughed, the sound genuine and boisterous, and, for the first time since he'd fumbled into wakefulness, Min realized why he'd invited her back to his bed the night before. He'd always fallen hardest for women who didn't put up with any bullshit. And Aiode's bullshit detector, Min guessed, was as finely tuned as his own.

Clearly he needed to never see her again.

MIN PARTED with Aiode in the street behind his lodging house and headed down the alley to the tavern. The Footbridge Tavern attracted a particular type of clientele: slummers. Spoiled sons of wealthy families who descended on the place after dark, eager to brush shoulders—and other body parts—with the unwashed, the uncouth, and the otherwise undesirable. And why not? The beer and the prostitutes were cheap, and hardly an hour went by without a fight breaking out somewhere. The slummers came for blood as much as anything else, too young and stupid to care it might be theirs.

In the day, the place was usually quiet. This morning, apart from the boy spreading fresh straw over the worst of last night's spills—beer, blood, piss, or a combination of all three—and a few of the regulars who possibly lived in the taproom, the Footbridge was almost empty.

Min sat at his usual table in the corner and watched a fat spider twirl and spin on a length of shimmering silk.

Freya, the wife of the owner, or at least one of Swann's wives—Min had never been brave enough to ask—approached him. She had her sleeves rolled up to show off her beefy forearms. Not a word of a lie, Min had once seen Freya arm wrestle a blacksmith into submission.

"Porridge or porridge?" she grunted.

"Porridge it is," Min said agreeably and set a coin down on the table. "Have you seen Harry?"

Harry was a skinny sixteen-year-old kid with gray eyes and a shock of untamable blond hair as soft and wild as dandelion fluff. He was sharp and clever, prone to going missing for long hours at a time, and could usually be found headfirst under the skirts of whichever young woman had caught his fancy that week. He had all the gentlemanly manner of a sewer rat, and it was a source of eternal mystery to Min how he somehow managed to stay on the right side of every girl he loved and left. The charms of youth, perhaps. Harry certainly didn't have any other charms he could lay claim to. Or, mostly likely, the young women he pursued were so used to being bought and sold in dreary transactions that they treated Harry's ardor as something of a happy diversion. They were flattered, bedded, and parted as friends.

"Not today," Freya said.

"Have you checked under all the beds?"

Freya grunted. It was as close to a laugh as Min had ever wrangled from her. She swept the coin off the table into her cupped hand and headed for the kitchen.

Min watched the spider for a little longer and wondered if the day would bring him anything more interesting than porridge.

As it happened, Min had only just finished his breakfast when a young man entered the tavern. The man looked around apprehensively before apparently deciding that Min looked like the least threatening option and approaching his corner table. He was thin and pale, with soft curls that spilled down to his shoulders. His clothes were plain but clean and well-made. He had a pinched look to his narrow features that gave him an air of a slightly dissatisfied weasel and would probably be the cause of at least one black eye by the time he left the tavern. It was that kind of place.

He looked hesitantly at Min and lowered his voice so much that when he spoke, Min could hardly hear him. "Are you Aramin Decourcey?"

Min used his foot to shove the other stool out from under the table. "That's me."

The young man sat, pulling the edges of his cloak around him as though it would offer him some sort of protection. "Ludin gave me your name. He says that…." And here the young man trailed off.

"He told you I'm the best thief in the eastern quarter?" Min asked. "That I'm a filthy son of a whore with lower morals than a sewer rat, but I've never yet double-crossed a customer?"

"Y-yes. Something like that." The young man flushed. Of course the poor fellow had no idea how to parse that as a compliment, but it was high praise indeed from Ludin.

"Well then," Min said. "How can I be of service to you?"

The young man stuttered and stammered for a moment, and Min tried desperately not to roll his eyes. He had rent to pay, and money, like always, seemed to trickle through his hands as easily as sand. He couldn't afford, literally, to alienate a paying customer.

Whatever the bright little popinjay was going to say, however, was lost in the sudden commotion when, in a flurry of skinny limbs, a boy burst through the tavern door. It was Auric, or Aulus, or whatever the little grub's name was. He had gap teeth, smelled like he'd never seen a bath in his short, miserable life, and for some reason thought that he was on first-name terms with Min.

"Min!" the boy exclaimed, gasping for breath. "Min! Come quick! The Sabadines are going to kill Harry!"

And then he burst into tears.

THE SABADINES were an old family. A rich family. A family that wielded a lot of political influence in Amberwich. Edward Sabadine, the entire world knew, sat at the elbow of the king. And he was not the sort of man, Min suspected, who saw the funny side of finding a common guttersnipe hiding under his granddaughter's blankets. In fact, he looked apoplectic when Min arrived at the Sabadine house and was shown into the hall.

"Aramin Decourcey, at your service," Min said and inclined his head at Sabadine.

He was an old man, but not a frail one. He had sharp features, a narrow beak of a nose and a thin mouth. He was balding, but not vain enough to try to disguise the fact by wearing a hat. Min knew better than to underestimate a man of his status just because his advanced age meant his knees creaked when he walked. This man was dangerous.

Edward's gaze flicked over Min quickly, as fast as the tongue of a serpent. Then, obviously judging Min to be no threat whatsoever, he waved his servants away with a liver-spotted hand.

Min watched them go out of the corner of his eye. It seemed as though they took all of the day's warmth with them. Only one remained in the room, staring firmly at the floor.

Min gazed at the wall for a moment.

The Sabadines, like all the great families, made their money on the land and spent it in the city. Somewhere far beyond the protection of the city walls, men and women labored in the field so that Edward Sabadine could keep his coffers full. Min doubted the man had stepped foot on his own lands in years. Despite the fact that the hall was decorated with friezes of pastoral scenes, Sabadine was as much a farmer as Min was a gentleman. At least Min didn't pretend to be better than he was.

Min ran a hand over his well-worn jacket.

Well, how could he?

He might have been a king in the eastern quarter, but here, in the shadow of the Iron Tower, he was a beggar.

"I know your reputation," Sabadine said after a while, his voice gruff.

Min jolted a little in surprise. Best thief in the eastern quarter? Certainly. Uncannily lucky and devilishly handsome? Of course. But that a man of Edward Sabadine's station had heard of him? The chill that ran down his spine was not a pleasant one. The problem with being the big fish in the little pond was that sooner or later some sharp-eyed hawk would spot him.

"And I know yours, sir," Min replied.

That won a humorless smirk from the old man. "Let's talk about the—" His mouth curved down again. "The boy."

"My nephew," Min said, although Harry wasn't. It had always just seemed a convenient label to use. Min would never claim Harry as anything closer, because Min was way too young to have fathered a sixteen-year-old boy, thank you very much. Also, nephew seemed to imply the perfect distance between them. Familial, but distant enough that Min could deny all accountability when it came to Harry's many faults.

"Your nephew has dishonored my granddaughter's name," Sabadine growled.

And probably given her the ride of her life, Min thought.

"I assure you, sir, that no dishonor was meant." Min kept his tone respectful, since Edward Sabadine would be well within his rights to demand blood. Harry's and Min's both, probably.

Sabadine snorted and folded his hands behind his back. "He has offered to *marry* her."

Min tried not to wince. Of course he had. Because he was an idiot and had probably read enough of his silly books to actually think that a guttersnipe could win a lady with nothing to offer her but his heart. Because he was sixteen and had no fucking common sense at all. Because he was *Harry*.

"Talys may be the mere daughter of my youngest son," Sabadine said, "but she is still a Sabadine. I could marry her to any younger son of a House or wealthy merchant in the city, and he would be honored to take her. Your brat has nothing to recommend him."

Min inclined his head.

"Except," Sabadine continued, "that I know your reputation."

Wariness and relief warred in Min's gut. "Sir?"

"I have a job for you, Decourcey," Sabadine said, eyes narrowing. "You will accept it."

Min bridled a little but inclined his head again. "And my payment?"

"If you do your job," Sabadine said with a grin like a death's head, "then the boy lives."

Min opened his mouth to speak, and at that moment a scream rang out from somewhere nearby in the house. It was high-pitched and filled with pain, and Min's stomach twisted.

Harry!

Sabadine huffed. "Calm yourself. He's not dead yet."

Min fought the urge to grab the old viper by the throat and choke the life out of him.

"Come with me," Sabadine said. "There are matters we must discuss."

He swept out of the room, the skinny little servant scuttling in front of him to open the door. Min followed him, his heart in his throat.

HARRY.

Fucking Harry.

Min should have left the little troublemaker where he'd found him five years ago, but even now he didn't fool himself that it had ever been an option.

"Want to get out of here, kid?" Min had asked him.

And Harry had wiped his eyes, squared his shoulders, and followed Min through the window and into a new life. Not a comfortable life. Not a safe life. But better by far than the miserable one he would have lived if Min had ignored him. And Min had never seen him cry since.

So perhaps Harry was more trouble than he was worth, and perhaps there were times when Min could gleefully strangle him, but there was always a part of Min that would forever see Harry as he'd appeared that first night: eleven years old, small for his age, with tears running down his pale face. None of Harry's teenage brashness would ever erase that image.

The scream had long died away now, but there was nothing comforting in its absence. Where the hell was Harry?

Min clenched his fingers into fists and tried not to panic as he followed Sabadine and the servant through the shadowed corridors of the house into what appeared to be a study or a library. Certainly the room contained more books than Min had read in his life. Which, to be fair, was only three. More books than Min had *seen* in his life, then. Entire shelves of them, arranged around the walls. And, in the center of the room, a large table surrounded by high-backed chairs. A man rose from one of the chairs as Edward Sabadine and Min entered.

He might have been a decade or so older than Min. He was tall and well-built. A neat, dark beard enhanced the sharp angles of his handsome face. His hair was gray around the temples and combed into well-coiffed waves. He looked distinguished, like a scholar, but no scholar carried himself like that. This man was undoubtedly a solider.

"My son, Robert," the old man said.

"Aramin Decourcey," Min said.

Robert's eyes were blue or gray. Min couldn't be sure. His gaze was speculative, clever, and cold. That seemed to be a family trait of the Sabadines. They probably beat all warmth out of their children from birth.

"Take a seat," Sabadine said.

A servant darted forward from some shadowed corner, pulling back one of the heavy chairs.

Min sat.

He listened for more screams that never came and hated Harry for ruining his morning—and his entire life—while hoping desperately that he wasn't hurt. There were gods and spirits he could petition, naturally, but Min had nothing to offer them except the lint in his pockets. Anyway, if he'd had anything of value to barter with, he'd have offered it to Edward Sabadine, not some insubstantial entity. Min was a practical man.

Sabadine sat across from Min, with Robert at his side. "There is something that has been taken from me, and I wish it to be returned."

Min glanced from Sabadine to Robert and back again. He found both their faces unreadable. "Do you know who took it?"

"Yes." Sabadine pressed his lips into a thin line. "A hedgewitch called Kallick."

So Sabadine wanted him to steal from the Gifted. Any mage or wizard worth their salt—and Min knew that a family like the Sabadines would have several in their service—could take a common hedgewitch in a heartbeat. The only reason Sabadine would refuse to use his own Gifted against this Kallick was because he needed to be able to deny all knowledge of the action if things went wrong. Criminality and plausible deniability. Two of Min's favorite things. They both fitted him as comfortably as an old boot.

"And what did Kallick take from you, sir?" Min asked.

Sabadine's lip curled. "My *grandson*."

That was unlike any answer Min had been anticipating.

Robert leaned forward slightly. "How familiar are you with the traditions of prentices?"

Min shifted his gaze back to Sabadine. "Your grandson is a prentice?"

He liked this less and less. What a damned shame, then, that Harry's life depended on it.

"He was born Gifted," Sabadine said. "Sent as a prentice to Kallick when he was…." He trailed off, frowning.

"Eight," Robert supplied for him. "As the law requires."

"Kallick was supposed to send him home when he was fourteen," Sabadine said. His voice had a sudden edge to it that sounded almost like a growl. "He did not. It has been five years."

"The law is with us," Robert said quietly, as though he thought that mattered to a man like Min. "Kallick ignores our petitions."

Min felt a sudden flash of admiration for any man, even a hedgewitch, who dared to ignore the Sabadines. He wasn't stupid enough to smirk at the idea, though.

"I want the boy returned," Sabadine said, the corners of his mouth turning down sourly. "It's a fair exchange. Your boy for mine."

And there it was, of course. The reason Min couldn't refuse. Which didn't mean he couldn't be at least a little intractable. "What if your boy does not wish to come home?"

"He has no choice," Sabadine said. "My claim on him is stronger than Kallick's."

Still, if the boy was unwilling…. Min's uncertainty must have shown on his face.

"And so is Robert's claim," Sabadine grunted.

Min turned his gaze back to Robert, and saw, for the first time, an expression of discomfort on the man's face.

"Robert's wife is dead," Sabadine said. "It's time he took another spouse."

Perhaps it was Min's hangover that caused his brain to stumble over that connection.

"Robert is your son," he said in an attempt to clarify the situation. "And the boy is your grandson? The marriage is between your son and…."

"My nephew," Robert said, his expression stony once more. "I am betrothed to my nephew."

No, not his hangover that caused the stumble at all. His sense of decency.

"Ah," Min said.

Ew, said his brain.

Sabadine smiled grimly. "Do we have a deal?"

"Yes," Min lied, because to hell with this. The second he had Harry, he was out of here, and he was never coming back. "We have a deal, sir."

Of course, he should have known a snake like Sabadine would have made refusal impossible. He realized it the moment the door to the study swung open and a man in a blue robe entered. A sorcerer. The Sabadines were wealthy enough and powerful enough to have a sorcerer in their employ. The man was dragging a sniffling Harry along with him.

"Harry!" Min exclaimed.

Harry looked up. His eyes were wide, and his face was tear-stained. And a black sigil the size of a coin had been burned into his cheek.

Min's heart froze.

They'd cursed him.

The Sabadines had cursed Harry.

Well, fuck.

CHAPTER 2

THE SHRINE of the Sacred Spring was located on the very edge of the eastern quarter of the city, in the cleft of a shallow valley that lay between two hills. From the east, the haphazard crowded streets threatened to spill their workshops and taverns and tenements into the valley. That'd certainly pollute the sacred waters. The houses on the other hill, where the western quarter began, were larger. Narrow lanes gave way to wide streets, and dusty shutters gave way to glass windowpanes. The residents were wealthy, certainly, but not quite wealthy enough to escape their neighbors.

The Shrine of the Sacred Spring was the heartbeat of the city. According to legend, it was here the founder of Amberwich, Rus Cardor, had built his hut. Min didn't have much time for legends. The Shrine was what it was. A squat, unimpressive collection of buildings with a temple in the middle. The path to the temple was bordered by trees tended by the hedgewitches who served the Shrine. Temple servants collected the fallen leaves and offered them to petitioners in exchange for coins. Min curled his lip at the display, but if he actually thought a few dead leaves would help Harry, he'd be flinging money at the servants right now.

Harry's heaving sobs had trailed off into sniffles on the walk from the Sabadines' house, but Min kept a hand on the boy's shoulder all the same. Harry was wearing his hood pulled up over his scruffy dandelion-fluff hair and had a hand clapped to his cheek for good measure. Min steered him around the line of people waiting to get inside the actual temple and headed for a green-robed acolyte instead.

"Hey," he said, and the acolyte clutched his basket of leaves to his chest protectively. "I need to see Aiode Nettle. Where is she?"

The acolyte looked him up and down warily. "Is Hedgewitch Nettle expecting you?"

"No," Min said, showing his most charming smile. "But, like the mild showers of spring, I find that although I arrive unannounced, I am always most welcome."

Usually something like that would make Harry snort with a laugh. Today, nothing.

The acolyte seemed just as unmoved.

Min dug a coin out of Harry's pocket—his own were empty—and handed it over.

"Follow me," the acolyte said.

Instead of heading for the temple and the sacred shrine inside its walls, the acolyte led them to one of the many side buildings. He pushed open the door. Inside it was dark and cool, a stark contrast to the heat of the day. Sweat cooled on Min's back, making his shirt feel clammy. He and Harry followed the acolyte past several closed doors and then up a set of stairs.

"Hedgewitch Nettle?" the acolyte asked when they reached the first door at the top. He rapped gently. "You have visitors."

The door was wrenched open, and Aiode stood there. Her expression of surprise morphed into one of suspicion. "Thank you, Dar. You may leave us."

The acolyte scuttled away.

Aiode narrowed her eyes at Min. "What do you want? I'm supposed to be at the ritual blessing in a moment. And, believe me, you didn't acquit yourself well enough last night to earn another attempt."

Clear and to the point. Min could respect that. He tugged Harry's hood back, then gripped his wrist and pulled his hand away from his cheek. "This is my nephew, Harry. He's in trouble."

Aiode's eyes widened as she took in the sigil burned into Harry's cheek. "I can see that." She drew a breath. "You'd better come in."

AIODE'S ROOM was small, neat, and clean. A window overlooked what appeared to be a private courtyard in the temple complex and let the sunlight in. Min paced up and down while Harry spilled the entire sorry tale, and tried not to growl at the boy, or possibly grab him by the throat and shake some fucking sense into him. Because clearly it was too late for that.

He had met Talys Sabadine at the Beltane festival. She had been wearing yellow ribbons in her hair. Harry had bought her an oatmeal cake and—

Min raised his brows a little at that. Stolen her an oatmeal cake, more likely, but why muddy the waters with that?

—and later that night she'd taken his hand and they'd jumped over the bonfire together. Harry's voice grew higher pitched as he talked. He hadn't known she was a Sabadine, and she hadn't known that he was a… a….

He flushed.

Aiode made a sympathetic noise.

"A nobody," Harry finished at last. He sniffled. "But that didn't matter to either of us. We met up a few times. Then, last night, we got caught. It wasn't the first time I'd been to her room, but her servant came in without knocking." He shuddered at the memory and twisted around to look at Min. "I told them I'd marry her and make it right!"

"Oh, sweetheart," Aiode said, catching Min's gaze.

It was something of a strange miracle that Harry was still so naïve in so many ways. That he seriously believed there was any possible way the Sabadines would toss Talys into the gutter to be with him. Because *love*. Harry thought love was the answer. Min wished he could laugh at him for it, but he couldn't even summon a regretful smile.

Aiode raised her hand and traced the sigil on Harry's cheek. "This is…." She sighed. "This is a very complicated, very expensive curse. If I'm not mistaken, this is moon work."

"What does that mean?" Min asked.

"It means you have until the next full moon until it kills him," Aiode said.

Harry blinked, and tears slid down his cheeks.

"Do you know of any way to remove the curse?" Min asked.

"This is the work of a *sorcerer*," Aiode said.

Well, that answered that. Min had suspected it, but Aiode's confirmation still felt like a blow. Sorcerers were incredibly powerful. Most worked directly under the king, using their Gifts to defend Amberwich from attacks by the Hidden Lord. They were feared, even by the other Gifted.

"It's a blood curse. It can only be removed by the one who placed it. This curse…," Aiode said, her brows drawing together, and then shook her head. "Using this curse on Harry is like using an anvil to crush an ant." Her gaze sharpened. "What do they want you to do?"

Min stopped pacing for a moment. "They want me to get back Sabadine's grandson. He's a prentice to a hedgewitch and is apparently years overdue his return. He's supposed to come back so he can marry Robert Sabadine. His uncle."

"Makes sense," Aiode said, and shrugged at Min's expression. "A way to bind the boy to both his grandfather's will, as head of the Sabadine household, and his uncle's, as his betrothed. A child submits to the head of the household, and an adult submits to their spouse. If those two are in accord, the little bird is caught twice in the same snare."

Without being given even a moment of freedom between one snare loosening and the other slipping tight, Min realized. No wonder the boy was refusing to come home.

"Well this little bird apparently enjoys his freedom as a prentice and doesn't want to come home," Min said.

"So that poisonous old toad is sending you to fetch him."

Min nodded.

Aiode looked thoughtful. "A hedgewitch, you say?"

"Some fellow named Kallick."

"The name is familiar to me," Aiode said. "I'm not sure I can recall...." She frowned and shook her head. "What is of greater concern, of course, is why a family with a sorcerer in their employ would want you to go and collect the boy."

"I have a reputation for discretion," Min said. "And I have a feeling that Edward Sabadine doesn't want the entire city to know he arranged to have his own grandson abducted. The law might be on his side, but what of his reputation? One of the most powerful men in all Amberwich, and he can't even summon his own grandson home?"

Of course, it wasn't that simple at all.

"Kallick!" Aiode exclaimed suddenly. "Kallick Sparrow! I remember now!"

"Remember what?" Min asked, a sense of dread crawling over him.

"Kallick," Aiode repeated, her eyes widening. "Kallick lives in Anhaga!"

A chill ran through him.

Ah. So that was it. It wasn't that Min was more discreet than a sorcerer. It was that he was more expendable.

A COOL breeze shuddered through the leaves of the trees lining the path as they left the shrine complex. Acolytes darted here and there like frantic squirrels, gathering up the leaves as they were shaken free. They laughed and chattered as they worked.

Behind them, a line of hedgewitches made their way from their quarters to the temple building where they would perform the daily Blessing of the Waters. The priest who had tutored Min had dragged him along once as a child. The ritual had involved a lot of chanting, singing, and an unexpectedly exciting finale when saltpeter had been tossed onto the braziers inside the temple, and flames had fizzed and sparked and burned. At eight, Min had been very impressed and even a little scared. These days it took more than flash-and-bang tricks to frighten him.

Some things still did, though.

Like Anhaga.

Min pushed his thoughts away from that and wondered instead how his name had come to the attention of a man like Edward Sabadine. He had taken jobs from representatives of noble Houses before, but they were the sort of jobs Min had assumed his employers would wish to keep secret. Min's crowning glory had been two years ago now. He'd returned to a nobleman a family heirloom—the ugliest necklace Min had ever seen, for the record—that had made its way to another noble family courtesy of a cheating husband enamored with a daughter of the second House. Messy all around, but the sort of mess that, if exposed, would have led to mutual mockery of both Houses.

The necklace had been kept under no special guard but the existing magic wards of the household. Min's client had been unwilling to send his own Gifted against those of another household and risk escalating a private affair into what amounted to a declaration of hostilities, and Min had a reputation for being able to bypass all kinds of security, even magical. His services weren't cheap.

A routine job, all in all, but maybe audacious enough that someone must have talked, and word had gotten to Edward Sabadine. At the time Min had been too drunk on his own success to consider that perhaps he might one day become a victim of it.

Or that Harry would.

He tightened his arm around the boy's shoulders as they walked.

At the crest of the hill, he looked back. The Shrine of the Sacred Spring was an inviting swathe of green in the shallow valley. Behind it, in the distance, rose the Iron Tower. If the Shrine of the Sacred

Spring was the heart of Amberwich, the Iron Tower was... well, it was the dick, wasn't it? It jutted proudly from the top of the King's Hill in the western quarter of the city, arrogant and bellicose and demanding attention. The tower was surrounded by the king's private parklands, which contained the barracks and the stables of the Royal Guard, the fortified Treasury, the Sorcerers' Guildhall, and the old palace. The king lived in the Iron Tower, and who could blame him with a bunch of sorcerers as neighbors? In the Iron Tower, the king could command his sorcerers without fear of one of them putting him in thrall. The purpose of the Iron Tower had always been twofold: it protected the king from his own Gifted as much as it protected the city from the fae.

The Iron Tower dominated the King's Hill. It was six stories high and topped by a sharply pitched red roof that gleamed in the sunlight. The walls of the tower were white, the paintwork weathered by the years. Barred windows overlooked the parklands. Under the roof, a parapet extended out from the tower wall. The tower was hundreds of years old. There were grander buildings now in Amberwich, but none as fortified as this. None as solidly imposing.

Min turned his back on it.

The streets grew narrower and more crowded as they passed farther into the eastern quarter. Clouds were moving in, the sort that promised just enough gentle rain to make the way slick and to sharpen the stench of the streets. Skinny dogs nosed in the gutter, accompanied by skinny kids. People went about their business in the stores and workshops that lined the way. Min's fingers itched out of habit as they passed a vendor's cart loaded with apples, and his stomach growled, but he kept moving. They passed a painted booth set up on a corner where the pedestrian traffic was forced to slow and watch the show: a puppet, its smirking face painted green and a silver crown on its head, pulled tufts of knotted red wool out of another puppet's belly. The older children laughed and jeered at the spectacle. The younger ones wailed.

Min's stomach clenched as he and Harry passed.

Anhaga.

The word was as sharp as a curse in his mind. Anhaga was a fishing village. It lay several days north of Amberwich. Min had never been there. And nobody in their right mind wished to go there. It was said the Hidden Lord walked in Anhaga. There had been a time when the village had been full and prosperous. A time when Min could remember his mother proclaiming proudly that she served her guests nothing but the finest snipe eels fresh from Anhaga. And then the Hidden Lord, king of the fae, had come. Anhaga sat on the edge of his shadow kingdom now. The Hidden Lord walked its streets at night. Those who had fled Anhaga had come to Amberwich with nightmares clinging to them like wraiths. Those who had stayed... well, Min didn't know why anyone had stayed. He wondered if they were in the thrall of the Hidden Lord now, and if he summoned them to dance with him until they died and then feasted on their entrails like his puppet counterpart did.

"Min?" Harry's voice was thin.

"Yeah?"

"We're being followed."

Min squeezed the boy's thin shoulder. "'Course we are, kid. You think the Sabadines will let us out of their sight? They've been following us since we left their house."

Harry's mouth turned down, and his shoulders stiffened. His gaze sharpened, and Min slowly let his arm slip away from him. When Min sidestepped a pile of horse manure in the street, Harry was gone.

Min continued on, smiling at the thought of the confusion that must have caused in the men following them. Harry was fast on his feet and had the ability to vanish in a crowd. He was as quick and clever as a fox. A fox with a ridiculously large blind spot when it came to a beautiful girl, but a fox all the same. Min had been sixteen once, and not *that* many years ago, but he'd never been a fool for a pretty face. Perks of being raised in a brothel. The mysteries of sex had never been even remotely mysterious, and by the time Min had been old enough to get the accompanying urges, he'd already developed a well-honed sense of cynicism and the ability to *not* think with his dick. Harry had yet to learn that lesson. Min hoped he lived long enough.

Harry was clever, though. He looked the part of a boy who was still soft around the edges and used that to his advantage. Older men often overlooked Harry and always underestimated him. He'd saved Min's skin more than once with his sharp eye, his quick mind, and the knife he carried hidden under his shirt. Well, the knife he usually carried. Min doubted the Sabadines had let him keep it.

Now, as Min continued down the street, he had no doubt that Harry had doubled back and was getting the measure of the men following them.

Harry was back again within three blocks, falling into step beside Min as though he'd never left.

"Two," he confirmed. "They walk like soldiers. One has yellow hair and pockmarked cheeks. The other one is a brown dog."

Min snorted at that. Harry's description of anyone particularly nondescript was *a brown dog*. The streets of Amberwich were full of mutts indistinguishable from one another. Both the four-legged and the two-legged variety.

"You can do better than that, Harry."

Harry grinned. "Fine. A pale fellow. Pointy chin. Eyes like piss holes in the snow."

"That's my boy," Min said and put an arm around him again.

The gesture of comfort was perhaps mistimed, serving only to remind Harry of the curse burned into his skin. Harry's grin faded as quickly as it had appeared, and he ducked his head.

When Min had first found him, Harry had been so desperate to prove himself useful and so afraid of being cast out that he hadn't dared raise his voice in dissent. It had taken a long time for Harry to realize Min wasn't going to ditch him if he talked back, or hoarded all the blankets on a cold night, or ate the biggest half of a stolen pastry. It took a long time for him to realize that Min expected loyalty, but that there was a lot of wriggle room between loyalty and abject deference. Of course, Min had never been deferential to anyone in his life, and so it seemed an unrealistic standard to hold somebody else to, particularly a child. And Harry had looked so terrified the moment Min had seen him first, he had no wish to ever see an expression like that on the boy's face again.

He hadn't, until today.

He hugged Harry a little closer. "Let's go home, kid."

Harry nodded.

SABADINE'S MEN followed them to the Footbridge Tavern. There was no harm in that. Anyone who ever tried to reach Min found their way to the tavern eventually. Min and Harry entered via the front door, then slipped out through the kitchens and into the narrow alleyway behind that stank of refuse. They made their way quickly to the house and trudged up the uneven, squeaking steps. The stairs were dark even in the middle of the day, but Min and Harry were surefooted on their home territory. Min unlocked the door to the garret room, and Harry slipped in underneath his arm.

"I'm sorry, Min," he mumbled, flinging himself down onto the bed.

Min crossed the floor to the window. He watched the alley for a moment to be certain they hadn't been followed and then pulled the shutters closed on the sunlight.

Harry lay curled up on the bed, his right cheek pressed into the lumpy pillow.

"I know," Min said. There was no point assuring the boy it wasn't his fault. It was, and they both knew it, but even Harry couldn't have foreseen that falling in love with the wrong girl would lead to a death sentence. For them both, probably. Because as much as the small, selfish part of Min wanted to just ignore the problem until it went away—next full moon, according to Aiode—Harry was family. He couldn't just let him die without at least trying to get Edward Sabadine's grandson back.

Min sat on the end of the bed and tugged his boots off. Then he stood again and padded across the gritty floor to the table. There was half a loaf of bread left. Min picked it up to inspect it. It was stale, but not yet moldy. He tore a corner off and chewed it into softness before swallowing.

Harry watched through red-rimmed eyes.

"Hungry?" Min asked.

Harry shook his head.

Min tore some more bread off and then stretched out on the bed beside Harry. Harry kept his back to him, his skinny body a tense line. He held himself stiffly for a moment longer and then abruptly rolled over and flung an arm over Min's stomach.

Harry smelled faintly of something floral. The lingering notes of a girl's perfume, perhaps. Min wondered if she was very pretty, this Talys Sabadine, and then smiled ruefully. Of course she was very pretty. Harry had impeccable taste. He wondered if she was clever, too, and if she liked to laugh. He wondered if she loved Harry in return, in that desperate, all-consuming way of the very young and the very stupid. Min hoped she did. It seemed a shame to die for just a pretty face.

A little under a fortnight until the full moon, until the sorcerer's curse killed Harry. A little under two weeks to try to abduct an unwilling prentice from under the watch of his hedgewitch master and haul him all the way back to Amberwich from Anhaga.

Fucking Anhaga.

Well, Min had never backed down from a challenge before, right?

When this was done, though—in the unlikely event he and Harry survived—Min was going to tear Edward Sabadine's scrawny old throat out and then piss on his bloody remains. Nobody fucked with Min like that. And nobody—*nobody*—fucked with Harry.

"What are we gonna do, Min?" Harry's blue eyes brimmed with tears.

Min ignored the twisting in his gut and forced a cocky smile. "What else? We're going to go to Anhaga."

CHAPTER 3

MIN SAT at his usual table in the back corner of the Footbridge Tavern and nodded at Freya as she slid a drink in front of him. The beer at the tavern was thin and bitter, but it was cheap. He also had an understanding with the owner, Swann, that if he didn't always pay his tab immediately, he'd pay it eventually and add in a little extra for the inconvenience. That arrangement had been borne out of years of frequenting the place. Min doubted Swann offered the same latitude to many of his other regulars.

"Was that Harry I saw you with earlier?" Freya asked. "You two swept through here like a whirlwind."

"Had a couple of dogs snapping at our heels," Min confirmed.

Freya pursed her lips and nodded. She knew better than to ask for details. "Harry all right?"

Min wondered how much Auric or Aulus had blurted to the neighborhood about Harry's run-in with the Sabadines. "We're working on it."

Freya was about as warm and comforting as an iron spike through the guts in the middle of winter, but she had a soft spot for Harry. She nodded at Min, her thick brows drawing together in concern, and then stomped back through the gathering crowd toward the kitchen.

Min stuck his finger in the layer of thin foam on top of the beer and then sucked it off. Swann might be waiting a little longer for his money this month. Anhaga wasn't just a dangerous proposition, of course. It also didn't pay a single copper. Because fuck Edward Sabadine, that's why.

Min watched the customers for a while. A girl strutted around, showing her ample cleavage and her saucy smile in equal measure to the young men who'd come to gape wide-eyed at the combined spectacle of poverty, low breeding, and bad manners. Good luck to the girl. Min hoped she stole their purses after fucking them.

A fight erupted in the doorway and was broken up by a glaring Swann and his glaring son. The combatants were ejected forcefully from the premises and left cursing and muttering.

It didn't take long at all for Robert Sabadine to find him.

Min pushed the opposite stool out with his boot and then studied Robert Sabadine over the rim of his mug. The stirring of heat in his gut wasn't entirely down to his aversion; Robert was a handsome man, with sharp edges Min might have enjoyed testing in all sorts of interesting ways. He set his mug down and then wiped the back of his hand across his mouth, scraping stubble. "Figured I couldn't get rid of you. Like dog shit on the bottom of a shoe, aren't you?"

"Are you this polite to all your clients?"

"My clients don't usually threaten to kill my nephew if I refuse them." Min leaned back in his chair and shrugged. "I mean, I love that boy." He raised his brows. "Not enough to *marry* him, of course, but it takes all kinds to make a world."

Robert pressed his lips into a thin line.

"I need horses," Min said. "And provisions. And coin."

"You're in no position to make demands," Robert said.

"Actually," Min said, "I am. You think I have no leverage here because your pet sorcerer put a curse on Harry? Oh, that ensures my compliance, but I promise you it doesn't ensure my success. If you actually want your little prentice hedgewitch returned to you, you'll make sure I have horses, and provisions, and coin."

Robert inclined his head.

"But you were already going to agree to that before you came here," Min said, taking another sip of his beer. "In fact, the only reason you even argued was because I caught you by surprise. You didn't expect me to know I'd need horses. How disappointing for you to come all this way only to find out that I already know your nephew is in Anhaga." He tilted his head curiously. "I'll bet you're the sort of man who really enjoys seeing the flash of fear in another man's eyes."

"You make a lot of unfounded assumptions, Decourcey." Robert narrowed his eyes. "Yes, I am here to tell you about Anhaga and to offer you whatever you need to travel there. I'm also here to tell you that I'll be going with you."

Min almost choked on his beer. "No. Harry and I work alone."

"That's not acceptable," Robert said.

"What's not acceptable," Min growled, "is expecting Harry to spend any more time with some fucking asshole who had him *cursed*."

Robert had the grace to look slightly uncomfortable. "That wasn't my idea."

"I'm sure," Min agreed. "If it had been up to you, he'd be lying in a gutter with his throat slit, right? All because he dared get his grubby paws on a Sabadine."

A muscle in Robert's jaw twitched.

"Harry and I work alone," Min repeated. "That's not negotiable."

"I will ride with you as far as Pran," Robert countered. "I have business to attend at my family's estate."

"As far as where?" Min asked.

Robert looked at him askance. "Do you even know the way to Anhaga?"

"No," Min said and drained his beer. "I just figured we'd turn north and follow the stench of the fae all the way there."

"You *joke* about the Hidden Lord?"

Min shrugged. "Not much fucking else I can do about him, is there?"

Afterward, he liked to imagine it was grudging respect that flickered briefly across Robert Sabadine's expression.

It probably wasn't, though.

THE NEXT morning dawned cold. A customary haze of smoke lay across the city. Min and Harry dressed and headed to the tavern for breakfast. Harry wore his hood pulled up and rested his chin in his hand as he ate. His thin fingers covered the curse mark on his cheek. He was pale and quiet and chewed his lip more than he chewed his breakfast.

"Eat," Min told him quietly, even though his own food sat heavily in his gut.

After breakfast they returned to their garret room to pack their scant spare clothes and a book or two for Harry. Harry struggled with the straps of his satchel and watched Min haul the iron collar and shackles out from underneath the bed. Harry's mouth turned down in distaste. Min didn't blame him. Min had once spent two weeks wearing the contraption in the debtors' prison after a small misunderstanding over an unpaid bill and a large misunderstanding about how willing his mother would be to drop everything to secure his immediate release. Apparently she'd thought those two weeks would teach him a lesson.

The collar and shackles should have been removed once Min's debt had been paid. They hadn't been, because technically Min hadn't been released. Instead, he'd charmed his way out. Well, out of his cell and into the warden's wife's bedroom. From there it was only a short drop to the street below. Min's next stop had been a friendly blacksmith. Then he'd gone immediately to visit his mother, in order to repay her the only way he knew how: petty revenge.

"Want to get out of here, kid?"

It wasn't altruism that had saved Harry that day. It was coincidence.

Min wrapped the collar and shackles in his spare clothes and packed them into his own bag. The chains rattled as he hefted the bag onto his back.

They headed back down the stairs. Min found himself trailing his fingers along the thin walls of the house, as though he was trying to leave his mark on it, or say a silent farewell. He wasn't sure which. He wasn't sure it mattered.

They walked down the alley toward the Footbridge, their boots kicking up dust.

"Have you ever been outside the city, Min?" Harry asked worriedly.

"No. Do I look like a farmer to you?"

Harry's mouth quirked in a smile.

Min saw plenty of trees on his brief visits to the Shrine of the Sacred Spring, thanks, which he generally only used as a shortcut through the valley anyway. Min was a creature of the city, of brick and stone and narrow streets. He had no desire to leave the protection of the city walls, and of the Iron Tower. Min might have hated the Gifted, but he recognized the truth: it was the king's powerful magic-users who protected Amberwich from the Hidden Lord. Beyond the reach of the Iron Tower, it was said the Hidden Lord moved unhindered throughout the land.

Min and Harry cut through the tavern and walked out the front door into the street. They waited there in the shade, watching people moving up and down the street and going about their business. Min saw a few faces he recognized and a few he didn't.

They hadn't been waiting long when they heard the sound of hooves and saw Robert Sabadine and his men approaching on horseback.

"Holy shit," Harry whispered.

At first Min thought he was worried about the horses. Min himself wasn't exactly confident of his ability to climb on one of the animals, let alone control one. Then he caught a glimpse of the girl riding alongside Robert. She was dark-skinned, with twists of brown hair falling down past her shoulders. She was lovely.

"Talys," Harry said, eyes wide.

Min put a hand on his shoulder. "Don't."

Because whatever Harry was thinking, it was bound to be a bad idea.

Except Talys was evidently capable of coming up with her own bad ideas. She swung down from her horse while it was still ambling forward, dodged her father's abortive attempt to grab her, and rushed forward.

"Harry!" She skidded to a stop in front of him, her eyes widening at first and then filling with tears. She reached out with a shaking hand to trace the curse mark on Harry's cheek, while Harry wrinkled his nose and blinked rapidly.

"Talys!" Robert snapped.

Talys stepped back from Harry, regret written across her face. She put space between them, their linked fingers falling away. Min wished he could hate her, except she was exactly as heartbroken as Harry. And then he remembered she would have an entire lifetime to regret Harry and found that she wasn't impossible to hate after all.

"You brought your daughter," he said, staring up at Robert as he drew closer.

Robert's mouth thinned, and he jerked his head in a nod toward the rest of the group. "Pick a mount."

There were two riderless horses. One brown with white patches, and one black. They were big. And tall. Min was suddenly certain he'd be dead of a broken neck before they even left the city. His heart thudded.

"Here," Talys said. "Put your foot in the stirrup, hold the saddle, and pull yourself up."

One or two of the men in the party snorted.

Min took a breath, followed Talys's instructions, and more or less managed to sprawl into the saddle. When he finally dared look around, he saw Harry blinking back at him from atop his own horse, looking just as nervous. Although that might have had more to do with the human company.

"Talys," Robert said curtly. "You ride by me."

Talys shot Harry a sad look as she swung herself back into her saddle.

"She's beautiful, right?" Harry whispered.

"Yeah," Min said. He'd never seen a prettier death sentence.

MIN HAD never been past the gates of the city. Neither had Harry, and he almost fell off his horse when he leaned his head back as they passed underneath the old portcullis on Stanes Street. There was nothing dramatic about it. The city didn't immediately stop at the wall. It fell away in dribs and drabs instead, crowded blocks giving way to space for scrubby grass to grow, for goats to wander and bleat, for lines of washing to be pegged up.

Min noticed the smell at first, or the lack of it. The haze of smoke was lighter here and gave way to the earthier and not unpleasant smells of mud and livestock. When Min twisted in his saddle, he saw that the city had receded behind him, those crowded, chaotic streets and alleys becoming something smaller, something cohesive. From this distance, from the outside, there was no difference between quarters, between streets or buildings. Min knew parts of the city well, and in close detail, but for the first time in his life, he had the sense of Amberwich as a whole. He saw the walls of the city. He saw the Iron Tower high atop the King's Hill. Everything else had bled together.

He wondered if he would pass back this way and watch the city reveal itself piece by piece as he drew closer, or if this was the last time he'd ever see Amberwich.

THE DAY drew on. They broke the journey to eat at the side of the road, and Min took the opportunity to stretch his legs and momentarily ease the ache in his thighs, ass, and back. Fuck horses. Fuck them all. Harry stuck to his side like a limpet, only ducking off behind a screen of bushes when he needed to piss.

When Min approached Robert, Robert shooed Talys away. Harry turned his head to watch her go.

"We'll reach Pran by nightfall," Robert said. "You may stay the night and continue on alone to Anhaga in the morning."

"How far is Anhaga from Pran?"

"If you leave early, you'll make it by dark." Robert's mouth turned down at the corners. "It's unsafe to travel at night."

Of course it was. Except Min didn't know what hazard of the darkness Robert was referring to. Bandits and cutthroats or the fact the veil between the worlds was thinnest at night.

"And people still live in Anhaga?" Min asked.

"Apparently." Robert's gaze followed Talys for a moment as she moved among the men and then fixed on Min again. "Though what kind of lives they lead, I can't say."

Harry jutted his chin out. "Why'd you even send your nephew there, then?"

Min felt a rush of pride for Harry's nerve. That was the disrespectful little guttersnipe he knew and loved. He'd missed him.

"It was over ten years ago," Robert said at last. He frowned. "The Hidden Lord hadn't claimed Anhaga at that time."

When Min was a child, the Hidden Lord had been no more frightening than the puppet show he'd seen in the street. A story and some songs. The fae had not troubled the world of men for generations, since the Iron Tower had been built. But then the Hidden Lord had taken Anhaga, and Min no longer laughed at puppet shows.

"Says something, doesn't it?" Harry asked Min. "How the guy would rather risk running into the Hidden Lord than come home to his family?"

Min shrugged and smirked.

"Watch your mouth, boy," Robert said coldly.

"Why?" Harry asked. "What are you gonna do? Curse me twice?"

And possibly that was just a tad too much of the disrespectful little guttersnipe Min knew and loved. He gripped Harry by the shoulders, turned him, and pushed him gently away. Harry huffed and stalked away.

"Stay away from my daughter," Robert said.

Min didn't quite catch what Harry muttered in return, but it sounded a lot like "Been there, done that."

Robert scowled after him.

"Nephews," Min said with a shrug. "It would help me if I knew something of yours."

Robert shook his head. "He was eight when I saw him last. He was an odd child. Quiet. I paid him little mind."

Min let his silence draw Robert out further.

"He's a bastard," Robert said at last. "My sister was unmarried. She died in childbirth. It was obvious from very early on that he was Gifted. My father believes that Gift would be better used to benefit the family than in service of the order."

Ah. So Edward Sabadine didn't want the boy to indiscriminately encourage crops to grow, or rain to fall, or the other nature-focused specialties of the hedgewitches. The House of Sabadine was old, and like all of the oldest Houses, its fortunes were tied to the land, to agriculture. Why should the boy expend his energies ensuring a good harvest for others when he could be doing it exclusively for his own family?

"His name is Kazimir," Robert said at last, almost like an afterthought.

Kazimir.

Min felt a stab of sympathy for the boy and then turned to watch Harry tentatively patting his horse's snout and flinching back with a surprised huff of laughter when the horse snorted. Min folded his sympathy away again and tucked it deep inside. He had no use for it when it came to Kazimir Sabadine.

THE DARKNESS was drawing in as they reached Pran. It was a small, well-kept village with just a few houses clustered around an unimpressive shrine. The Sabadines' lands lay a little to the north of the village, and Min wondered if they picked up pace on that final stretch because Robert was eager to be on home territory again or because of the gathering shadows that seemed to grow and stretch behind them. Min kept his gaze fixed ahead, half-afraid of what he might see if he stared too long into the trees that lined the road.

The magic of the fae was said to be different from the magic of the Gifted, though both were weakened by iron. Min hated all magic. He had done ever since he was a child and saw a mage put a man into thrall for nothing but the crime of knocking against him in the street. The man had jerked and twitched like a cheap dancing puppet while the mage had pulled his strings. Min had heard stories, too, of the Gifted who kept people in thrall for years and years on end, turning them into nothing more than mindless, dull-eyed slaves. And it was said the fae could do in a heartbeat what even the most Gifted took years to learn. A hedgewitch might take days to summon a gentle rain. One of the fae could command a tempest with a single word.

Ahead, Min could see servants moving out of the manor house. Some of them carried lamps that flickered dimly in the strange liminal light of the dusk. From somewhere behind them, Min fancied he heard the echo of hoofbeats, as though unseen horses followed hard on their heels.

Min refused to look back.

His horse slowed at last, and someone caught the reins to pull it to a halt. The servant boy had a freckled face. His brow was puckered in a frown.

"Your foot, sir," he said, offering Min his cupped hands to step into.

Min slithered awkwardly out of the saddle, the horse skittering sideways. The boy tugged it at a jog toward what must have been the stables.

Robert led the way into the house.

Min pulled Harry with him.

The doors were shut behind them, and the heavy bolts slid into place.

Min looked around the hall. Glass-eyed stags' heads stared down at him from the wall.

"Decourcey," Robert said, shrugging his cloak off into the waiting arms of a servant. "With me."

Min and Harry followed him into a small room off the entry hall.

Robert opened a narrow drawer in a bureau and pulled out what looked to be a scroll. He set it down on the table and raised his eyebrows at Min. "Can you read a map?"

"Of course."

Robert rolled it open and jabbed at a point on it. "This is Pran. Tomorrow you'll follow the road north. It will take you directly to Anhaga."

Min leaned over the table. It took a moment to orient himself. His gaze followed the road north, and he discovered Anhaga settled in a sharp little bite in the wide curve of the coastline. It seemed so close, but then so did Amberwich. Barely the length of Min's thumb away.

"And we'll reach it by nightfall?" Min clarified.

"Yes. If you leave at dawn."

"Then we leave at dawn," Min said, glancing at Harry.

Harry nodded.

"We're a long way from Amberwich here," Robert said. "We no longer fall under the protection of the Iron Tower. The servants will tell you it is unwise to leave the house before light."

"What's out there?" Min asked and then wished he hadn't.

"The people hereabouts are credulous and simpleminded," Robert said, his voice even. "I believe there is nothing outside but that which is conjured by baseless superstition." His mouth twitched in what was almost a smile. "I also choose not to test that belief."

A woman appeared in the doorway and hovered there.

Robert nodded at her and rolled up the map again. "Show our guests to their room, please."

Min and Harry followed the woman. She led them up a set of steps to their room. It was a narrow room but clean. The woman left them with water for washing and a plate of meat and cheese to share. She checked the shutters were secure and then turned to face them. She dug into the pocket of her apron.

"Mistress Talys asked me to give these to you." She held up two little bundles of twigs fastened with ribbon.

Harry took his eagerly, eyes lighting up as though it was a love token.

"Rowan," the woman said. "It will protect you on your journey."

"Tell her thank you," Harry said reverently.

The woman ducked her head and scurried away.

"Excellent," Min said. "Twigs. I'm sure they'll make all the difference."

"Shut up," Harry said, setting his tiny bundle carefully down on the small table beside their food. He peeled his breeches off. "Ouch."

Fucking horses. Min's chafing had chafing.

They washed and ate and climbed into the bed.

"Do you think Talys's room is close to here?" Harry asked after a while.

"Don't," Min said in a warning tone.

"I wasn't going to!" Harry insisted, the dirty little liar.

"Don't." Min closed his eyes and let his body's aches and pains drag him into a well-earned sleep.

CHAPTER 4

THE VILLAGE of Anhaga clung to the cliffs above the coastline like a cluster of barnacles on a rock. In the golden light of the late afternoon, it looked almost picturesque. Gray gulls arced through the salt-sharp air, calling to one another in desolate tones. Smaller birds that Min couldn't identify flurried from one rooftop to the next. The village seemed to be built along several steep streets that led down the cliffside to the ocean. Wooden docks bristled into the water, and boats bobbed in their moorings. Min had been expecting something more from a village caught in the shadow of the Hidden Lord. Something dark, disquieting. Instead, children played on the cobbled streets, and men and women went about their business just as they would in the streets of Amberwich.

In the town square—which in reality resembled no shape found in either nature or geometry—Min asked for directions to the inn, and an unassuming building with sagging eaves was pointed out to him. It wasn't until they were closer that Min saw the sign swinging from the post above the door: three faded fishes fanned out like a hand of cards.

Harry waited outside with the horses while Min went to enquire about lodgings.

The taproom of the Three Fishes was small but pleasant. A fire was already burning in the hearth, sending waves of warmth throughout the room. The innkeeper introduced himself as Heron, seemed surprised that Min actually wanted to stay, and then sent his daughter to go and stable the horses around the back.

Harry slipped inside a few minutes later, lugging their bags. He was wearing his hood pulled forward again, to hide his curse mark.

"And what brings you to Anhaga, sir?" Heron asked as he showed them upstairs.

"We are traveling," Min said.

Heron raised his eyebrows. "We don't get many travelers up this way nowadays."

Min shrugged and showed him an easy smile. "Ah, well we are not so much traveling as we're taking account, as it were."

Heron's eyes widened. "You are a reeve, sir?"

"Yes," Min said, because why not?

"From *Amberwich*?" Heron's mouth worked for a moment before he found his next words. "Why, sir, it's been over ten years since the king sent a reeve to the village!"

"Ah, but reckoning does come to us all," Min told him piously.

"Oh, yes, sir," Heron agreed. "Indeed it does, sir."

Really. The deferential titles were coming thick and fast thanks to that one mention of taxation, weren't they?

Heron flung open the door to a room and ushered them in.

"Tell me, Heron," Min said. "I'm afraid our travels have left us a little saddlesore. It's no urgent matter, but is there a healer in the village? A hedgewitch, perhaps?"

"Ah!" Heron exclaimed, eager to help. "Yes, a hedgewitch called Kallick! He can charm the fish from the oceans, can Kallick."

Which, in all fairness, was probably a skill set very much in demand in Anhaga. And how amusing that Heron was so eager to push Min's attention toward the hedgewitch.

"He is good with farmers too," Heron said. "There was Gredar, a few years ago, who had a plot of land that refused to yield. The soil is very full of salt in these parts, you see. He asked for Kallick, and now he has one of the best barley harvests in the district, year in, year out. We brew our beer from Gredar's barley."

"I shall have to try some," Min said.

Heron looked grateful for the reason to escape. "I'll make sure to have some waiting for you, right away."

He thumped off back down the stairs.

"A reeve, really?" Harry asked, raising his eyebrows. "Can you even count beyond your fingers and toes, Min?"

Min grinned and thwacked him on the back of the hood. "I had an abacus as a child, and everything."

Harry looked dubious.

"My mother tells me I took it apart and tried to eat the beads," Min mused. "But I like to think the potential for mathematical greatness was still there."

Harry huffed out a laugh and set his satchel down. He headed for the window of the small room and looked out into the square. "This is not what I was expecting."

Min joined him, his smile fading. "Me neither."

They gazed at the square a moment longer.

When they returned to the taproom, Heron, as promised, had a beer each waiting for them. It was far better stuff than Min had ever been served in the Footbridge Tavern. They took seats at a bench by the door and watched the pedestrian traffic outside in the square.

Heron pointed out a few landmarks. The entrance to the local shrine. The shop that sold the best eels, both salted and fresh. Kallick Sparrow's house.

"He doesn't answer to visitors," Heron said. "But you'll find him at the market every morning."

"Yes, I think we can wait until morning," Min said. "Harry?"

"Morning," Harry agreed.

Min was more interested in whether or not his prentice wandered about the town, but to ask would be to raise questions he wasn't prepared to answer. He watched the hedgewitch's house for a while instead. It was a narrow house with two stories and an attic, almost identical to its neighbors on that side of the square. There was no sign on it to proclaim that a hedgewitch lived inside, but in a village this size, who wouldn't know? The door was painted green, which might have been a subtle sign. It might also have been coincidence. The windows on the ground floor were shuttered. On the upper floor, a drab curtain swayed in the breeze, but there was no sign of life from inside.

A few villagers stopped by the Three Fishes for a quick drink, and their conversations with Heron seemed friendly but unremarkable. Min eavesdropped more out of habit than anything else.

Harry, careful to keep his right cheek turned to the wall, drank his beer slowly.

Dinner was bread, cheese, and fish, in quantities generous enough to overcome the blandness of the meal. Min was equally generous with Robert Sabadine's money, waving away Heron's thanks. Min rarely got the chance to play the munificent stranger. He quite enjoyed it.

"Min!" Harry whispered urgently at one point, nodding at a table in the corner. "That man's pie is *looking* at him!"

The man was digging into a pie with gusto. Fish heads poked out of the crust, as though the fish were staring up at him.

"Oh!" Heron said, passing the table. "Would you like some stargazy pie, young sir?"

"No," Harry said firmly. "No, thank you."

Min couldn't blame him.

At dusk, as though it signaled some sudden calamity, the square cleared quickly. Even the children hurried for home, the smaller ones dragged by their older brothers and sisters. A strange quiet seemed to settle over the village. Min watched, his skin prickling with unease, as Heron's daughter carefully carried two small jugs of milk out from the kitchens and onto the street. She was back moments later, empty-handed. She shut and bolted the door behind her.

Heron pulled the shutters closed.

The last thing Min saw before his view was obscured was the hedgewitch's curtain still flapping in the breeze.

AT NIGHT the wind howled through the narrow streets of Anhaga, rattling the shutters of the Three Fishes. Harry, who had started off on the side of the bed closest to the window, somehow migrated to the other side and curled up like a pill bug against Min's back. Min lay awake for some time. He thought once that he heard the echo of hoofbeats in the street and the sound of voices that held the cadence of strange music. He told himself it was the wind, but a shiver still ran up his spine. It took a long time for sleep to claim him.

THE SUN rolled in on the mist, sinking into it and shrouding the village in salt-sharp droplets that seemed to hang in the air and cling to Min's stubble when he pushed the shutters open to greet the day. Across the square, the drab curtain in the hedgewitch's window sagged under the weight of the damp. Shop doors and shutters were being thrown open up and down the square, the barrage of noise swallowed in the heavy mist. Horses clopped into the square, pulling squealing carts behind them. The carters leaned heavily on the brakes as they navigated the steep streets that fed onto the square.

Min shivered in the cold but left the shutters open when he went to dress. What *was* the appropriate wardrobe for a reeve? Hopefully not too dissimilar from that of a scoundrel and a thief. Min tugged on a clean linen shirt and buttoned a blue tunic over it. Countless lovers had told him before that blue brought out his eyes, and who was Min to go against popular opinion like that? He knew he was handsome enough to be vain about it. Fortunately he had Harry to keep his conceit in check.

"How do I look?" he preened, shoving the bundle of blankets that was his nephew.

Harry appeared, squinting, his face creased and his hair doing wild things. He looked Min up and down and grunted. "Like you're trying too hard to get laid."

"I never have to try hard," Min reminded him. "Now hurry up and get dressed. We're going to meet our hedgewitch today."

Harry rolled out of bed in a flurry of scrawny limbs and a shock of blond hair. He climbed into his pants and tugged his shirt and tunic on. Harry didn't have the eye for color Min did, despite Min's best efforts to educate him. His yellow shirt and black tunic, both worn a size too large for his frame, made him look like a sloppy bumblebee. One day the boy might grow into himself, but today was not that day.

Min's gaze caught on the curse mark on Harry's cheek.

He hoped, if their luck held, to see that day.

Harry pulled the hood of his tunic up and then grumbled and muttered to himself as Min led the way downstairs. They didn't stop in the taproom of the Three Fishes but headed out into the square instead. The air was heavy and tasted like salt. Min drew a breath, gazed around the square, and followed his growling stomach toward the scent of hot bread. The sign hanging over the door of the nearby bakery showed either a rye loaf or a mildewed one.

Min dug into his purse and dropped a few coins into Harry's hand. He did enjoy being generous with the Sabadines' money.

"Keep your eye out, kid," he said.

Harry nodded and slunk away.

Min visited the bakery first and bought a round roll of bread. He picked at it while he made a slow, curious circuit of the square and eventually doubled back to a cart selling elvers cooked in oil and garlic. Min stood in the street and ate a bowl and wished his mother was here in Anhaga to see him eating elvers like they were a cheap street food. She would seethe with jealousy. Also, if she were here to get tormented and killed by the fae, Min would be totally fine with that.

Slowly, the mist began to dissipate.

Min cleaned his bowl with the remainder of his bread and watched the square come alive with people. He smiled and nodded at those not too wary to meet the gaze of a reeve, or of a stranger, or whichever one it was they found they liked less. He was close to Kallick Sparrow's green front door—close enough to see the paint peeling away like scales—when it opened and the hedgewitch stepped outside.

An unremarkable man. A brown dog, Harry would consider him. A long face with a longer nose, skin sagging with age. Loose folds of it hanging from his jowls like a chicken's wattle. He was balding, and what little hair remained on his crown was gray. He wore a green kirtle that was stained with wear.

"Good day, Kallick," a woman said in passing.

The hedgewitch blinked his dun-colored eyes and jerked his head in a nod. The corners of his mouth quirked up in a smile not unlike rictus. His voice, when he spoke, sounded like it had been pushed through bellows. "Good day."

Min stepped toward Kallick. "Sir?"

The hedgewitch stopped, his expression almost totally blank for a moment before a long blink brought it back into focus. He tilted his head to look Min up and down. "Who are you?"

"Aramin Decourcey," Min said, hoping a name that sounded as impressive as his was some form of currency in a place like Anhaga. He then balanced the truth with a lie. "I am a reeve."

The hedgewitch's blank gaze flicked over him again.

"Heron recommended I seek you out," Min continued. "I came from the south yesterday. I was in the saddle all day and am suffering chaffing."

Kallick's gaze met his and yet somehow failed to connect. "The cure will cost you a quadrans. Be waiting in the square at noon. I will bring it to you."

"I could collect if from your house, if that is more convenient," Min offered.

"No," Kallick said. He turned his head, gaze falling on something on the other side of the square, and stepped away from Min. "Good day."

"Good day." Min watched him walk away, an uneasy weight settling in the pit of his stomach. There was something very strange about Kallick the hedgewitch. Something about the way he moved and spoke, his reactions just a fraction too slow, too perfunctory. Something hollow and cold.

Min was halfway back to the Three Fishes when he felt it: the warm frisson of magic prickling his skin like an unasked question. Fucking Gifted, always poking around where they weren't invited. Min pretended not to notice. Kallick's interest may have been simple curiosity. Few strangers came to Anhaga, after all. And Min was as uninteresting as a blank slate and unthreatening as a kitten. Kallick wouldn't find even a hint of magic in him.

Min headed inside the Three Fishes and climbed the stairs. Harry was sitting on a stool by the window, his feet up on the sill.

"Well?" Min asked.

"He's buying bread," Harry announced. "Just an ordinary, boring old man buying bread and milk, but something about him stinks like a three-day-old fish."

"I thought so too."

"What now?" Harry asked.

"We watch," Min said.

Harry nodded and scratched idly at the curse mark on his cheek.

THE NIGHT drew in, cold and close.

The hedgewitch's salve sat unused in a little clay pot on the table by the bed. Min wasn't stupid enough to ignore every instinct in him that warned him not to trust Kallick.

Harry was red-cheeked and bleary-eyed from too much beer. He sat cross-legged on the bed, squinting at the pages of a book. He followed the crowded lines of text with a bitten-down fingernail for a few minutes and then shut the book. "What's the plan, Min? You know if you don't start doing reeve things soon, they'll all begin to wonder about us."

"Reeve things?"

Harry wrinkled his nose and shrugged his skinny shoulders. "Inspecting things? *Counting* things?"

Apparently Harry was as vague on the details as Min. It wasn't as though either of them had ever paid taxes or intended to.

Min took one of the stools out from under the table and moved it close to the window. He sat and regarded the closed shutters quietly for a moment and then reached out and unlatched them.

"Min?" Harry's voice wavered, hardly a whisper.

Min pushed the shutters open, just wide enough that he had a narrow view of the square and of Kallick's house. The sky was cloudless and the moonlight was bright. Kallick's window was open, the curtain flapping in a desultory way. The square was empty except for a few seagulls inspecting the rough cobbles for scraps and a thin black cat that streaked across the open space before being swallowed by the darkness of the houses. In front of every doorway Min could make out, except Kallick's, sat a saucer, or a mug, or some other small container that caught the shine of the moonlight. Min thought of Heron's daughter, carrying jugs of milk out into the square before night fell.

"Min!" Harry hissed in an undertone, scrambling off the bed and rummaging through his satchel. He sat up clasping the little bundle of rowan twigs he'd been given in Pran, holding them in front of him as though they were a shield or perhaps a weapon.

Min watched the square.

It was hours before anything happened. The night air, sharp with the taste of salt, pinched cold into Min's cheeks. Harry had long since fallen asleep, forsaking the bed for the comparative security of keeping his back to the wall and keeping Min between himself and the open window. He'd dozed off with his head resting on Min's thigh, one hand still clutching the rowan. Min sat in the darkness of the room, watching the moonlight illuminate the square, watching that curtain flap-flap-flap in the breeze. He listened to the sound of the ocean below the village, the tiny waves breaking endlessly against the shore, the rhythmic push and pull that lulled him ever closer to sleep.

Min had slipped deeper than he realized when the clip of hoof beats on cobblestones and the jangle of trappings ringing like bells jolted him properly awake. His heart pounded fast as the riders approached his narrow field of vision.

They were luminous. More luminous than the moonlight should accord. Riders on pale horses. Some walked too. Tall and lean and sharp-featured. Min thought he saw both men and women, but such a distinction seemed petty. They were beautiful and terrible at the same time. They were the sickening moment right before the dream twists into a nightmare.

Min watched as the fae paused in front of Kallick's house. He heard them speak in a language he didn't recognize but resonated deeply in the part of his mind he usually reserved for music. One of the riders dismounted and approached Kallick's door. He raised a hand to it—

A flash of blue light sent him stumbling back.

Holy *fuck*. Kallick had warded his house against the *fae*. That was… that was impossible! Surely it was impossible. Min wouldn't have believed it if he hadn't seen it for himself. He scarcely believed it as it was.

The voices of the fae took on a harsher note, and Min leaned away from the window, suddenly afraid of being seen. He heard them move on again, hooves clopping and trappings jingling, and sat for a long time without moving. When Min finally looked out on the square again, it was empty.

"I DON'T like this plan," Harry said the next morning as they wandered the street behind the square. Behind Kallick's house. "This is a shit plan."

Min's gaze slid over the curse mark on the boy's cheek. "It's the only plan we've got, kid."

The thing with kidnapping—and Min was by no means an expert, despite his mother's insistence he'd stolen Harry—was that it was a crime best carried out under the cover of darkness. Except in Anhaga, of course, where the fae walked the streets at night. Min didn't want to attract the attention of the fae, but he also didn't want to attract the attention of the townsfolk who set up in the square every morning at a little past dawn and stayed all day.

As far as they could tell, Kallick's house had no exit into the back street. It meant Min would have to go in the front door and out the same way. And it meant he had to be leaving, with Kazimir Sabadine tucked under his arm, before dawn. Which meant entering the house at night when the fae were still abroad. Which meant that Harry's assessment of the plan was entirely accurate.

"I'll go in an hour before dawn," Min said. "The fae were long gone by then last night."

He stepped around a mound of rubbish that had been dumped in the narrow street. It stank of rotting fish. A cloud of excited flies hovered over it.

"Last night they were," Harry said, "but how do you know it's the same every night?"

Min didn't. But he also didn't have much of a choice. Usually he liked to take his time to study his mark, to note patterns, to note opportunities, and to consider all of his options, but every night the moon rose meant another day closer to Harry's death. Min needed to act now.

"Harry," Min said, and put a hand on his shoulder. "We don't have *time*."

For a moment he thought Harry would say something typically blunt, but abruptly his blue eyes filled with tears and he looked younger than his sixteen years. "I'm *sorry*, Min."

"I know," Min said and pulled him into a hug. "I know you are, Harry."

He couldn't help looking around him just to make sure—even if nobody in Anhaga knew them—that this spontaneous expression of affection went unwitnessed. Min had a reputation to uphold, after all.

CHAPTER 5

THE FAE came at night, moving through Anhaga wreathed in the strange, ghostly light they carried with them. Min watched through a crack in the shutters as they again stopped at Kallick Sparrow's door and were again repulsed by whatever wards the man had worked. It was powerful magic that belonged more to the dark arcana of the sorcerers than to the nature charms of simple hedgewitches. It unsettled Min, but no more than anything else that had come before. The sooner he and Harry were back in Amberwich, the sooner Min could pluck the Sabadines free like the burrowing ticks they were. And then he intended to spend a lifetime dreaming up ways, both magnificent and petty, of fucking them over for hurting Harry.

In the hour before dawn, Min prepared. He slung the bag carrying the iron shackles over his shoulder and tucked his knife into his belt. Min had always felt that simplicity was the key to a successful plan, although it was a philosophy formed as much by laziness as anything else. He'd unhooked the collar from the cuffs, given there were two of the Gifted to deal with in the hedgewitch's house.

"Get packed," Min said to Harry in a low voice. "Have the horses ready to leave before dawn."

Harry nodded. He was wearing his rowan twigs tucked into the laces of his shirt. "Be safe," he said.

Min forced a smile. "You too, kid. Watch you don't let one of them kick you in the skull."

"Would hardly make a fucking dent," Harry said, lifting his chin.

Min grinned at him, checked the weight of the satchel wouldn't pull him off-balance, and then pushed the shutters open and climbed out the window.

The windowsill was damp and slippery and the footholds were few and far between, but Min had always been surefooted. He dropped to the ground, the iron in his satchel clinking, and looked around the moonlit square. Fear froze him for a moment—what if the fae returned?—but he was out in the open now with no choice but to move.

He straightened up and darted across the square.

The strange itch and tingle of magic crawled over his skin as he reached Kallick's door and ran his fingers down the peeling paint.

The lock was flimsy, and Min made easy work of it with his knife. Typical of the Gifted. They never did expect attack via such mundane methods as a broken lock. Arrogant fuckers.

Min pushed open the door of Kallick's house and stepped inside.

It was dark and smelled of dust and damp and pungent unidentifiable herbs. Min blinked for a moment, waiting for his eyes to adjust to the gloom. The room he was in appeared to be a storefront, with a counter dividing it and shelves against the back wall. There was a doorway behind the counter that Min assumed led into the rest of the house. With any luck he could head upstairs and find where Kazimir Sabadine was sleeping, without even waking his master. Of course, Min should have known better than to count on luck.

"Who are you?" a creaky voice wheezed, and Min saw the shape of the hedgewitch looming up in the doorway.

Min squinted at him in the gloom, brushing his hand against the knife in his belt just to reassure himself it was still there. Min wasn't a violent person by nature. He preferred flight to fight every time. But he knew how to snap and bite if he was cornered.

Kallick raised his hand to make some sign, and a faint green light illuminated the room. It flickered briefly and then grew stronger, bathing Kallick in its glow. The old man's saggy face was blank. "Aramin Decourcey," he said in a monotone.

"The very same," Min said, and wondered if there was any way he could actually bargain with the old man.

"What do you want?"

"I want your prentice," Min said. "His family sent me to bring him home."

A flicker of some unknowable emotion passed over Kallick's face, and he raised his hand again. A ball of light appeared in his palm. Fire.

"Now that's very impressive for a hedgewitch," Min commented, dodging as the hedgewitch flung the fire toward him. Too impressive for a hedgewitch, in all honesty, but it made no difference to Min if the man was a hedgewitch or a wizard, or a mage, or a sorcerer. The hierarchy of the Gifted was pure semantics to Min, although it rankled that the Sabadines had lied to him. No common hedgewitch should be able to create fire.

Except if the Sabadines had lied, then so had Aiode Nettle. And it wasn't as though Min trusted her or anything—he trusted nobody; it saved time and inevitable disappointment—but he couldn't think of any reason she would lie. Which meant that whatever was going on with Kallick Sparrow, his fellow Gifted were just as much in the dark.

The ball of fire hit the wall behind Min and vanished into nothing. Kallick raised his hand again.

Min lunged forward. So few of the Gifted expected a physical attack. He hit Kallick with his shoulder, hard, and the old man stumbled backward. Min caught his wrist and dragged his hand back down before he could pull some more magic out of the air, and then they were falling. Min heard the crack of Kallick's skull as they hit the floor together.

"Oh *shit*."

Dark blood spread out underneath Kallick's head. His blank eyes stared up at Min.

Min pressed a hand against the man's chest to push himself away. He felt no heartbeat under his palm. The hedgewitch was dead. Min had killed him.

Shit shit shit.

Kallick blinked slowly. "Who are you?" he asked again tonelessly.

Min's blood ran cold.

YEARS AGO now.

The man in the street.

Min had watched in horror, unable to tear his gaze away as the man in the mage's thrall shuffled and jerked. The mage had directed every muscle, every sinew with a lazy flick of his fingers, smiling thinly. And the man had danced and danced and danced, mouth open in a silent scream, and Min couldn't look away.

THE HOUSE was lit with the strange green light still, like something eldritch, liminal, out of a dream or a slow-creeping nightmare.

Min hurried up the stairs, his boots breaking lines of rowan ash as he moved, sending tiny clouds into the air. His skin prickled as he passed indecipherable sigils painted on the walls. He threw open the door of the first room he came to and found it in darkness. The second too. The third, though... in the third room—it appeared to be both a workroom and a bedroom, with the window that opened onto the square—a boy fumbled with a knife, eyes wide.

The stairs creaked as Kallick climbed them slowly.

"Well now," Min said. "You must be Kazimir."

"Wh-what—" The boy edged around the table, putting it between them. His shoulders rose and fell as he breathed heavily, quickly, like a frightened little rabbit. It made Min want to laugh.

Oh, but this boy. This contradictory, *impossible* boy. Min liked the look of this boy. He was pale, whip-thin, and the very air around him seemed to thrum with energy as though the boy's body was too paltry a vessel to contain it and it overflowed. He had unruly dark hair and dark eyes too—as stark as mud thrown up from the wheels of a cart onto a whitewashed wall. The boy was not conventionally handsome, but when had Min ever enjoyed the conventional? His snub nose and wide mouth might not catch the eye of some artist chasing beauty worthy of worship, although his cheekbones, Min allowed, would be the envy of any sculptor. The boy reminded him of nothing more than a half-grown pup, all awkward long limbs, and Min couldn't decide if he would grow into devastating beauty or into ugliness. Min found both equally appealing.

Of course, he'd always had problems differentiating between the people he'd like to punch and the people he'd like to fuck. They were so often the same people.

"How did you get in here?" the boy asked, one shaking hand holding the knife and the other twisting the fabric of his nightshirt into a knot.

"Through the front door," Min told him, quirking his mouth in a sharp smile. "How else?"

The boy's eyebrows shot up. "But... but the...."

The boy looked down at his hands for a moment, as though doubting them. He was charmingly discombobulated.

Min softened his smile into a sympathetic pout. "The wards? The runes? The little lines of rowan ash? Truly prentice-level stuff. I'm disappointed, actually."

The boy took a step back. "The... the *barrier*!"

"The barrier?" Min asked. "Shiny blue burst of light that keeps the fae from your door? I walked right through that. Sorry."

He watched with interest as the realization dawned.

The boy gasped. "You're a void!"

"And you," Min said as Kallick lurched into the room behind him, "are a fucking *necromancer*."

The boy took another step back, coming up hard against a shelf. Something rattled and clinked. A pestle rolled in its mortar, stone scraping against stone.

A necromancer.

It seemed incredible. Impossible. And yet here they were.

Min opened his satchel and pulled out one of the shackles. "Drop the knife."

The boy clenched it tighter reflexively.

Min moved quickly forward.

Subduing the boy was easy enough. He might have had the power to animate the dead, but he couldn't fight to save his life. Min ended up kneeling on his back, with one of the boy's arms twisted and held easily. The knife lay discarded well out of reach of the boy's free arm, although his long fingers strained toward it. The boy squirmed and bucked as Min closed the first of the shackles around his wrist.

"No!" the boy exclaimed. "Kallick!"

Min turned his head to watch.

Kallick collapsed slowly like an empty sack as the boy's Gift was bound by iron. His mouth opened and closed once, and then fell open again. His skin seemed to slough off him like a snake's, now that the will to hold it in place had been severed. There was no blood now, no gore. Just a dry, brittle husk that crumbled into nothing. A dandelion seed head torn apart by a puff of air. Kallick's outstretched hand fell away like sand. His green kirtle folded in on itself and floated to the floor in a cloud of dust. For a moment there was no more movement, and then, with a rattle, Kallick's yellow skull rolled out from under the hem of the kirtle.

Ew.

"Exactly how long has he been dead?" Min asked, unable to keep the surprise from his voice.

"I was ten," Kazimir said, his voice ragged and his eyes shining with tears.

Incredible.

Impossible.

By all rights the boy should have been at least unconscious on the floor with the effort it took to animate Kallick. To have him walk around the town and buy his bread and milk. To have him speak and respond to questions. Min had never even heard of such a thing, and the tales of necromancers' magic were full of exaggeration and horror. He had once heard the story of a man from a powerful House who had been murdered long ago, and the king at the time had ordered his necromancer to find the identity of the killer. It had taken weeks for the necromancer to prepare. Weeks, and the blood sacrifice of a score of beasts. The effort to compel the dead man to speak the name of his murderer had almost killed the necromancer. Which in Min's opinion was a fitting end to a man with a Gift so grotesque.

"And you didn't even give him the honor of a burial," Min commented, twisting the boy's other arm back to shackle that wrist as well. "Don't tell me you're upset. Friends don't reanimate friends' corpses."

Kazimir turned his face away, only flinching slightly when Min fastened the collar around his pale throat. He didn't attach the chains. Without his Gift, the boy was no physical threat.

"There," Min said, climbing off him at last. "That should keep you out of trouble."

"Why do you even bother?" the boy muttered. "I can't do anything to *you*."

To be born without a Gift wasn't uncommon. Most people couldn't do any magic. But only a very few were immune to it. And Min kept the fact he was a void very much to himself. He preferred his clients to think he was clever enough to work his way around the trickiest magic, not walk straight through it like it wasn't even there. The bastards would probably try and argue his fee down to a pittance if they knew the truth. And, given the scarcity of voids, Min knew it would attract a lot of attention he didn't need if it became common knowledge. Possibly even attention from the Iron Tower.

"And I wasn't born yesterday," Min told the boy, standing again. "You can't curse me or put me in your thrall, but, *oh look*! A storm! A flood! A rampaging herd of wild boars! Let's not pretend you're not clever enough to find a way to kill me indirectly."

Kazimir's mouth pressed into a thin, stubborn line.

"Come on, then," Min told him. "Up!"

Kazimir climbed slowly to his feet. He raised his hand to his throat, and iron clanked softly against iron. "This hurts."

"You get used to it, trust me."

"It's *heavy*."

"Don't worry about that, sweeting," Min said, relishing the flash of anger in the boy's eyes at the endearment. "It's the horse that has to carry you."

"Carry me where?"

"Back into the loving bosom of your family," Min said. "Where else?"

"No! I can...." Kazimir looked around desperately. "I can pay you!"

Min followed his gaze. "In what? Dust and bones?"

"In... in magic!"

Min huffed out a laugh. "Nice try, but the iron stays on." Even if he trusted the boy's word—which he didn't—there was no way for a curse like Harry's to be removed except by the sorcerer who'd placed it on him. It wasn't a question of power. It was a question of *blood*. The sorcerer had used his own blood to bind the curse, and only his blood would remove it. "Now get dressed."

Kazimir jutted out his chin. "No!"

"Then wear your nightshirt all the way to Amberwich. I really don't care either way. This leverage you think you have here? It doesn't exist."

Kazimir's lower lip trembled, and he turned away quickly. He pulled open the drawer of a dresser and began to drag clothes out. He sniffled.

Min glanced out the window. The darkness was softening slowly into the gray light of predawn. "Come on, kid. Hurry it up."

Kazimir stepped into his breeches first, pulling them up under his nightshirt in a display of modesty Min found almost charming. Of course, Min had been born and raised in a brothel, and modesty had never been one of the values instilled in him at a young age. Kazimir even kept his back turned to Min while he pulled on an undershirt. When he turned around again, his face was set. He hesitated for a moment before picking up a green kirtle and tugging it over his head. His fingers trembled with the laces. The kirtle was cut short in the style of a prentice, more like a shirt than a robe.

Min raised his eyebrows. "Shouldn't you be wearing something in black?"

Kazimir ignored the barbed question and knelt down to pull his boots on.

"That everything?" Min asked.

Kazimir picked up a somewhat threadbare cloak from the end of the bed and jerked his head in a nod.

"Let's go, then," Min said and gestured toward the door. "You first."

He stepped over Kallick Sparrow's dusty remains and followed the boy down the stairs.

MIN KEPT a hand on Kazimir's shoulder as they stepped outside into the square, half expecting the boy to be stupid enough to try to run. There was no mist today. It was still dark enough that there were no people around, but the dawn was beginning to paint swathes of pink and orange in the sky. The last of the stars were fading into nothing. Min was pleased to see Harry was waiting outside the Three Fishes, his hood pulled up and the reins of the horses looped in his hand.

"Please don't," Kazimir said, his voice faltering.

Min tightened his grip on his shoulder. "Come on."

He wondered if the boy had ever used the word *please* in his life before tonight. Min had certainly never known the Gifted to be generous with it. And not forgetting Kazimir was a Sabadine as well, which just added a whole other layer of assholery to that entitled equation.

Harry led the horses toward them. His face was pinched with nervous relief. "Min! You did it!"

"Did you ever doubt me, kid?"

"Every second of every day," Harry said with a grin that belied that.

"Harry, this is Kazimir Sabadine. Kazimir, Harry Decourcey. My nephew. He doesn't look like much, but he's scrappy and can fight like a cornered tomcat."

Harry's grin widened.

"Stone," Kazimir said.

"What?"

"My name is Kazimir Stone."

The boy had traded in his family name for a hedgewitch name.

"My apologies," Min lied. "Harry, this is Kazimir *Stone*."

He might as well enjoy the name while he still had it.

Min mounted his horse with what he felt was more precision than the first time he'd tried it, and then reached a hand down for Kazimir.

"You only have *two* horses," the boy said blankly.

"So much for your plans to ride off alone," Min told him.

Kazimir grimaced and took Min's hand. With the aid of a leg up from Harry, he seated himself in front of Min, hunching forward in what Min assumed was a useless attempt to keep some space between them.

"Keep wriggling like that, sweeting, and you might not like what happens," Min told him.

Kazimir froze.

Harry snorted and swung himself into the saddle with more grace than Min had managed.

"Ready?" Min asked, sliding an arm around Kazimir's waist.

Harry nodded. "Let's get the hell out of this shithole."

Min smirked and ignored the way Kazimir's body shuddered with silent sobs as they left Anhaga behind. Above them, gulls circled the lightening sky, crying mournfully to one another as the dawn slowly bloomed.

CHAPTER 6

THE DAY grew steadily brighter as the light chased down dawn's extravagant tapestry and bleached the colors out of it. Min's back grew warm. He felt sun-dozed and indolent, like a cat stretched out on a sunny stair lording over his dominion. And why not? He'd captured a necromancer, a task that even a sorcerer would struggle to complete without being killed in the process. The Gifted. So damned smug about their magic and their power, so damned arrogant, and they were as weak as kittens where Min was concerned. Kazimir Stone could certainly vouch for that.

Against the pale nape of Kazimir's bowed neck, his scruffy dark hair curled around the iron collar. Min resisted the urge to brush it away.

They stopped after an hour or two to stretch their legs and ease their aching muscles, in a place where the road dipped and forded a shallow, clear stream. Min swung awkwardly down to the ground—more like sliding off the back of the horse than anything that could be classified as an actual dismount—and then held his cupped hands out for Kazimir to step into.

"I don't need your help," Kazimir said.

Min was almost disappointed when he didn't stumble and break his neck.

"Don't wander too far," Min instructed him. "If I have to hunt you down, I'll be very annoyed."

Kazimir shot him a baleful look and slunk behind a tree. It didn't offer enough cover for Min to worry the boy was trying to run. He glanced at Harry as Harry walked toward him, leading his horse.

"Doesn't look like much, does he?"

"A milksop," Harry agreed, stretching.

Min smirked. "And a necromancer."

Harry's eyes widened. "Are you serious?"

"*Deadly* serious."

Harry narrowed his eyes. "That's a terrible fucking joke."

"Shut up," Min said. "It's true, by the way. He's a necromancer."

Harry looked dubiously at Kazimir as he reappeared, adjusting his pants.

"The old hedgewitch?" Min shuddered. "Came apart like a dry husk the second I got the iron on the boy."

"Fuck," Harry said mildly, raising his eyebrows. "But he's safe now, right?"

Kazimir shuffled over toward the stream. He crouched down and dipped his hands into the water. The iron gleamed dully on his wrists. Min remembered the weight of it well.

"He's safe," he confirmed.

Harry led the horses over to the stream to drink, and Kazimir watched him warily for a moment before moving to the shade of a wind-twisted tree and staring unhappily into the water. In the daylight he looked pale and pinched, like some barefoot winter's urchin begging alms. Min didn't fall for it from the big-eyed brats who hung around the city shrines, and he wasn't going to fall for it with Kazimir Stone either.

He walked over to the horses, damp earth and pebbles crunching under his boots. He opened Harry's saddlebag, trusting him to have them as well stocked as any larder. He pulled out a wrapped package and was pleased to discover it was a stack of small barley cakes.

"Help yourself," Harry said, rolling his eyes.

Min didn't bother responding. Please. As though it hadn't been Min's money that had paid for the barley cakes in the first place. Well, Robert Sabadine's money, but Min felt that was splitting hairs. He bit into a barley cake and crumbs rained down.

Kazimir looked toward him.

"Hungry?"

Kazimir shook his head and looked away again.

Min finished half his barley cake before Harry claimed the other half. Min took the opportunity to cuff Harry gently around the head. Harry pressed close for a second, closer than usual. Harry was made of narrow gazes and sharp edges, all angles and points cultivated to belie the gentle cast of his features. He didn't like to show his vulnerability to anyone. Even Min rarely saw it. But Harry had been terrified these past few days. Too terrified to handle things with his usual brash confidence, at least. Min couldn't blame him for that.

Harry flashed him a quick smile before he busied himself with the horses again.

Min stretched, rolling his shoulders to ease the twinge in his back. He caught Kazimir's gaze and motioned him over. "Time to go, then, necromancer."

It took a moment of jostling to get Kazimir seated in front of him again and the horses pointed in the right direction. Harry took the lead, looking more at ease on horseback with every passing mile. Min's horse, fortunately, was placid enough to fall into line behind Harry's.

"Your nephew has a curse mark," Kazimir said once they were underway, his voice low.

"Thanks to your family, yes."

Kazimir turned his head slightly. The sunlight caught in his lashes and sparkled like raindrops. Like tears. "That's the reward, then. His life."

"That's the reward," Min agreed.

Kazimir made a small noise that sounded something like defeat, or at least like resignation. He bowed his head and didn't flinch away when Min circled an arm around his waist.

Good, then.

He understood the stakes.

He understood that it didn't matter what he offered. There was no way Min would ever choose him over Harry.

THE DAY wore on. Min watched as Kazimir's pale nape became pink and then red as the sun beat down. The boy swayed in the saddle once, and then twice, jerking himself upright each time. He was fighting sleep, Min thought. When the boy's shoulders slumped again, Min pressed his hand against his chest and applied enough gentle pressure to encourage him to lean back. He was obviously too tired to argue, possibly too tired to even register what Min was doing. He sagged back against Min, his head resting on Min's shoulder, pale face lifted to the sun. His eyes were closed. His dark lashes rested against his cheeks. Min felt his heart thumping under his palm. The boy's muscles would be knotted up like an old string when it came time to stop, but Min didn't wake him. A slumbering abductee was a lot easier to manage than a conscious one. Min assumed. It wasn't as though he kidnapped people regularly.

Kazimir twitched a little in his awkward sleep and made a series of nonsensical little noises. What did necromancers dream of? Min wondered if there was anything in all of creation that could give them nightmares. Puppies and sunshine, probably, and the carefree laughter of tiny children.

It was difficult, even though Min had seen the evidence, to think of Kazimir as a necromancer. Necromancers were things of legend. They inhabited nightmare worlds and horror stories. They walked the paths known only to the dead and breathed easily the bad air of rot and decay. Min had always imagined necromancers to be as grotesque and cadaverous as their victims. Not so… baby-faced. Snub-nosed. Kazimir was soft in sleep, almost pretty.

A snort from Harry drew Min's attention.

Fine, yes, Kazimir was exactly Min's type, and Min was as transparent as water and had been studying the boy's face for too long.

"Keep your hands out of his pants, Min," Harry said. "He's not yours to fuck, remember?"

"Why are you such a vulgar child?"

"I blame my upbringing," Harry said, which was a completely fair call.

Now might have been a good time to bring up the fact that Min had raised Harry smarter than to even think about fucking a Sabadine and that Min would never do something so stupid, but it would have been a low blow. If needling Min made Harry feel better about this whole mess, then Min could take a little.

"Looking isn't touching," Min reminded him.

"You're touching him," Harry pointed out.

"Touching isn't fucking."

Harry raised his eyebrows.

"Which, by the way," Min said, "are words to live by."

Harry's grin was wry.

Kazimir twitched again, and Min tightened his grip slightly. He liked the weight and the warmth of Kazimir leaning back against him. And why not? Kazimir was a good-looking boy, and Min had always enjoyed those. It was a shame Kazimir had been promised to Robert. A shame he was a necromancer as well. Those were two very good reasons for Min to keep his distance. But today, for a few more hours at least, Min could enjoy this for what it was: the warm body of a good-looking boy pressed against him.

It lasted only as long as the next dip in the road, when Kazimir jolted awake and immediately leaned away from Min again. He hunched forward, the back of his neck suddenly pinker than his sunburn.

Min smirked and glanced over at Harry only to find that Harry's forehead was puckered with a frown as he stared at the road ahead.

"Min, do you remember any of this?"

Min forgot Kazimir and gazed at the landscape. The road. The trees. The scrubby ground. Every mile looked much the same as the last. That was the tragedy of nature.

"I think something's wrong," Harry said.

"Nothing's wrong," Min told him. "There's one road south and we're on it. It is literally impossible for us to be lost."

"Right," Harry said and pointed ahead to where the road forded a little stream. "So why is that the exact same place we stopped this morning?"

Min felt a sudden rush of sickening dizziness.

Oh fuck.

KAZIMIR STRUGGLED when Min hauled him off the horse, twisting to try to dig his elbows into Min's stomach. Min shoved him to the ground, ignoring the boy's yelp of pain as he hit the dirt.

"I didn't do anything!" he protested. He shook his shackled wrists in Min's direction. "How *could* I?"

"I don't know," Min said with a sneer. "Maybe the same way you could animate a fucking corpse for the past nine years and still be breathing yourself!"

A Gift, he'd once heard someone say, was like a tiny spark inside a person, an ember. Sometimes, with the right training, that spark could be nurtured into a flame. But there was a very fine line between a controlled flame and a conflagration. And from what Min had seen of Kazimir's Gift, the boy was long overdue being burned to a crisp from the inside out.

"I didn't do anything!" Kazimir yelled again, his cheeks red with indignation and his voice breaking. He hugged his right arm to his chest, cupping his left hand over his elbow. Min saw blood soaking through the sleeve.

"Min!" Harry wrenched him away and then dropped to his knees beside Kazimir. He wrinkled his nose. "Sorry. He's not *always* such an asshole."

Min turned away, refusing to feel guilty about knocking Kazimir into the dirt. He busied himself with the horse instead, scratching its mane in a way it seemed to enjoy enough to lean into and enabled Min to keep safely clear of both the kicking end and the bitey end. He concentrated on that for a few minutes. When he glanced over at Kazimir and Harry, they were crouched by the stream, and Harry was dabbing Kazimir's bleeding elbow clean with the wet end of his sleeve.

Min squinted at the sky, trying to guess how long they had until dusk. Long enough to get back to Anhaga? It was doubtful, even if Min could trust they weren't trapped in some sort of... of whatever the fuck this was.

He stalked over toward the boys. "If it wasn't you, then what is it?"

"The veil," Kazimir said, voice shaky. "The fae have pierced the veil. Usually it only happens at night, when it's thinner, easier to pass through."

"Why now?" Min asked, taking another step toward him. "Why *today*, Kazimir Stone?"

Min didn't believe in coincidences.

Kazimir flinched, losing his balance. Harry reached out to steady him, but it was too late. Kazimir's arms windmilled, and he toppled backward into the shallow stream, landing on his back in a flurry of limbs and an explosion of water.

"Kaz!" Harry exclaimed, wide-eyed. "Fuck, Min! Can you stop pushing him around?"

"I didn't even touch him!" Min pointed out. "That time."

I don't get to be his friend, kid. Because if we somehow survive this night, I'm the one who has to turn him over to the Sabadines. Not you. Me.

Which was really too much to convey in a single glance to an unreceptive target.

Harry held a hand out to Kazimir and helped him to his feet. Kazimir half turned away, wiping at his face with his hands. Water dripped from his clothes. The weight of it tugged his scruffy curls straight.

That's when Min saw it: the tip of one pale ear protruding from behind a wet, flattened shank of dark hair.

He stepped forward, tugging Kazimir from Harry's grasp. He held the boy's chin in one hand and tilted his head. With his other hand, he wiped the wet hair away from the boy's ear.

His *pointed* fucking ear.

It made a terrible sort of sense. The incredible power of Kazimir's Gift. The way the fae stopped at one door in Anhaga and one door only. The way the Hidden Lord had only claimed Anhaga once Kazimir Stone had been sent there to prentice with Kallick Sparrow.

Min felt the pieces slotting in together as inextricably as the tumblers in a lock. Every single one falling into place.

"You're *fae*."

Kazimir lifted his gaze long enough to meet Min's, his eyes shining more gold than brown in the sunlight, and then looked away again. "It's only blood."

Min rubbed his thumb along the pointed ridge. "What?"

Kazimir's tongue flicked out to swipe his lower lip. "Just because I'm half fae doesn't mean I'm an enemy of the king."

"I'm the last man in the world to care about your loyalty to the king," Min told him. "But I find it interesting the first thing you do is protest your innocence."

Kazimir pressed his mouth into a tight line.

"Interesting," Min explained slowly, "means, in your case, unconvincing. You say you are loyal to the king, but you did not come home when the king's law required it. You made the Sabadines look bad. And the Sabadines don't like to look bad, little necromancer." He narrowed his eyes. "Ask Harry."

Kazimir glanced warily in Harry's direction.

"Your poor old grandad," Min said. "Whose only crime is to serve the crown."

"He serves himself," Kazimir said, gaze catching briefly on Min's again.

Min huffed out a humorless laugh and released Kazimir's chin. "And you thought you'd hide in Anhaga where he couldn't reach you? Looks like he found a way to pull you into the game after all."

"By pulling you in too." Kazimir glanced at Harry and at the curse mark on his cheek.

"That doesn't mean we're on the same team, kid," Min warned him.

"I know that," Kazimir said and hugged his arms to his chest. "I know."

Min resisted the urge to reach out and touch his hair again. To grab something out of his bag and offer it to Kazimir to wear. To get him dry, get him warm. "You reanimated Kallick to protect yourself."

It was clever, Min supposed. Kazimir didn't want to be a pawn of either the Sabadines or of the king they served. Pretending to be Kallick's prentice had offered him the perfect solution, but not forever. Kazimir was overdue his return home. What a shame that binding him with iron had also served to destroy whatever wards Kazimir had wrought to protect himself from the fae. And what a shame—no, what a fucking *tragedy*—that Min was only discovering this now.

"No. Well, yes." Kazimir shook his head slightly. "But I was *ten* as well."

Harry made a humming sound. "You didn't want to be alone."

Kazimir nodded, staring at the ground. "He was different, though, when he came back. It wasn't him anymore."

Min closed his eyes briefly. He hated feeling like he was being played. And, oddly, he didn't get that feeling from Kazimir right now. But the stench rolling off Edward Sabadine, all the way from Amberwich, was as putrid as always.

"Your grandfather doesn't know you're a necromancer, but he knows you're part fae. The second your mother spat you out with ears like those, of course he knew. Why the hell does he want you home so badly?"

"I don't know," Kazimir said. "I don't know anything about the war between the king and the Hidden Lord, but I think I might make a good hostage."

"For which side?" Harry blurted, wide-eyed.

Kazimir squinted at the ground and shrugged. "Either? Both?"

He sounded a lot younger than his nineteen years. Min wondered how much of it was artifice and how much was Kazimir's self-imposed isolation. How much could anyone learn about the world through an open window and the glassy eyes of a dead man?

"Not a hostage," he said thoughtfully. "Leverage. If the Hidden Lord claims you for whatever dark purpose because you're one of his, then if the king holds you, you become leverage. And if you are of use to the king, then you are of use to the Sabadines. No wonder they want to make sure of you, to bind you with both blood and marriage."

Kazimir jerked his chin up. "What marriage?"

Whoops.

"Didn't they tell you? You're marrying your uncle."

Kazimir's face went slack, pale. "What?"

"You're marrying Robert." Min suddenly hated the way Kazimir's eyes shone with tears and his bottom lip trembled. "Cheer up, sweeting. I'm sure it'll be a beautiful wedding."

Harry smacked him in the chest.

"What?" Min asked. "There'll be *cake*."

Kazimir turned away, shoulders rising and falling as he struggled to breathe.

"You're a fucking asshole sometimes, Min," Harry said softly.

Yeah.

Point taken.

"What's the problem?" Min asked. He'd always believed the best form of defense was attack. "He's not getting married, is he? Because we're not going to make it back to Pran before the Hidden Lord catches us and takes our flesh apart with his teeth. So here we are, Harry. We rode for fucking hours, and yet here we are. And unless you read somewhere in one of your damned books about how to escape the shadow realm, then we're fucked, aren't we? We're well and truly fucked."

Harry didn't say anything. Just pushed past him and flung an arm around Kazimir's shoulders. Muttered something that sounded half-soothing, half-accusatory in his ear—Min was sure the accusatory portion was for his benefit—and ran his fingers through Kazimir's damp hair. He made a small noise of surprise and tugged a tiny black feather free. He released it, and it spiraled to the ground.

"Harry," Min said.

Harry turned his head, scowled at him, and murmured something in an undertone to Kazimir.

Min curled his lip.

The scowl stung more than Min wanted to admit. He had a ridiculous soft spot for his adopted nephew. It's why he was here, after all. A colder man, or a smarter one, would have cut his losses and let the curse take its course. Well, it's not like they had to worry about the curse anymore either, did they? After tonight they wouldn't have to worry about anything ever again. Eternal rest and all that. Min might have been more open to the idea had he not been absolutely certain of the horrific agony that would precede it.

And the fact necromancers existed.

Kallick the hedgewitch hadn't rested, had he?

"Iron," Harry said suddenly. "We have iron and the fae hate iron. It causes them to sicken!"

"Harry…."

"No, it *does*," Harry insisted. "The fae are creatures of magic, and iron weakens magic. Why else does the king live in the Iron Tower?"

"To stop his own Gifted from stabbing him in the back, probably!" Min threw up his hands. "And clearly iron doesn't hurt the fae much since Kazimir is still standing!"

It was a logical deduction worthy of any scholar, and Min was proud of it. So of course that was the moment when Kazimir proved him a liar by shivering, stumbling, and keeling over facedown in the mud.

IT TOOK Min and Harry a long time to get Kazimir back in the saddle, where he slumped forward, unconscious. Harry gathered up the reins of the horses, and Min walked alongside Kazimir, hoping to catch him if he had the good sense to fall off on the correct side. The iron shackle around Min's wrist was heavy and reminded him of the weeks he'd spent in debtors' prison. A time that, in retrospect, really didn't seem so terrible after all.

Harry wore the other shackle.

Kazimir still wore the collar.

"Which way?" he asked, wrinkling his nose.

Min shrugged. "Does it matter?"

"Probably not," Harry admitted. "But we know going south doesn't work, and we know we don't have time to get back to Anhaga before nightfall." He gazed along the shallow stream. "Inland?"

"Why the hell not?" Min agreed.

It was a motto that had always served him well in the past.

They splashed through the water, heading west into the golden light of the late-afternoon sun.

CHAPTER 7

THE SETTING sun had never seemed so ominous. Min could feel the darkness behind him, gathering like the clouds of a coming storm. He tried to keep one eye on Harry, leading the horses, and one on Kazimir, still slumped forward in the saddle. Kazimir's arms hung at his sides. Min could see a thick ring of abraded skin around his wrist where the iron cuff had been removed. It looked almost like a burn. Min had no doubt his other wrist was similarly marked and that the collar, still locked around his throat, was hurting him.

Min had never thought of himself as a cruel man, just a practical one. But here, in this moment, he let Kazimir suffer. He could not risk removing the collar and giving Kazimir back his Gift. He wouldn't have risked it even for a hedgewitch's prentice. To do so for a necromancer would be suicide. Even if Kazimir could not work his Gift directly on Min, he could work it on their surroundings—and on Harry.

Kazimir murmured something into the mane of the horse. He shuddered, and Min put a hand on his thigh to steady him. If he noticed, he didn't respond.

And behind them, the darkness gathered.

Harry drew the horses forward, having forsaken the stream for the narrow path that cut alongside it. It was a thin trail of dirt framed on either side by stringy grass. The path had clearly been formed by repeated use, but Min didn't know if it was humans or animals who had made it. The way their luck had been so far, they'd follow the path all the way to a rabbit warren. Which a horse would then step in and snap a leg.

"Come on, kid," Min said to Kazimir as the boy swayed alarmingly. "Hang in there."

Kazimir made a small noise that might have been an answer and might have been a fluke.

"Min!" Harry called out from ahead, his voice thin with excitement. "Min, look!"

In front of them, in a clearing just above the bank of the creek, was a dwelling. It wasn't much more than a hut, Min supposed, and the rush of relief that flooded through him—shelter, safety, *sanctuary*—was absurd. What were a thatched roof and a wooden door to the Hidden Lord?

Still. Better than dying in the dirt, Min supposed.

Slightly.

Harry tugged on the reins of the horses, urging them toward the dour little hut.

"Hello?" he called as they approached. "Hello?"

Harry looped the reins around a scrubby bush and darted toward the door of the hut. He pushed it open—"Hello?"—and stepped inside.

Min's shoulders ached from keeping Kazimir more or less upright in the saddle, and with every passing minute, Kazimir was leaning more heavily to the side.

"It's empty!" Harry called out.

"Let's get you down," Min said to Kazimir, encouraging him to slip farther over until he was essentially breaking the boy's fall. The horse huffed and danced sideways a little as Min braced himself under Kazimir's weight. He slung the boy's arm across his shoulders, gripping his wrist tightly to hold it in place, and put his other arm around his waist. He shuffled toward the hut while Harry hurried back to see to the horses.

The hut was small and dark. It took a moment for Min's eyes to adjust before the light slanting through the gaps in the walls—*wonderful*—illuminated the place enough for Min to get a sense of it. It was a single room only, and not the dwelling he'd initially taken it for. The smell was the first thing that gave it away: stale and smoky and *meaty*. The dirt floor had been dug into a firepit that took up most of the space, and a series of hooks hung from a crosshatch of narrow beams inside the pitched roof. It wasn't a hut at all. It was a smokehouse. Judging from the mass of spiders' webs in the roof, it hadn't been used in some time. The wood in the fire pit had long ago burned into ashes. Still, spending the night here was a slightly better option than spending it in the open.

Surviving the night… well, that was another matter entirely.

Min eased Kazimir down onto the ground, where he curled up like a pill bug. Min knelt beside him and pressed a hand to his forehead. He was burning up.

"Kazimir," he said. "Kazimir?"

Kazimir snuffled and blinked his eyes slowly open.

Min slid his fingers down the boy's hot neck and felt his pulse beating rapidly under his touch. He pinched the edges of Kazimir's shirt and pulled them up, threading them through the collar. Putting some small barrier between Kazimir's skin and the iron that burned him. He hoped it was enough.

Kazimir blinked again.

"Better?" Min asked.

Kazimir nodded, his eyes slipping closed once more.

Harry stepped inside the hut, dragging their saddlebags. "How is he?"

"Not dead," Min said, which seemed to be the best any of them could wish for, frankly.

"I'm sorry, Min," Harry said softly. "For everything."

"Don't," Min told him, sitting down on the floor and stretching his legs out. "Apologies are for lesser men than us."

Harry's mouth quirked in a quick grin, and he settled down beside him.

Min leaned against the wall and drew Kazimir closer. He let the boy curl into him and rest his head on his thigh. He kept one hand on the iron collar, making sure the fabric of Kazimir's shirt stayed in place. Harry sat close, their shoulders bumping, until Min relented and put an arm around him.

"There are worse things to die for than love, I suppose," Min said at last.

Harry nodded.

"Not that I'd know," he added.

He wondered, as the darkness began to settle, if that was something he ought to regret.

MIN HAD more or less resigned himself to certain death and had just started to doze off when he felt Kazimir move. He glanced down. In the slanted lines of moonlight cutting through the gaps in the wall of the hut,

Kazimir seemed almost to glow. Possibly it was his pale complexion, and possibly it was something to do with his fae blood.

"You're out of your depth here, aren't you?" Kazimir asked, his voice a little rough with sleep.

"Story of my life," Min told him softly, aware that Harry was asleep against his shoulder. "And, apparently, my death."

"Mine too." There was a touch of amusement in Kazimir's regretful tone.

Min wondered if at some point he ought to stop carding his fingers through the curls behind the boy's ear. But then, he wasn't getting any complaints, and there was something about the repetitive gesture he found soothing.

Kazimir's shirt and kirtle had ridden up, and Min gazed down at his pale hip. He caught a glimpse of something underneath the scrunched-up fabric. Lines inked into skin. "Is that a tattoo?"

Kazimir shifted, tugging his shirt up to look. "Mmm. It's my cat."

"You have a tattoo of your cat?"

Kazimir frowned and blinked up at him. He pulled his shirt back into place. "No. The tattoo is a cat, I mean, and it's mine. So it's my cat."

"Fair enough," Min allowed. "Less annoying than the real thing."

"I wouldn't know." Kazimir finally moved, shifting his head off Min's thigh and sitting up. He leaned back against the wall and rolled his shoulders.

"Are you feeling better?" Min asked.

Kazimir nodded. "It helps, I think, not to have it touching my skin."

Min pressed his lips together tightly.

Kazimir's expression seemed soft in the gloom. "I know you're not doing it to be cruel."

Min met his gaze. "That's irrelevant, don't you think?"

Kazimir's brows drew together in a slight frown. "Motive is never irrelevant."

"It is, actually," Min said. "Motive is the most irrelevant thing in this entire scenario. You should know that better than anyone. You're the one being abducted, after all. Besides, don't fool yourself. If I wasn't doing this for Harry, I might have done it for the money."

"Would you really?"

Min sighed. "Maybe not *this* job. I didn't like the smell of it from the start. For good reason, right?"

Kazimir's mouth twitched in a quick, bitter smile.

"But people living in poverty can't afford luxuries," Min told him. "And foremost amongst those luxuries is conventional morality."

Kazimir shifted slightly and peered at him intently. "You have a gentleman's name, though?"

"I did not come by that honestly," Min told him with a grin.

"What do you mean?"

"My mother is a whore," Min said. "There's a certain tradition in her particular circle to take the name of their first paying customer. Decourcey it was. She swears it was the lord of the House himself, but my money's always been on some younger bastard by-blow. It makes no difference to me, certainly. Whichever Decourcey he was, he had no input into my existence. I came along years later." He smiled at Kazimir's wide eyes. "So, there you are. People like me pick up our names where we find them. Whereas you, Kazimir, discarded yours for a lesser one."

"Stone is a hedgewitch's name," Kazimir said, stumbling over the words a little. "A-a name from nature."

"You were never a hedgewitch, though."

"I wanted to be one." Kazimir scratched his scalp and then sighed. "I wanted to be one."

"Enough to give away the name of your House?"

"They never wanted me," Kazimir said.

"They want you now."

Kazimir huffed and shook his head. "Now I'm some use to them. My grandfather wouldn't even look at me when I was a child. All of my cousins called him Grandfather. I had to call him *my lord*."

Min had no answer to that.

"I don't know why he thinks I am useful to him," Kazimir said, frowning into the gloom and chewing his bottom lip. "It doesn't matter, does it? As soon as he finds out what I am, he'll keep me in iron for the rest of my life."

"There you go again," Min said. "Assuming we won't die tonight."

Kazimir gave him a sideways look. "You have a strange way of looking on the bright side, Aramin Decourcey."

"You're not the first to comment on it," Min said. "And it's Min, by the way."

"Kaz," Kazimir replied with a slight smile.

They settled into silence as the night drew on.

FIREFLIES, MIN thought as he jolted awake with a start.

The tiny dancing lights froze as Min moved, and Min's blood turned to ice. He could make out figures in the soft green lights. Sharp faces, clawed hands, and the rapid burr and whirr of dragonfly wings. There were two of them to begin with, and then those two dipped close together, and when their light parted again, there was a third creature with them, bobbing around like a wasp in a bottle.

Beside him, Min heard Harry's breath catch.

The fae made chattering, clicking noises like insects and floated closer to them. To Kazimir. Their green light illuminated the pale planes of his face and was reflected in his dark eyes. As Min watched, he thrust his hand into one of the saddlebags and pulled it out again. Then he opened his fist and scattered something all over the dirt floor. For a moment Min wondered if the iron had somehow failed and the boy was attempting to use his Gift, but then he realized what the tiny pale flecks on the floor were: oats. Oats for the horses.

The tiny fae buzzed down toward the scattered oats, needle-sharp teeth clicking as they chattered away.

"Count them," Kazimir said, his voice shaking.

The fae buzzed like angry bees, and Min remembered old stories of impossible tasks the fae were compelled to attempt if asked. Hammering a curly hair into straightness, making a rope out of ashes, carrying water in a sieve. He just wasn't sure how impossible a handful of oats was to count. The fae seemed to be having no problems, until Kazimir leaned down close to the ground and blew at the oats, enough to send them scattering again.

The little fae flashed toward him, green light pulsing, and hovered close to his face.

"Count," he rasped.

Their wings whirred as they buzzed around the tiny space, jostling into one another and bouncing away again.

Min heard the scrape of another saddlebag on the dirt floor as Harry dragged it closer. One of the fae, no doubt suspecting further treachery, zipped toward him, and Harry held up his bundle of rowan twigs. The fae made a tiny sound that seemed almost incensed, and flitted back toward its fellows again.

Shit.

Was it possible this was *working*?

Were they really defending themselves from the fae with iron, twigs, and *oats*? Or at least the fae equivalent of insects, because these creatures were nothing like the ones Min had glimpsed in Anhaga, tall and stately and terrifying.

Harry flung another handful of oats to the ground.

"Count," Kazimir said again to the furious little creatures.

Count.

Count.

Count.

Min lost all track of time. He felt as though he was trapped in some nightmare. Between them, Kazimir and Harry kept blowing the oats around or adding to them. Once, Harry darted out a pale hand and stole some back while the tiny fae shrieked at him in outrage. Min felt as though he was caught in some intricate balancing act with no end in sight and that a stumble was inevitable. How much longer could they last? And what would happen if the fae completed their task?

It took Min a long while to notice dawn was creeping in, softening the brilliant moonlight into muted tones of gray. The light of the fae seemed dimmer as the dawn slowly brightened. When the first glimmers of sunlight filtered in through the walls, the little fae seemed to fade suddenly. They swooped toward Kazimir, chirping and gesturing wildly, tiny faces pulled into fierce expressions, and then, abruptly, they were gone.

Outside, Min heard birdsong.

"Holy *fuck*," Harry said at last, his voice pitched higher than usual.

"We should go," Kazimir said. "Before the Hidden Lord learns we were here."

Min blinked at the oats scattered on the floor. "I think it's highly likely that he already knows, don't you?"

"Those were wisps," Kazimir said. "Only fools believe the words of wisps."

Min felt a sudden chill. To his knowledge only the most Gifted sorcerers in the Iron Tower could speak with any certainty about the fae. To hear Kazimir announce it so casually, as though it were something everyone knew, was unsettling. It reminded him that not only was Kazimir a necromancer, a practitioner of the darkest sides of the arcane arts, but he was also part fae. Min wondered if his knowledge of the fae had been obtained from the moans of the mouthless dead or if it was blood-born. Both were terrifying in their own way.

Harry climbed to his feet first and held his hand down to pull Kazimir up. Kazimir's shirt and kirtle rode up a little as he stood, and Min caught a glimpse of the cat tattooed on his hip. Its tail trailed around to Kazimir's lower back, and—perhaps it was in part a trick of the early morning light—Min swore it flicked a little from side to side as Kazimir stood and his muscles shifted under his skin.

Min's knees ached as he stood, and he rolled his shoulders to ease the stiffness in them. Then, laden with saddlebags, they headed outside to see if the horses were still there or if the fae had driven them off in the night.

To Min's relief, they were still there, reins tied around the scrubby bushes outside the hut.

They seemed unharmed and unfazed, but, Min saw, sometime during the night tiny fingers had woven pretty little flowers into their manes.

THEY STOPPED at the place where the road forded the creek and let the horses drink. Harry picked the tiny flowers from his horse's mane and let them fly away on the breeze.

"Flowers," he said when Min caught him watching. He wrinkled his nose and shrugged his skinny shoulders. "I wasn't expecting flowers."

Min snorted. For all they knew, the fae liked to decorate their victims before tearing them to shreds with their teeth and claws.

Kazimir squatted down by the creek and reached out to dip his hands in the water. His wrists were still red and raw from yesterday's iron shackles. He cupped his hands and raised them to wash. Water slid down his face, his throat, catching the sunlight and making his pale skin gleam.

"Does it still hurt?" Min asked him in a low voice.

Kazimir blinked up at him, droplets glistening like tears in his dark lashes. "What?"

"The collar."

"A little." Kazimir shrugged. "It's not so bad if I keep my shirt pulled through."

Min hated the guilt that rose up in him. He nodded and turned his gaze away. When he looked back, Kazimir was holding a small black feather by the quill between his thumb and forefinger, twisting it around. As Min watched he flicked it into the creek, and the shallow water carried it away.

THEY HAD been riding for hours when Harry spotted the riders—or at least the haze of dust they conjured on the road ahead.

"Min!" he called, twisting around in the saddle.

Min straightened up and peered ahead.

Fear twisted in Min's gut. Had the fae discovered them after all? The riders were approaching from the south, but what was geography to the fae? They'd proved yesterday that the shadow realm operated under none of the usual rules. Direction and distance were as meaningless to the fae and to their world as they were in those places shaped by dreams.

The knot in Min's stomach loosened as he saw the glint of sunlight on graying hair. As the riders drew closer, Robert Sabadine's sharp profile became clearer.

"It's Sabadine!" Harry called back, the relief in his tone swamped quickly by a guilty, hangdog expression as he looked at Kazimir.

Kazimir's heart beat fast under Min's palm. When had he slipped his hand higher? Min was shocked when Kazimir raised his own hand and curled his trembling fingers around Min's palm. A futile gesture. An unbearably pathetic one. What a miserable fucking life Kazimir had stretching out ahead of him if he sought comfort from his kidnapper in this moment.

Kazimir must have realized it too. He dropped his hand quickly.

"Decourcey!" Robert called as he and his men drew close. "We thought you must be dead."

"Not dead," Min said, resisting the urge to tighten his grip on Kazimir. "Just detoured."

Robert nodded, reining his horse in. He looked Kazimir up and down, some expression that Min couldn't read crossing his face before he schooled his features. "Kazimir?"

Min could feel Kazimir shaking as he lifted his chin to meet his uncle's gaze.

"You will ride with me," Robert said.

For a moment Kazimir didn't move, and Min thought he would refuse. And then he was slipping awkwardly down onto the dusty road, fingers digging into Min's thigh to steady himself.

Robert hauled him up onto his horse as though he was no more than a chattel. Which, well. Min had no right to judge Robert for that when he was just as much a part of the ugly transaction, did he?

Robert said something in an undertone to Kazimir that Min didn't catch. Kazimir's scruffy curls bounced a little as he nodded in response. He kept his head bowed.

Robert and his men turned their horses and pointed the way south again.

Min and Harry trailed along behind them.

There was nothing to say.

There was nothing to be done but hope to hell they made it back to Pran tonight and then Amberwich. And then Min could demand Edward Sabadine have his sorcerer remove the curse mark from Harry's cheek, they could put this whole sordid business behind them, and Min could fall into a barrel of beer for a week and not come out until he'd forgotten all about Kazimir Stone and the misery Min had helped heap upon him.

The sooner Anhaga was well and truly behind him, the better.

Min slouched in the saddle as they headed south and didn't dare look over at Harry.

He could hear him sniffling for miles.

CHAPTER 8

MIN WAS almost shocked when dusk found them not at the creek ford with its wind-twisted trees, but at the Sabadines' manor house outside of Pran. Like the first time they had approached the manor, the gathering dusk urged the company faster, and like the first time, there were servants waiting to take their horses.

Harry and Min dug their belongings out of the saddlebags and were amongst the last of the men to enter the house before the doors were bolted.

The small entry hall was illuminated by candlelight.

"This way, sirs," a servant woman said and drew them up the stairs. Min tried to catch a glimpse of Robert and Kazimir, but they had already vanished somewhere else into the house. The woman led them along to the same bedroom they had shared the last time they had stayed here.

"Master Robert requests you join him for dinner when you are ready," the woman said, looking their travel-stained figures up and down pointedly. "I shall send up hot water."

"Thank you," Min said, flashing her his most rakish smile and bowing slightly.

That seemed to mollify her somewhat, or at least fluster her. She retreated pink-cheeked.

Harry slumped down onto the bed, tugging his boots off. "Fuckers."

Min didn't know if he was talking about his boots, about the Sabadines, the fae, or the universe in general. With Harry it was sometimes better not to ask.

Min sat down beside him and pulled his own boots off. Then he stood and shoved his breeches down, and sat again to unlace his tunic. He sat around in nothing but his shirt until a boy came with the promised hot water, then pulled that off and began to scrub himself down. He stank of sweat and dust, and *horse*. Then, the water dripping from him, he rummaged through his things for some clothes that, although not clean exactly, were at least a little less ripe.

When he was finally dressed, Harry was washing, his skinny body angled awkwardly away from Min's gaze. Min lay on the bed and flung his arm over his eyes.

"So, we're alive," he said.

Harry snorted. "So far."

Clever boy. No way were they out of the figurative woods yet. Edward Sabadine seemed like the exact sort of asshole who'd go back on his word, just because he could. It made Min uneasy that he had no leverage over the old man now Kazimir had been delivered into Robert's custody. It had rankled from the beginning, though. Min hated to be powerless, precisely because men like Edward Sabadine relished it so very much.

Min heard Harry drop the washing cloth back into the basin.

"We're doing a lot better than I thought we would," Min said.

"Tell that to Kaz."

Min almost pulled his arm away from his face. "Harry. Don't."

Clothing rustled, and then the thin mattress dipped, and Harry jabbed a finger into Min's ribs. Min lowered his arm. Harry's wide eyes were full of misery.

"Harry, someone has to lose," Min said. "You or Kazimir. And it's not going to be you. Fuck them, but it's not to be you."

Harry nodded, his mouth pressed into a trembling line. "It's not *fair*, though, Min."

He sounded so young that Min's heart clenched.

Min sat up. "Come on, let's go and eat."

He kept a hand on Harry's shoulder all the way down the stairs.

MIN HADN'T been expecting a family dinner. Robert Sabadine sat at the head of the table, with Talys on his left and Kazimir on his right. There were two more places set, one on either side of the younger Sabadines.

Well, how fucking awkward.

Min steered Harry firmly in Kazimir's direction and took the seat next to Talys himself. She looked at him almost reproachfully. Fucking teenagers. It was getting too close to Harry that had got them all in this damn mess to begin with.

Min didn't need to glance at Harry to know he was looking at Talys with hopeless longing. He turned his gaze on Kazimir instead. Kazimir was wearing a clean white shirt, with the edges pulled up through the iron collar like a ruff. He sat with his hands folded on his lap, his eyes downturned, and didn't look at Min. Min thought of the boy from the hut last night, eyes bright with fear, voice shaking, who still found the courage to demand the wisps count. Perhaps the shadow realm was a dreamscape after all; there seemed to be no trace of that boy in the Kazimir who sat across from him now.

"Decourcey," Robert said with a nod.

Min nodded back.

A small parade of servants brought dinner: a cabbage and leek pottage, roast chicken, and turnips and carrots glazed with honey. The wine was thin but sweet and tasted of rose hips. Min couldn't decide if this was how the rich ate or how country people ate. Possibly it was a combination of both.

Robert sipped his wine. "Kazimir didn't give you any trouble?"

"Not at all," Min lied pleasantly.

Robert gestured at his nephew vaguely. "And the iron?"

"A precaution," Min said, stabbing a chunk of carrot with his fork. "Even a common hedgewitch might have a few nasty tricks up his sleeve."

Kazimir raised his gaze at that and met Min's.

Harry said nothing. Good boy.

Let the Sabadines discover Kazimir's necromancy themselves. They'd kept enough secrets from Min.

"And because of his fae blood, of course," Min added with a lazy smirk.

Robert's expression shuttered.

"Ears like those," Min said. "They stand out like the balls on a dog. Still, it might have been useful for me to know something like that before I went to Anhaga."

"His blood is irrelevant," Robert said.

Min doubted that very much, actually. Not when the fae had stopped at Kallick's door every night on their eerie ride through Anhaga. "Is it?"

He gave his fork a jaunty twirl. "I suppose I'd tell myself the same thing, in your shoes."

It was unfair, probably, to needle Robert about the fact he was marrying his own nephew when Kazimir was listening as well, but when was Min going to get the chance otherwise? He met Kazimir's dark gaze and felt queasy guilt stirring in his gut.

"It is irrelevant," Robert said, a hard enough edge to his voice that Min figured it was time to shut his mouth. Min was a slow learner at times, but he usually got there in the end.

In the silence that followed, Talys cleared her throat and leaned across the table toward Kazimir. "Cousin, I hope—"

"Don't call him that," Robert snapped.

Talys's eyes widened, and she sat back quickly. Min had the impression her father rarely took such a harsh tone with her. He could see the moment her surprise transformed into mulishness. She set her fork down and jutted out her jaw. "What shall I call him, then? *Stepfather*?"

Oh yes. Min could see why Harry had fallen so hard for this girl. She was clearly his mouthy, disrespectful soul mate.

Robert slammed down his knife and stood so quickly that for a moment his chair seemed in danger of toppling. He cast a withering look at Kazimir before turning his icy gaze on Talys. "You will not speak *of* him, and you will not speak *to* him. He is no family of yours. He is nothing more than the spawn of the creature that raped my sister."

He flung his napkin down on the table and stormed from the room.

The door slammed shut behind him.

"Well then," Min said awkwardly. "I can see why you didn't want to come home."

Kazimir didn't reply. He sat, his head bowed, while tears ran down his cheeks.

"YOU'RE SUCH an asshole, Min," Harry said as they climbed the stairs to the bedroom.

"I am very aware of that, thank you."

Dinner hadn't lasted long after Robert's abrupt departure. Within moments servants had appeared to escort Kazimir and Talys away. There had been no offer of dessert.

"You shouldn't have said that thing about blood. I know you hate the Sabadines, but making Robert angry will just make things worse for Kaz!"

Min sighed. "Yes, thank you again, Harry. I do realize that now."

When they entered their room, Harry closed the door behind them and rounded on Min quickly. Min had expected to see anger blazing in the boy's eyes. Not… not something that was quite so calculating and curious.

"You didn't tell Robert that Kaz is a necromancer."

"Why should I? He didn't tell us he was fae."

Harry narrowed his eyes. When he spoke, his tone was thoughtful. "You want him to surprise them. You want him to get out of this somehow."

"I don't," Min said. "But so what if I did? What he does and doesn't do is their problem, just as soon as we get that curse mark off you."

"You *hate* the Gifted."

"Maybe I hate the Sabadines more." Min sat down on the bed and eased his boots off. "Anyway, what does it matter? They never wanted him back for his hedgewitch powers. They wanted him for his fae blood, and they'll keep him in iron because of it. He won't be given another chance to reanimate the dead or whatever else it is necromancers do."

"It's not *fair*, Min."

Min didn't reply to that. Of course it wasn't fair. And of course Harry already knew that. He didn't need Min to confirm it or, worse, to demand he grow the fuck up. Min had no idea where Harry had picked up the notion that life ought to be fair or just in any way—his damn books, probably—but he wasn't going to be the one to knock the last of the shine off Harry's improbable naivety. Life was already proving itself well and truly up to the task.

He lay down, and Harry flopped onto the bed beside him.

"It's not Kaz's fault he's a necromancer," Harry said at last. "People don't choose their Gifts. It's not his fault he's half fae either."

"No, it's not his fault," Min agreed, although it seemed the sort of crime Robert Sabadine would make him pay for. Bad enough that Kazimir was being forced into an incestuous marriage with the man, but Robert clearly hated him as well. Min wondered if the best Kazimir could hope for was cold indifference from his uncle.

"I hate them," Harry muttered. "I hate the Sabadines."

Min smiled slightly at that, because he knew it wasn't entirely true. There was one Sabadine at least that Harry didn't hate. And, Min suspected, if Harry had made it all the way to Anhaga and back, curse mark burned into his cheek, and hadn't managed to summon up any resentment at all for Talys Sabadine, he doubted there was very little that could change that now.

"Go to sleep, Harry," Min said, because there was nothing else to say.

MIN DREAMED he was back in Anhaga, this time on one of the fishing boats in the harbor. He looked up at the village clinging to the cliff face like a tick on a dog and tried to see Kallick's house. It was impossible, though, with the boat rocking and rocking and rocking....

Min opened his eyes. "Oh, for *fuck's* sake!"

Two faces peered back at him in the gloom.

"I don't have many rules, Harry," Min said. "But if I did, I like to think that fucking a Sabadine under her father's roof while sharing a bed with me would be somewhere at the top of the list. I also like to think it would go without saying, but, well, here we all are."

"We were just talking!" Harry whispered indignantly.

Min snorted. "Next time take your hand out of her underwear before you try and feed me that bullshit." He rolled away from them and rose to his feet. "I'm going for a walk. When I get back, you'd better be alone, Harry."

He was sure they were sharing a soulful gaze in the dark.

"Because," Min said, tugging his tunic on over his shirt, "now we've brought Kazimir back to the warm embrace of his loving family, not only do we have no actual leverage left to make sure they lift your curse, there is also no reason to stop her father from slitting your throat if he finds her in bed with you." He shot Harry an intense glare that he knew was wasted in the darkness. "But I'm sure you already thought of that."

He left them whispering frantically to each other and slipped outside the room.

The house was dark, and Min worked his way carefully toward the stairs. His thoughts drifted toward Kaz, and he wondered where the boy was sleeping. If he was sleeping. A knot of guilt as heavy as lead sat in his stomach. The guilt was to be expected. Min would learn to live with it, and gladly, as long as Harry survived this. And yes, perhaps there was a small part of him that hoped Kaz could somehow escape the clutches of his family. It was out of Min's hands, in any case.

Min felt his way downstairs.

Of course, the guilt of handing Kaz over to the Sabadines might actually be negligible compared to the guilt of knowingly unleashing a necromancer onto Amberwich if Kaz did find some way to slip his iron chains, but Min couldn't bring himself to care. If Kaz did somehow manage to slaughter the entire Sabadine family, good luck to him. Min was sure the king's sorcerers could band together and take him down before he came after anyone else. Anyone who, say, might have helped in that whole messy abduction thing.

Besides, after seeing Kaz crying at dinner, it was somewhat difficult to imagine him as a crazed necromancer, filled with darkness and flame and burning with the need to take bloodthirsty vengeance. Not exactly impossible, but somewhat difficult.

Min probably wouldn't feel so blasé about the possibility if he weren't a void.

A faint glow of flickering light came from the dining room. Min turned and climbed the steps again. He had no wish to disturb whoever was still awake.

He reached the top of the stairs and saw a slim figure darting away in the darkness: Talys, with her robe billowing around her as she moved. She looked a little like a wraith, or some insubstantial creature conjured from mist and winter's breath.

Min took a step forward and was almost brought down by the cat that suddenly curled around his ankles.

When his heart had stopped trying to hammer its way out of his chest, Min bent down and scooped the cat up. He regarded it narrowly in the gloom. "Is there nothing in this house that doesn't want to kill me?"

The cat was gray. Most cats were gray in the darkness, Min supposed. He saw patches of what might be color under a better light. A speckled little tortoiseshell, possibly. Its rib cage rumbled under his fingers.

Min set it down again. "Go on. Piss off."

The cat gave a plaintive mewl and vanished down the stairs.

Min was about to return to the room he shared with Harry when he saw a faint glimmer of light spilling from underneath a door at the end of the passageway. His breath caught and his skin prickled before he realized this was nothing more than ordinary candlelight and not the same eldritch light that heralded the presence of fae magic.

The light grew for a moment, and Min saw a figure silhouetted briefly in the doorway before the door was closed again. Robert Sabadine. There was no mistaking the way the man carried himself.

Sons of Rus. The passageway was busy enough tonight to feature in a particularly bawdy comedy about young bed-hopping wives, ardent student lodgers, and oblivious old cuckolds. Any moment now someone would wave their naked ass at the laughing audience.

Min stood still in the darkness, silent and unmoving—a particular skill of his honed over years of practicing burglary—and waited until Robert vanished. Fortunately in the opposite direction of Min. There was skill, but there was also luck.

Min was about to return to the room he shared with Harry when he was brought up short by the sound of a muffled sob.

Fuck.

Min treaded quietly down the passageway, forcing his trepidation away. He was no doubt stupid for seeking out Kazimir now, and Min was usually the opposite of stupid, but… but he was *guilty*. And guilt was as strange and uncomfortable to him as this total lack of common sense.

"Kaz?" he asked in a whisper, twisting the latch and pushing the door open.

Kazimir was lying in his narrow bed, arms at his side, wide eyes fixed on the ceiling. A lamp burned on the little table beside the bed. The room was otherwise bare and even smaller than the guest room Min shared with Harry.

"Kaz?" he asked again.

Kazimir turned his head slowly. His dark eyes shone, and his cheeks were damp. His throat bobbed as he swallowed, and then he looked back at the ceiling again.

"What did he do?" Min asked, hating himself as soon as the question was out. Because Kaz could regale him with a litany of crimes against Robert Sabadine, and Min could do nothing about it except share in the blame. Still, he stepped fully inside the room and closed the door again.

Kazimir turned his head again and blinked at Min. "Did you ever think you had a destiny?"

Min couldn't help his sudden smile. "No."

"Not ever?"

"Only children believe that," Min said. "Children, and lovesick teenagers, and possibly men born in powerful Houses."

Kaz's smile was brief. "Oh, so you're letting me have it on a technicality?"

Min snorted.

"And which am I?" Kaz asked. "A child or a man born in a powerful House?"

"Not a lovesick teenager?" Min asked, stepping closer to the bed.

"No." Kaz quirked his mouth in something not quite a smile.

"Well, you're half Sabadine, half fae, and you're a necromancer," Min said. "On the balance of all that, how can you not have a destiny?"

"I think that rather than a destiny of my own, I'm to be a footnote to my grandfather's." Kaz exhaled slowly. "It would be better, I think, if my uncle didn't hate me."

"Yes," Min agreed quietly.

"He must have loved his sister very much," Kaz murmured. He shifted slightly, and Min heard the rattle of a chain. Of course. Of course Robert had chained the boy to the bed to keep him from running, although Min knew there was no way he would. Not with the threat of the fae hanging over him. Kaz was a little fox caught between two traps, and this one just happened to be the less terrible. "I wonder if she would have loved me."

Min had no answer for that.

"I used to watch them from my window," Kaz said, a wistful tone creeping into his voice. "Mothers and children."

"Not all mothers are the same."

Kaz's brow furrowed. "Are you saying that because your mother is a, um, a...."

"A whore," Min said with a soundless laugh. "You can say the word, Kaz. And no. That's not the reason. I don't hate that she's a whore. It put food in my belly when I was a squalling little brat, after all."

Kaz's eyes widened. "I meant no offense."

"I took none," Min assured him, and for a while they regarded each other in the silence.

In that moment the shutters rattled suddenly, and Kaz all but flew out of bed, only to be brought up short by the chain connected to the iron band around his neck. He made a choking sound and dropped to his knees. Min hurried forward to support him; the boy could hang himself if he wasn't careful.

He knelt in front of Kaz, shuffled him back a few inches to put some slack in the chain, and put his hands on his shoulders to ease him into a more upright position. He stared over Kaz's shoulder at the window, at the rattling shutters, and willed himself to believe it was nothing more than the wind.

"Just the wind," he said with more confidence than he felt.

"The wind," Kaz echoed back, his breath hot against Min's throat.

"The wind," Min promised him, and how was one of his hands now at the nape of Kaz's neck, fingers twisting elflocks into his dark curls? He eased his hand away, heart beating fast, and forced a smile. "Go to bed, Kaz. Get some sleep."

Kaz couldn't quite meet his eyes. He nodded and shuffled on his knees back toward the bed. He climbed back onto the frame, chain clanking and straw in the mattress rustling, and tugged the blankets over him.

"Good night," Min said and then, seized by a rush of sudden dangerous affection for the boy, reached into his shirt to withdraw the rowan twigs Talys had given him and Harry. He still doubted their power. Certainly the wisps hadn't liked them, but it had hardly driven them away. Still. Min crossed to the window and set the twigs on the latch of the shutter.

"Thank you," Kaz whispered.

Min nodded and left the room. He closed the door carefully behind him.

"WHERE THE hell have you been?" Harry muttered when Min finally crawled back into bed. Then he wrinkled his nose, and his expression softened into something like sympathy. "Oh."

Min ignored him.

It didn't stop Harry from giving him a consoling pat on the shoulder and curling up closer than he usually did.

Min didn't have the energy or the inclination to tell Harry that he had it wrong.

Totally and *utterly* wrong.

CHAPTER 9

THE STORM broke sometime before dawn. The wind bashed at the doors and shutters of the manor house, and the rain lashed against the roof. Min, woken by a sharp crack of thunder that seemed to shake the house to its foundations, lay awake and watched as the black of night gave way fraction by fraction to a bleak, dark day. At last, when it became apparent that the day would grow no brighter anytime soon, Min climbed out of bed and dressed.

Harry snored on, curled up in a lump under the blankets, his head wedged under a pillow.

Min left the room and headed down the dark passageway toward the stairs. The day was cold too, colder than yesterday, and Min's fears seemed to seek out all the shadowed corners of the house and multiply rapidly. The gloom was oppressive. Laden. Min half expected a knot of tangled little wisps to buzz out of the darkness, sharp little teeth and claws bared, or, worse, the Hidden Lord himself, his face terrible and beautiful in all its cold-blooded glory.

He hurried down the steps, cursing his own imagination.

Like any smart stray, Min was drawn to the warmth of the kitchens and to the smell of baking bread. A maid shooed him away, but not before he helped himself to a still-hot knot of bread. He ate half at once and, accustomed to putting something aside for later—or for Harry, if he was feeling charitable—slipped the other half of the roll between his undershirt and his tunic. He headed farther into the house, the bread cooling slowly between his clothes.

The lamps in the library were lighted, tiny flames flickering away behind the small panes. Robert Sabadine, as immaculately presented as always, stood leaning over the table in the center of the room studying papers, like a warlord strategizing over a map.

"Do we attack the Iron Tower at dawn?" Min asked.

Robert looked up sharply.

"A joke," Min said mildly.

"Treason is no joke."

"And a fish is no bird," Min said agreeably.

Robert straightened up and rolled his shoulders. "What the hell are you even talking about?"

"Harmless nonsense," Min said. "You should give it a try once in a while. It does wonders for the humors."

Robert looked him up and down. "I cannot decide if you are a snake or a fool."

Min shrugged. "And you would have had no reason to ever ponder such mysteries if your family hadn't put a curse mark on my nephew."

Robert's mouth turned down at the corners. "Your guttersnipe nephew was found in my daughter's bedroom."

Min raised his eyebrows. "Well, perhaps your daughter shouldn't have been so eager to open her—" He gave Robert a moment to bristle. "—*window*."

Robert stared at him, the moment taut with tension, and then shook his head. "You will find my humors more balanced than you think. I am not so easy to rile as you suppose." His gaze was steely. "And you, sir, are a fool."

Wrong, Min thought. *I am a snake.* But he smiled and bowed slightly. "We leave for Amberwich today, then?"

"I would rather wait and see if the weather passes."

"Indeed," Min said. "But I would rather return home a drenched rat with a living nephew than bone-dry and bereft."

Robert's mouth tightened like a cat's bum. "There is still over a sennight until the full moon."

"Yes," Min said, "but I would rather the skein runs out of thread at the end of the matter, not the middle. In my line of work, sir, I like to press what advantages I have. And I have so few in this case that I would prefer not squander that of time. Particularly when time means nothing to the Hidden Lord."

Robert held his stare for a moment. "I have not met many men who can say his name without flinching."

Min shrugged. "Perhaps you have not met as many men as you think."

Was that a hint of a smile that twitched at the corner of Robert's mouth? Doubtful. It was probably indigestion. Men like Robert Sabadine were most likely prone to all sorts of digestive ailments. A side effect of being so uptight they couldn't unclench their sphincters in order to take a shit. It was bound to lead to intestinal distress.

"Perhaps." Robert shrugged. "If you wish to leave today, then I will not object."

"Thank you," Min said, and the sentiment was even genuine.

"Make yourself ready, then," Robert said, and turned his attention back to the papers he had been perusing before Min's interruption.

Min knew a dismissal when he heard one.

He turned on his heel and headed for the stairs again.

He ate the rest of his bread roll on the way. Harry could beg for his own.

IF MIN had thought riding a horse a wretched enough experience in good weather, then the misery of it was multiplied a thousandfold when it was pissing down rain. He was cold and wet. His cloak had barely managed to keep the rain off him for a few minutes before it was soaked through, and now it was just an added weight dragging at him. His ass made a squelching sound against the saddle every time the horse took a step forward, and every one of Min's muscles was tense. His seat felt twice as uncertain as it normally did with the leather slippery underneath him, and the horse, surefooted as a mountain goat in dry weather, skidded every few steps as the road did its damnedest to wash away under the assault of the rain.

Somehow, Kaz was riding next to him. His balancing act was even more precarious than Min's: the boy's wrists were lashed to the reins. If he were to fall, he'd be dragged. It also left him unable to brush the rain out of his eyes. His hood was pulled forward, the fabric stuck to his forehead, and the water ran off the tip of his nose and the bow of his mouth as if he were a gargoyle perched on the roof of a shrine. He squeezed his eyes shut and shook his head every few moments, trying to shake the water free.

Min looked away.

It was very easy to hate himself for his part in relieving Kaz of his freedom, but it was even easier to hate the Sabadines. Poisonous as vipers, the lot of them.

The rain grew heavier. It fell around them in a thick, gray shroud that hid the world. Even the sound of the horses' hooves splashing in the mud, and the grunts and the coughs of the men riding them, were muted by the rain. It was dark. It felt more like night than day. Min twisted around once in the saddle to see if he could tell how far they'd ridden from the manor, but all he saw was rain. It was impossible to tell if they'd ridden half a mile or several leagues. Harry, his horse keeping close behind Min's, was wearing a saddle blanket over his head like a shawl, for all the good it did him. As far as Min could tell, he was as soaking wet as the rest of them. Talys was riding beside Harry, something Min was sure her father would disapprove of if he weren't currently attempting to lead them on this miserable slog through the mud. Her wet hood was plastered to her head, and her mouth was pressed into a thin line. She appeared more stoic than peevish, unlike Harry. She rode with her spine straight and her shoulders back. A soldier's stance, Min thought, like her father's. He could imagine her holding her own in a battle.

Min had grown up surrounded by women. He wasn't enough of a fool to underestimate them.

A few of Robert Sabadine's household men brought up the rear—a sodden little vanguard. They appeared to Min as insubstantial as ghosts, fading in and out of the curtains of rain.

Min was wet and cold and miserable. He thought longingly of his bed back at the manor house and then cursed himself for his lack of imagination and thought even more longingly of the attic room he and Harry shared back in Amberwich. The old bed was lumpy and the mattress sagged into the middle, which always led to Min and Harry rolling into each other and subsequently fighting with elbows in the middle of the night, but it was warm, and it was free of bugs and lice, which was more than a lot of people had. And each minute now, however miserable, brought Min closer to home. That seemed like a thought worth holding on to.

Home.

It was hard to think of the word without forcing down the unasked-for flash of guilt that accompanied it. Because while Min was looking forward to being back in Amberwich, master of his own fate and king of his own grubby little quarter, Kaz was facing a much unkinder future in Amberwich, wasn't he? He would be bound in iron the rest of his life probably, forced into a marriage with his own uncle, and both of them ground under the heel of Edward Sabadine.

Min stole another look at Kaz, guilt stabbing him when he discovered Kaz looking back. Min turned his face away and stared into the dark shroud of the rain.

Then, in an instant, the world was torn apart.

A burst of light and a crack of sound louder than the crash of iron on iron. Blinding. Deafening. The scream of a horse, although Min wasn't sure if he heard it or if he felt it, and then he was falling, thrown to the muddy ground. A flash of hooves above him, but he rolled away, sliding down into a shallow ditch before scrambling to his feet.

It took a second lightning strike hitting the ground—this one a little farther away—for Min to even realize what had happened.

It was chaos.

His wasn't the only horse that had panicked and unseated its rider—
Shit.

Min darted forward to where Kaz was being flung back and forth like a puppet in the mud. He had fallen, but his wrists were still bound to the horn of the saddle. He was wrenched wildly every time the horse bucked, his cloak and hood flapping around him. He couldn't get his feet under him to remount, and Min was afraid the panicked horse would bolt and drag him, or tumble and crush him.

There was a scrambling throng of men and horses on the muddy road now, and as the ringing in Min's ears slowly faded, he heard Robert Sabadine bellowing orders as he attempted to impose order on the chaos. Typical fucking nobleman.

Min tugged his knife out of his boot, caught Kaz around the waist, and *slashed.*

He really, really hoped that was rope his blade was hacking through, and not muscle and tendon.

Something gave—again, Min really hoped it was rope—and then he and Kaz were tumbling backward into the ditch. Min was blinded for a moment by muddy water. He struggled to sit, one arm still wrapped around Kaz, his hand pressing against his chest. He could feel Kaz's frantic heartbeat and his heaving ribs.

Last time Min had held a boy in his lap like this, the circumstances had been a lot more pleasant. That boy, though? Nowhere near as interesting as this one.

"Are you hurt?" he asked, pressing his mouth close to Kaz's ear to make himself heard above the rain.

Kaz turned his head, leaning into him. "Min, I....." He closed his eyes and shivered.

Min wanted to smile at the idea that the little necromancer was frightened after a brush with death, but he was too cold and too wet and too shaken.

A hundred feet down the road, the lightning-struck tree burned in the rain.

Min was soaked and jittery and cold. He was more scared than he wanted to admit to any man, even to himself, and he just wanted to go home.

It wasn't until Kaz twined his shaking fingers through his that Min realized his wrists were still bound. He caught the rope, the ends ragged where he'd hacked through with his knife, and unwound it slowly from Kaz's wrists. His skin was ripped and abraded and slick with blood. He flexed his hands, though, and then rolled his shoulders, so perhaps nothing was snapped or torn out of place.

Boots splashed down into the ditch, and Min squinted up.

Harry.

A wave of relief flooded over him, followed by a short, sharp burst of recrimination. Harry was family, and Min's first thought should have been of him. But it wasn't enough to make him release his hold on Kaz.

Harry squatted in the ditch beside them while Talys hovered close by. Min didn't trust his shaking legs to stand, and fuck getting back on the road anyway. Let Sabadine and his men kill themselves trying to catch the horses. Min would rather drown in the mud than get close to another mad horse.

There were a hundred ways to justify his crazy dash to save Kaz. What the hell did Min know about horses? Not enough to have a healthy respect for how deadly they could be, probably. And if he hadn't darted in to save Kaz, then where would Harry be? A dead Kaz meant a dead Harry, so of course Min had acted. What other choice had he had? And there was his professional reputation to consider as well. Min was the best thief in the eastern quarter.

A hundred ways to justify it, without once admitting the truth. Min would go to his grave denying it, for what good it did. He was trapped as well. And the truth was, it hadn't been Harry he'd been thinking of when he'd leapt in to save Kaz.

"Cousin," Talys said above the sound of the rain, reaching down a hand toward Kaz. "Let me help you up."

Kaz's fingers twitched in the loose cage of Min's, and Min released him.

Talys drew Kaz to his feet.

"Are you all right?" Harry asked, wide-eyed.

Min nodded.

A horse backed down the road, rearing up, with a man wrenching at its bridle. He pulled it to a halt at last and turned, and Min saw that it was Robert. His hair was plastered to his skull, beaten flat by the rain. His hood hung from his back, water running in a stream from the sodden peak.

"Back!" Robert bellowed above the rain. "We go no farther today!"

Min wanted to hate him for forcing this delay on them, but not as much as he wanted to turn tail and get back to the manor house. They couldn't continue in this weather. It was not only miserable, it was dangerous.

The rain had defeated them.

They had no choice but to head back to Pran.

THEY MUST have made a wretched sight, Min thought, struggling back up the road toward the manor house in the teeming rain. He spared a brief thought for the men who had to see to the horses, but his sympathy wasn't deep enough to volunteer to stay and help them. Fuck that. Min never wanted to see another horse again, after his close encounter with Kaz's.

Talys was whisked away upstairs, leaving a series of wet boot prints puddling behind her.

"Come." Robert gestured to Min and Harry, one hand on Kaz's shoulder as he led them toward the kitchen.

Min balked when he saw the large tub set up on the stone floor, the water hot and steaming as a boy poured another kettle into it.

"No," he said, even though he wanted nothing more than to dive in headfirst.

Robert, unlacing his sodden tunic, paused. "Excuse me?"

"You may be a soldier, sir, but I am not." Min didn't care if Robert thought him arrogant, petulant, a beggar demanding to choose. Really, he couldn't sink any lower in Robert Sabadine's opinion anyway. "I prefer privacy when I bathe. Unless I'm with a companion of my choice, naturally."

Robert's eyes narrowed. "You want me to put the servants to the trouble of making you a separate bath?"

"Yes," Min said imperiously. He glanced at Kaz, and then back at Robert. Raised his eyebrows. "I think I've earned my small luxuries today, don't you?"

He swept out of the kitchen without waiting for a reply, Harry trailing behind him, and strode toward the stairs.

They headed for their room, stripped off their sodden clothes, and huddled under blankets until a tub was brought and a succession of annoyed servants trudged up and down the stairs until the tub was half-filled with hot water.

Harry had the first bath. He sat in the tub and hugged his knees, grumbling slightly when Min scrubbed a cloth across his shoulders and down his spine, but eventually uncurling a little. When it was Min's turn to wash, Harry repaid him by scrubbing his back in return and taking the time to dig his fingers into the knotted muscles of his shoulders and neck.

"I'm not sorry we're out of the rain," Min said, "but I wish we were in Amberwich."

Harry hummed in agreement.

The room was gloomy, lit by only a single candle that did very little against the darkness brought by the rain. It felt like night. Maybe it was; Min had no way of telling. Min closed his eyes briefly and tried not to fixate on the flicker of unease in the corner of his mind that whispered to him they wouldn't make it back to Amberwich in time. That Harry would never again climb the steps to their dusty attic room, or eat porridge at the Footbridge Tavern, or flirt with the girls who worked there.

Tomorrow.

They would set out again for Amberwich tomorrow, the weather be damned.

Min gripped the edges of the tub and lifted himself free. Water ran off him in rivulets, leaving his skin prickling with the cold. He dried himself off and dressed in his least-damp clothes—those that Harry had pulled out from the middle of their bags. The rest he and Harry draped around the room—onto the bed, over the edges of the table and the back of the rickety chair—in the vain hope they might dry by morning. After pushing his luck by demanding a private bath, Min didn't like his chances that any clothing he took downstairs to dry in front of the fire wouldn't end up in the flames courtesy of some vindictive servant. Min had a vindictive streak of his own and knew never to underestimate petty spitefulness in others.

He sat on the bed and tugged his damp boots back on, grimacing at the sensation.

"At least the food is good here, right?" Harry asked, quirking the corner of his mouth upward in a rueful smile. His cheek dimpled, and his curse mark shifted.

Min looked back at his boots so he didn't have to stare at it. "The food is fine. The company leaves much to be desired." He stood, his toes squelching. "Shall we go and hover in the kitchen like flies?"

They tramped downstairs, making for the kitchen.

The tub that Robert and Kaz had bathed in was still in the center of the room, in front of the kitchen fire, and Min felt a twinge of disappointment in his gut as he imagined Kaz, pale and long-limbed, water glistening on his skin and clinging to the bow of his mouth like dew. Instead of that particularly alluring fantasy, he had to settle for spotting a tiny black feather floating on the cloudy surface of the water and a trail of wet footprints that petered out before they reached the doorway.

"Food will be sent to the dining room," one of the maids said, mouth turned down at the corners.

Min and Harry headed that way.

Robert and Kaz and Talys were seated already. A fire flickered in the hearth, bleeding warmth into the room. Min took a seat beside Talys, and Harry sat beside Kaz. The food was served and they ate. The meal was as grand as the one from the night before, but Min took no delight in it today. There was no conversation, only the scrape and clatter of cutlery against their wooden bowls and the crack of the logs in the fire. Kaz didn't lift his gaze from his plate, Harry and Talys cast furtive, frantic glances at each other, and Robert glowered at them every time.

Min had been to merrier funerals.

He ate quickly, like a stray dog thrown an unexpected treat and wary of losing it again. He had no desire to spend a moment longer than necessary in this miserable company. He'd rather fill his stomach with more speed than grace and then go and wallow in his room for a while. Perhaps he'd entertain himself with fantasies of Kaz bathing, the water sluicing off his pale, glistening skin.

He glanced at Kaz.

In his fantasy, Min decided, Kaz wouldn't look so wretched.

"My lord!" The cry came from somewhere outside, startling Min out of his sordid daydreams, and Robert was on his feet in an instant in response. "My lord!"

The man who skidded into the room was soaking wet, pale, and shaking.

"What is it?" Robert asked, already striding for the door.

"My lord!" the man cried, and pointed toward the front of the manor, as though he could not find any further words.

Min rose, snatching up a knife from the table as he did so. He followed Robert out into the hall, the others at his heels. The candlelight from the sconces on the wall cast strange shadows and glittered in the glass eyes of the antlered stags' heads staring blankly down at them.

The front doors of the manor were open, and the wind was blowing the rain inside.

There was a woman standing in the doorway. She was dressed in white. She wore no hood. Her dark hair hung loose. She was pale and dark-eyed. She was beautiful. She was—

Min felt a chill slice through him.

She was *dry*.

Min was frozen with horror.

There was a hoarse whisper from beside him: "*Avice?*"

Robert.

And then the man was moving, striding forward to close the heavy doors. "Help me, you cowards! Help me!"

A servant, braver than Min, darted forward to assist.

They slammed the doors shut and slid the bolts into place just as every candle in the hall guttered and was snuffed out, plunging them into darkness.

CHAPTER 10

MIN DID not consider himself a superstitious man. He'd tossed a few coins toward a few shrines in his life whenever custom or whimsy dictated, but he wasn't sure he'd ever prayed. And now, fumbling in the darkness with the cries of the panicked servants ringing in his ears, he really wished he'd paid more attention to his lessons when his mother had sent him off to the priest down the street a few days a week so he could get an education. It was supposed to have been six days a week, but Min's mother had made the mistake of trusting Min with the quadrans a day it cost for his lessons, and Min had often managed to spend that before reaching the priest's house. It had been months before his mother had discovered his ruse, and a good few days before he could sit down without wincing in pain for all the bruises on his tender backside.

The point was, Min really wished right about now that he could remember a few of those prayers the priest had tried to teach him.

"Light!" Robert called imperiously above the noise. "Bring me light!"

The faint glow of the fireplace in the dining room drew Min back there. He caught Harry's wrist and pulled him along with him, realizing only when he was crossing the threshold into the dining room that it wasn't Harry he had grabbed at all, but a shivering Kaz.

"Did you see her?" Kaz whispered. He broke Min's hold and reached out and twisted his fingers in Min's tunic. "Did you *see* her?"

"I saw her." Min snatched a candleholder from the table, looking back at the door as Harry and Talys darted inside. They were holding hands, like scared little children. Min didn't blame them. He crossed to the fireplace and lit the candle from the flames there.

His efforts were in vain.

By the time he moved back to the hall, servants were lighting the candles in the sconces again, perhaps having rushed to the fireplace in the kitchen. Min returned to the dining room and set the candle down on the table and then went and stood in front of the hearth with Kaz and Harry and Talys. The warmth and the light from the fire did nothing to quash the fear that sat heavily inside his gut, ice cold.

"Who was that?" Harry whispered, wide-eyed.

Min clenched and unclenched his fists, trying to regain control of his trembling fingers. "Avice," he said. "He called her Avice."

Talys darted her gaze quickly to Kaz and then back to Min. "That... that was the name of my father's sister."

Kaz's breath tumbled out of him in a tiny gasp. "My mother? That was my *mother*?"

Oh, and there was a lifetime of heartbreak in his tone that Min couldn't even begin to untangle. It hung in the air like regret and hope all muddied in together, and it made Min's chest constrict with sudden sorrow. "Kaz."

Kaz reached up and touched the iron collar around his throat. His forehead creased with a frown. "But I didn't... that isn't what the dead look like, Min." He shook his head. "I didn't do this! He will blame me, but I didn't do this!"

Min gripped him by the shoulders. He kept his voice low. "He won't blame you. He *can't*. You are a hedgewitch, remember? Just a hedgewitch."

He caught Talys's gaze and saw the sudden understanding light in her eyes.

"He's bound by iron," he told her. "Whatever the true nature of his Gift, he didn't do this."

Harry looked at her beseechingly, and Talys jerked her chin in a nod.

"I didn't do this." Kaz squeezed his eyes shut tightly, brows knitting together as he mumbled. "Her hair wasn't wet and neither was her dress. No physical form, so she was not summoned from the grave. A spirit? A shade. Yes, a shade, an echo. But an echo only occurs when there has been noise, so what is the noise? I need—" He stopped suddenly, a visible shiver running through him. "I don't know. I don't know what caused this."

Min reached up and pressed a hand against Kaz's cold cheek.

Kaz opened his eyes again and looked suddenly, achingly uncertain. "What does she *want*, Min? Why is she here?"

Min didn't know the answer to that.

He wasn't sure he wanted to.

Because when the shades of the dead came unbidden into places where the living dwelled, how could that be a portent of anything but horror? And how fucked were they all when Kaz was looking to Min for comfort?

I kidnapped you, he wanted to say.

I'm the villain of this story.

And so are you, kid. You're a necromancer.

If there was one of them who *shouldn't* have been shitting himself right now, Min felt it should have been Kaz. Death was his Gift.

Min reached out and swept his thumb along the curve of Kaz's cheekbone and held his wide gaze. "I don't know either, sweeting." He could summon none of the usual sharpness he usually reserved for the word. "I don't know."

They might have stood there for hours, frozen still in that moment, if Robert hadn't strode into the dining room. Their little tableaux broke apart into pieces then: Min stepped away from Kaz and Harry from Talys. Kaz turned and stared into the fire, the glow bringing the dark shadows under his eyes into sharp relief.

"A trick," Robert said sharply, taking a seat at the table as though he meant to finish his meal. "An illusion, no doubt wrought by an enemy of our House."

Talys lifted her chin. "For what purpose, Father?"

Min didn't miss the way Robert's hand shook as he reached for his knife.

"To see if we frighten like children," Robert said, but Min knew he didn't believe it. "Sit. Eat. Put it out of your thoughts."

Of course. Because the shade of a dead woman turning up on the doorstep in the middle of a storm was nothing at all to fear, right? Because a mage or a sorcerer—the only Gifted ranks who could even begin to knit together an illusion as convincing as the apparition had been—just happened to be wandering the countryside waiting for an opportunity to fuck with the Sabadines. The lie was as brittle as Robert's strained composure.

"I will not," Talys said. "I have lost my appetite."

Robert glared at her. "Then go. All of you, go!"

Min stood his ground while the others scattered. He regarded Robert steadily for a moment and then sat back down in his seat and picked at the remains of his meal.

"He is bound by iron," he said at last. "And you know a hedgewitch could never do anything like that anyway."

Robert pressed his mouth into a thin line and then snorted. "You concern yourself too much with the boy. Do you think I haven't seen your interest?"

"It is my only interest that you don't snap and beat him to death before we get back to Amberwich," Min said.

Robert stared at him, as though searching for the truth behind his words. He said, at last, "He looks like her. Like Avice."

Pale-skinned, dark-haired, and sloe-eyed. The resemblance had been unmistakable.

"That was no illusion we saw just now," Min said. "That was your sister's shade."

If Robert hadn't been holding himself as stiff as a board, Min might not have seen the shudder than ran through him.

"She was kind," he said at last. "Sweet. Even after...." He clenched his jaw for a moment, and a muscle in his cheek jumped. "Our father had her locked away for her convalescence, to protect her from scandal. My brothers and I were forbidden to see her. The midwife said she asked to be buried here at Pran. She said she begged us not to hate the child."

Min wondered if Robert's guilt had been enough to summon her. Perhaps the shade of Avice Sabadine had risen from whatever place her bones rested and had come to her brother's doorstep for a reason. To accuse him. To shame him. To stare into his eyes and demand to know why he intended to marry his own nephew. Her son. That seemed the sort of transgression that might pull a soul from rest.

Robert's mouth twisted into a bitter smile. He raised his cup of wine and drank and then set the cup down again. "And yet, how can I not hate him? He is the spawn of the creature that violated Avice and the thing that killed her. I wish my father had left him to rot in Anhaga."

"So does Kazimir, no doubt," Min said. He grabbed the jug of wine on the table and poured himself a cup. "But since your father has us all trapped in the same web, I shall keep my sympathies for myself."

Robert grunted, lifting his cup in Min's direction, and Min took it as grudging agreement.

He drank, startling briefly when he felt a touch against his leg. He looked down to see a small gray cat bumping its head against his calf. Min dropped his hand down, and the cat butted his fingers and then vanished under the table.

Min brought his wine up to his mouth to take another sip and saw something floating in it. A leaf? He set his cup down and fished two fingers in it to pin the offending article to the side and drag it out. He set it on the table.

No. Not a leaf at all.

A small black feather.

Min stared at it, disquiet building in him. An omen? Min was not superstitious, but he'd already seen the shade of a dead woman walking the earth tonight, so at this point why the fuck wouldn't he feel disturbed by an incongruous feather? At this point, Min felt, it was entirely rational to think everything was a portent of disaster.

Except this wasn't the first time he'd seen a feather like this one, was it? He'd seen one floating on the surface of Kaz's bath, and before that as well, at the little ford in the stream on the road back from Anhaga when Harry had plucked one from the tangle of Kaz's hair.

Kazimir, he thought, his heart pounding faster. He rolled the shaft of the tiny feather between his thumb and forefinger. *You are the stone I wish I had left unturned.*

The wine barely disguised the bitter taste of the lie.

AVICE SABADINE'S shade was not the only one to haunt the manor at Pran. The whispers of the servants followed Min as he climbed the stairs toward bed, and the chink and rattle of a chain drew Min past the doorway of the room he shared with Harry and toward the room where Kaz slept. The hall was dark and shadowed, and the skin on the back of Min's neck prickled as his perverse imagination summoned a hundred more shades to stalk him through the darkness, their black voiceless mouths open in hunger.

Kaz's door was open. He was sitting on his bed in the darkness. He was unchained but was running the links through his hands, letting them puddle on the floor before drawing them up again like a fisherman bringing in his nets. His hands fluttered palely in the scant light, and Min thought of the large moths, as white as the moon, that used to tremble and shudder against the window of the attic room in his mother's house when he was a child, drawn by the light of his lamp.

"Does that burn?" Min asked quietly from the doorway as Kaz fed the links through his hands again.

"Not as much as it did." Kaz looked at him and then down again. "It feels like grasping a stinging nettle."

Min pushed away his disquiet. The iron had been strong enough to cause Kaz to faint the first day he'd worn it. Was there some impurity in this chain that made its effect weaker, or was Kaz developing a tolerance for iron? Min wasn't sure how he felt about the second possibility at all. "Then why do it?"

Kaz shrugged and let the chain slide to the floor. He looked up again, his face as pale as his mother's shade, his eyes as wide and dark as caverns. "Min…."

There was a note of despair in his voice, or perhaps it was a strange sort of longing. Min didn't trust himself to judge it or to respond to the plea he imagined there.

"I found a feather in my wine," Min said at last, when he could trust his aching throat to push the words out without mangling them. "I thought of you and of disaster."

He couldn't be sure in the gloom, but he thought he saw Kaz's mouth quirk. "Me and disaster. We are the same thing, I think."

It was truer than Min wanted to admit. He felt the cold shadows crowding at his back.

This boy.

This *impossible* boy.

This boy with a boot in both magical camps—both fae and human—and political too, with nothing to bind him but the iron around his throat. Kaz might have considered himself a footnote in his grandfather's history, but Min wondered if the boy was selling himself short. Wondered what might happen if he chose to unlock his collar. Kaz would be wilder than the storm still raging outside. A part of Min, that part swimming in sour guilt, wanted to unleash chaos. A part of Min thought the world, and the men like him who lived in it, deserved it. A part of him thought it would be magnificent to watch Kazimir Stone scourge the world with fire.

And then he thought of Harry and the curse mark on his cheek, and he pushed such dangerous thoughts away.

"Good night, Kaz," he said softly.

Kaz turned his face away. "Good night."

And Min wondered, as he walked back toward his room with the darkness swirling around and the storm howling outside, whether necromancers had dreams when they slept, or nightmares.

MIN TOSSED and turned with the storm. Harry's cold feet were pressed against Min's shins, and he snuffled into his pillow like a pup and snored like a wheezy pair of bellows. Harry could be quiet and watchful as a sentry in his waking hours, but when he slept, he was a danger to his bedfellows. Min had woken up covered in bruises in the past, and not even any sordid memories to make the getting of them worthwhile.

Min dozed uneasily, each rattle of the shutters and moan of the wind pulling him back into wakefulness. His eyes stung with grit, and he ached through to his bones. He needed sleep but was too unsettled to find more than a few passing moments.

He wanted this over. He wanted to be back in Amberwich, in a bed wider than this one so he could get some space between him and Harry's sharp elbows. He wanted to be done with this Sabadine business. He wanted to walk away from the machinations of powerful men from powerful Houses, with Harry safely tucked at his side. He wanted to slink back to the boltholes and rats' nests of the eastern quarter and drink enough gut rot to forget any of this had ever happened. He wanted to sink so deeply into his cups that he no longer had any memory of Kazimir Stone and the misery in his dark eyes that Min had put there.

Min had never pretended to be better than he was, but he was unaccustomed to feeling the stirrings of guilt in his gut and found he didn't like it much. He liked the fact that he was backed into a corner even less.

Min was no less trapped than Kaz.

He tugged some of the blankets back from Harry and closed his eyes. A gust of wind shook the shutters, and Min reminded himself that he was a grown man and unafraid of storms. Which he felt might have been more convincing if only he could forget the shade of Avice Sabadine wandering in the night and the dark specter of the fae hanging over everything, as omnipresent as the storm itself.

He barely registered the noise of footsteps on the stairs over the storm before the bedroom door was flung open and Min found himself squinting into lamplight.

"Is he here?" Robert demanded.

Sleep might have eluded Min, but his brain was addled with weariness. "What?"

"Kazimir." Robert drew the lamp back, the shadows shrinking over his drawn face. "Is he here?"

"No." Min stared blankly at Robert as, beside him, Harry snorted into wakefulness.

"Kaz is gone?" Harry asked, his voice tremulous.

"He's not in his room."

Min felt a chill. He flung the blankets back, scrabbling on the floor for his pants and tugging them on under his bed-rumpled shirt. He pulled on his tunic as well, for extra warmth, and his boots. He rose to his feet.

"The servants are checking the house," Robert said, raising the lamp as though he half expected Kaz to be burrowed into Min's blankets like a fat little bedbug. Which, in the normal run of things, Min wouldn't have been opposed to at all. But this was a long way from normal.

"He's not in the house," Min said with a sinking sense of certainty.

"My mother?" Kaz had asked earlier, a hundred different hopes balanced on the knife's edge of his heartbreak, just waiting to fall and to shatter. *"That was my mother?"*

Robert shot him a sharp look. "What do you mean?"

Min met his gaze and ignored the chill that ran down his spine. "Where is your sister's grave?"

IN A garden behind the manor house, a weeping willow sagged under the weight of the rain. There was no marker on the grave, no stone set there to counter life's transience with an attempt at something more lasting. And yet Kaz had known where to find his mother's grave. Min wondered if he had followed her shade here.

Kaz knelt under the tree, his fingers digging into the sodden earth, his head bowed.

Robert Sabadine strode forward, followed by a cluster of nervous servants brandishing lanterns. They knocked against one another like fireflies in a bottle. Their lamps guttered in the rain despite their care. Min kept his gaze fixed on Kaz. To look away from him was to acknowledge that the night was vast, and that the storm was wild, and that shades walked in the darkness.

Robert wrenched Kaz to his feet. "Get inside!"

"No!" Kaz cried out. He scrabbled at the iron collar Min had fastened around his throat in Anhaga. "Please, please take it off! Please! Please!"

Min's guts turned to ice.

"Please!"

Min winced as he saw it coming—Robert raised his hand and slapped his palm across Kaz's cheek. The sound of the blow was swallowed by the rain and the wind, but Kaz stumbled back, his hands flying to his face.

Robert gripped him by the wrist and dragged him toward the house.

Min and the servants followed. The servants scattered like rats once they were inside the shelter of the house again, and the doors were barred against the storm and whatever else lurked out there in the night. Min stayed on Robert's heels as he manhandled Kaz toward the kitchen.

"Sir," he called, sounding calmer than he felt. "You are right to be angry, but you are hurting him."

Robert flung Kaz to the floor. He huddled there, his wet hair plastered to his skull, his clothes dripping onto the stones in front of the fireplace. He cradled one arm to his chest.

"Get your clothes off, you fool," Robert said, "before you are stricken with the ague."

Kaz fumbled with the laces of his tunic.

Robert reached for the poker beside the fireplace. Kaz flinched back, but Robert only jabbed the poker into the fire and stirred the embers back to life. "What the hell were you thinking?"

Kaz swallowed, his chest heaving. When he spoke, his voice was ragged. "I wanted…." He shivered. "I wanted to see if she would show herself again. I wanted to be close to—"

Robert's grip tightened on the poker as he whirled on Kaz. "She is nothing to you. Not now, and not ever. You are the thing that *killed* her."

Kaz flinched as though Robert had struck him again.

"Sir," Min said quietly, stepping forward. "Let me tend to the fire."

He held his hand out for the poker, half-afraid Robert would strike Kaz before he even knew what he was doing. Robert thrust it toward him and paced back and forth on the stones.

Min knelt before the fireplace, feeding in a few pieces of wood from the basket beside the hearth. He was close to Kaz. He was aware of Kaz in his periphery, shifting, but kept his gaze fixed on the fire even as he heard the wet slap of clothing on the floor. He had imagined Kaz naked, hadn't he? That pale skin, that lean, coltish frame. Kaz was very much Min's type—to be fair, of course, everyone was very much Min's type—but he didn't dare turn his head. Robert already suspected his attraction, and Min didn't want to test his temper any further tonight. He worked in silence to rebuild the fire.

Silence was safest.

"Sir," Kaz said, and Min felt his stomach swoop. "Please, if you would just take the collar off so that I might talk to her!"

Min froze for the space of a heartbeat.

Oh, the fool. The stupid, reckless fool.

He rose to his feet, the poker still clutched in his hand. He stepped between Kaz and Robert and thought that well, if this were his last moment, he hoped someone would embellish his heroism when it came time to memorialize it in song.

Robert stared down at the naked boy, shock and horror written large across his face. "You are no hedgewitch."

No. Kaz was a lot of things. A lot of very stupid things. But he was not a hedgewitch. Min tightened his grip on the poker.

Robert's face twisted. "You are a necromancer!"

"A necromancer," Min agreed blithely, "and at no extra cost. Now step back, sir, lest I am forced to protect my investment."

Robert's gaze flicked from Kaz to Min. "You threaten me, scoundrel?"

"I may be no gentleman," Min said, "but I am also no fool. If you beat your nephew to death because of his vile Gift, then my nephew dies too. Kazimir is no threat to any man. He is bound by iron. Step away, sir, and take your rest if we are to leave for Amberwich in the morning."

"Are you mad? We cannot leave in the morning. The storm is barely easing, and—" Robert shook his head. And his nephew was a necromancer. And the shade of his dead sister was wandering the land. "It's *madness*."

"And who do you think sent the storm?" Min asked him. "Who do you think is trying to delay us from getting Kazimir to the protection of the Iron Tower? The fae have been snapping at our heels since Anhaga, and if we delay for much longer, they will be on us. We must leave in the morning."

Robert paled, his jaw tightening. He held Min's gaze for a long moment, as though he was searching for a falsehood there, and then nodded. "Very well. We will leave in the morning."

He turned on his heel and left the kitchen.

Min's heart rediscovered its regular rhythm, and he loosened his grip on the poker.

"Thank you," Kaz whispered from the floor.

Min couldn't bring himself to look at him. "You're a fool, Kazimir. They'll keep you in iron until you're dead now."

"I just wanted to talk to her." His voice was as small as a child's.

"You're a fool," Min repeated, but waited with him in silence until Robert returned with dry clothes for Kaz to wear and the chain from his bedroom folded into lengths over his shoulder.

CHAPTER 11

THE MORNING brought a respite from the storm. The lashing rain had eased to drizzle, and the dark clouds that had covered the night sky were breaking up in places now, like the glaze on old dinnerware, with faint light shining through the cracks. The morning was sharp with cold, and Min shivered as he and Harry tramped over the muddy courtyard toward the stables. Min had five hot bread rolls shoved between his shirt and his tunic, and the smell of them made his stomach growl out its hunger. He was saving them to eat in the saddle.

Harry's tunic was as suspiciously lumpy as Min's own.

"At least it's stopped pissing down," Harry muttered.

"Hmm." A more optimistic man might have taken some delight in that. Min couldn't help but wonder if the storm had ended because it had already served its purpose: it had allowed the fae to catch them. He cast his narrow gaze over the courtyard and over the men waiting with the horses but saw nothing out of place. A buzzing insect zipped past him, and Min's heart skipped a beat as he thought of the chattering wisps that had tormented them the night they'd left Anhaga, but it was only a horsefly.

One of the stableboys led Min's horse to him, and Min tried to suppress a shudder at the thought of getting back into the saddle. The horse, he thought, was probably just as reluctant.

The horse's trappings jangled, metal clinking against metal, and Min saw a pair of horseshoes hanging from the pommel. Iron. Enough to repel the fae, though? Min had no idea.

Amberwich was a day's ride away.

In a day this could all be over.

Min stood in the stableboy's cupped hands and hauled himself into the saddle. He tugged the hood of his tunic forward and cast an eye over the rest of the party. Robert Sabadine held his gaze for a moment and nodded. He looked like a man who hadn't slept; the shadows under his eyes were deep this morning.

Talys yawned in the early morning gloom and then craned her head to seek out Harry. The scant light caught her profile, and for a moment she glowed as though she had been painted by a scribe in some volume illuminated in gold.

Harry stared at her achingly, adoringly.

Kaz's hands were unbound today. Clearly Robert didn't want a repeat of yesterday's close call. Kaz sat in the saddle with his head bowed, hemmed in by Robert's men.

A day, Min reminded himself. In a day this could be over.

A day.

He tore his gaze from Kaz and tugged on the reins of his horse.

HOURS LATER Min's body was aching when Robert finally called for the party to stop. He had twinges in places he didn't have names for, his ass was sore, and his bladder was throbbing with the need to take a piss. His boots hit the ground, jarring his bones, and he hastily tangled the reins of the horse around a scrubby bush before stepping behind it to relieve himself.

There was woodland on this side of the road and fields, divided into patchwork by hedgerows, on the other. Min tucked himself back into his pants as Harry darted around the bush to join him, then turned his back on the boy and stared out into the trees. The road here followed a rise in the land; on either side it dipped away again. The trees were sparse at the edge of the road but grew thicker some distance back. The shifting light made it appear as though there was movement in the woods, and Min's skin prickled with unease. He wanted to be back in Amberwich, where the city was close and crowded and stank, but Min understood it in a way he would never understand the countryside.

He waited until Harry nudged against his side like a tick trying to burrow in, and slung his arm around the boy's shoulders.

"Fucking trees," Harry muttered, squinting into the woods.

Min smiled despite himself. Harry was an annoying little shit, but he had always been a boy after Min's own heart.

He drew Harry back onto the road, releasing him with a slap on the back. Robert's men were walking around, stretching their limbs and taking the opportunity to eat. Min dug a bread roll out of his tunic and tore a chunk out of it with his teeth, his gaze seeking out Kaz as surely as Harry's sought out Talys.

Idiots, the both of them.

Kaz was standing at the side of the road, motionless while men and horses moved around him. He was not eating. His hands were tucked into his damp sleeves. He was looking out across the fields, and Min wondered if it was a hedgewitch's eye he used to survey them. Kaz had never been a hedgewitch, but he'd wanted to be one. He'd wanted an affinity with crops and seasons and growth and life, and instead his Gift was death.

Born to the wrong family, to the wrong blood, and to the wrong Gift.

Min watched as Kaz shifted his weight from foot to foot and then stooped down and picked a stringy dandelion from the muddy road. He held it as carefully as if it were precious as balsam.

"More rain coming," Harry muttered.

Min looked at him.

Harry nodded toward the fields. "More rain."

The farthest edge of the fields had already vanished under a shroud of gray. More of the fields vanished into the mist even as Min watched.

"That's not rain," Min said. "That's mist."

Except since when did mist roll in like the waves of the ocean, so quickly? Since when did it transform so rapidly into fog as thick as smoke? And—Min felt ice slide down his spine—since when did it carry on it the faint sound of *bells*?

Min and Harry weren't the only ones who had noticed the fog swallowing the fields.

Kaz, wide-eyed, his mouth open in horror, also stared. The dandelion fell from his twitching fingers into the mud.

"Ride!" Min called. "*Ride!*"

Dragging Harry by the elbow, he dashed back toward his horse.

And remembered, too late as it happened, to avoid crossing too near the end of the beast. The horse didn't kick but, in the sudden flurry of panicked motion around it, skittered backward and knocked Min solidly enough to send him tumbling to the ground. Harry reached for him, but the horse was still dancing, and somehow it got between them.

Min clambered to his feet. "I'm fine! Get on your horse!"

Harry scrambled into the saddle.

Min gripped the reins of his horse, wincing as pain cut through his shoulder. He tried to hold the horse in place and step into the saddle, and the contrary beast skipped away from him. Around them, the others were already on horseback, already fleeing down the road toward Amberwich.

And the fog was rolling in, closing the distance between the field and the road as surely as a flood.

Min tried to mount his horse again, and the objectionable animal reared back. The reins tore through Min's grasp and left his stinging hand holding nothing but air.

"Min!" And suddenly Kaz was there, reaching a hand down for him.

Min would like to say he swung himself up behind Kaz with actual finesse, but he felt more like a fat seal beaching itself on the rear end of the animal. It was clumsy and unbalanced. He lay on his stomach, in imminent danger of pitching all the way forward and breaking his skull open on the road. There was nothing to hold on to as Kaz nudged the horse into an ungainly trot.

Sons of Rus.

A canter would fucking kill him if he even stayed on that long!

"Min!" he heard Harry yelling above the rattling of his teeth in his skull.

And then the fog was on them, and they were blind.

Above the sound of panicked horses and men, Min heard again the jangling of bells. He was suddenly acutely aware of the sound of the bundle of horseshoes tied to Kaz's saddle clinking together in answer. The iron might have offered protection, but it was loud.

So too was Robert Sabadine. "Talys!" he bellowed from somewhere in the fog. "Talys! Kazimir!"

Min gripped Kaz by the back of his tunic as he felt himself starting to slide off the horse. He went backward, fortunately, not forward, and landed more or less on his feet. And Kaz slid down beside him. His face, his form were ghostly in the fog, made somehow as shifting and insubstantial as his mother's shade.

If the fae were on them, then they needed to be invisible, or at least more invisible than their companions. Let the fae tear Robert's men apart first. Perhaps that would buy Min and Kaz some time. And Min hoped that Harry, lost somewhere in the chaos, was smart enough to realize the same thing.

Min slapped Kaz's horse on the rump, sending it trotting away, its trappings and its iron shoes jangling. Then, gripping Kaz by the wrist, he pulled him onto the verge of the road and down into the trees.

"Kazimir!" Robert called again, already sounding fainter as the fog smothered his voice. "Kazimir!"

Min pulled Kaz close, his back to Min's chest, and put a hand over his mouth.

He pressed his other hand to the iron collar around Kaz's throat and hoped it would be enough to protect them both from the fae. It was quieter than horseshoes, at least.

"Shhh, sweeting," he murmured against the shell of Kaz's pointed ear.

Kaz's breath was hot and damp against his palm, and he nodded to show that he understood.

Min fixed his gaze on a damp curl of Kaz's hair. The fog shifted around them, and he was afraid of what he might see if he looked there instead—either the fae or whatever Min's imagination conjured in their place. No. He watched Kaz instead and held him close. Stole as much comfort as he offered.

He heard the distant thundering of hooves. He heard, closer than that, the sound of bells. And he heard, his blood turning to ice as he did, an exchange of voices somewhere close by that sounded like music plucked from some strange, unearthly instrument.

Kaz shivered, and Min closed his eyes.

And then everything went deathly quiet, and Min wondered if the fog had drowned him, pulled him under like a black ocean would a sailor, and left him senseless. He could hear nothing, see nothing. He couldn't say how much time had passed, and only the faint click of Kaz's throat as he swallowed—and the dip of the iron collar—convinced him that he wasn't frozen. He opened his eyes and turned his head.

Up on the rise of the road, a horse stepped through the fog. It seemed both taller and narrower than the horses Min had become unwillingly accustomed too. It was as white as bone. Its rider was tall, too, and as deathly pale. Min saw an angular profile: ageless, beautiful, terrifying. The fae wore a gold circlet around its head. Its ears were pointed. Its hair, the color of autumn leaves, fell in a smooth wave down its back. It wore robes that could have been cut out of a midsummer night's sky the moment before the darkness overtook the last shade of deepest blue.

And then the fog shifted again, and the fae rode on.

Min's heart hammered.

Sudden birdsong broke the silence and broke the spell of fear that had kept Min frozen in place. He jostled Kaz farther down the slope, deeper into the cover of the trees, away from the road and from the fae who followed it. He hoped the fae were trailing Robert and his men and not the sound of the damp leaves and twigs that crunched under his and Kaz's boots.

They hurried deeper into the woods.

"I DON'T blame you."

It felt like hours until Kaz broke the silence. They were picking their way alongside a narrow stream that seemed more sludge than water. Its surface was dappled with half-rotted leaves. Stringy grass bordered its edges, and Min's boots slipped more than once on the muddy bank.

"I don't blame you," Kaz said again, as though Min might not have heard him.

"No offense," Min said, his voice rougher than he intended, "but it wouldn't change a thing if you did."

"I know." For some reason that made Kaz's mouth quirk in something that was almost a smile.

Min slipped, his left boot dipping into the water. He caught a branch to steady himself. "We're lost, aren't we?"

"Better lost than caught by the fae," Kaz said wryly.

Min huffed. He rolled his shoulders and squinted up at the sky. It was bluer than it had been when they'd set out from Pran, but the day was still cool and damp. The night, when it came, would be cold. "True."

Kaz walked in front for a little way, and Min wondered if he had any idea where he was leading them. Did he know the way toward Amberwich? And would he lead them in that direction even if he did? If Min had been in Kaz's position, he wasn't sure he would. What was worse? To be out in the wilderness hunted by the fae or to be imprisoned in iron in Edward Sabadine's house? Kaz only had two choices, and they were both bad.

"Do you even know which way you're going?" he asked when they had left the little stream behind them.

"No," Kaz said over his shoulder. "But I think this way is southeast."

"You *think*?"

"I can't see the sun," Kaz said, rounding on him. He shrugged, and the coins of soft dappled sunlight on his shoulders rolled with the motion. "But I think it's this way. I did train as a hedgewitch, you know. Kallick taught me how to feel the leylines."

Min felt unease stirring in his gut. "But you're bound in iron."

"Iron blocks my magic," Kaz said. "Not the earth's. I can't use it, but I can feel it." He wrinkled his nose. "I was a terrible hedgewitch, though."

"Were you?"

Kaz looked down, as though he was embarrassed to admit it. "I was supposed to be able to follow the leylines, but usually I just found dead things instead. The first time it happened, I was nine. Kallick sent me to find the place where two leylines crossed, for part of a harvest ritual, and instead I found a dead badger." He looked up again, a rueful smile on his face. "That was when he knew for sure that I was no hedgewitch."

Min couldn't stop himself from mirroring Kaz's smile, though a more sensible man might have found more horror in the subject than amusement. Kaz was nothing if not contradictory, though. A shy, naïve boy without a whiff of guile about him, and he had been born with the darkest Gift known to the world. "He took it in his stride, though?"

"He did. He was a good man. He taught me what he could about my Gift. He taught me how to hide it from people who would fear it."

"He didn't fear it?"

"He said…." Kaz swallowed. "He said it was a Gift, the same as any other, and that no Gift is good or bad of itself. That was before I… before…."

Before you turned his corpse into a puppet, Min thought.

"Before he died," Kaz finished softly. "I just… I didn't want to go back to my grandfather's house. And I *couldn't*. I couldn't leave Kallick's house, because he'd shown me how to use our Gifts to ward it against the fae as best we could. He didn't think it would work, but it did. He said he thought it was my blood that did it more than our Gifts. When he died, I didn't know what else to do except to stay there and to keep the wards in place. I wanted to be safe, but it was more than that as well. I didn't want to be alone."

"Kaz," Min said softly. "You lived almost a decade locked in a house, watching the world through a window and the eyes of a dead man. I think you were very much alone."

A shudder ran through the boy, and Min might not have noticed it at all if he hadn't been watching him so closely.

"Yes." Kaz's voice cracked on the simple word. "I think I was very lonely."

The silence between them was heavy with expectation, and Min felt the urge to reach out and gently trace his fingertips along Kaz's jaw or the bow of his lips.

Kaz stepped back before Min could move, flashing him a smile. "There was a girl I liked, from afar. She came to Kallick once and asked for a poultice. She had freckles on her nose. I could see her from the window sometimes. She used to walk down to the harbor with the fishermen at dawn, with the food she'd made them wrapped up in oilskins to protect it from the spray of the ocean. She would watch them as they set out for the day, and I would watch her." He flushed. "And then, a few months later, I realized I was watching her brothers more than her and the way their shirts stuck to them when they got wet."

Min laughed, delighted at the revelation and at Kaz's pink cheeks. "I do love the taste of salt."

Kaz laughed, too, although he dropped his gaze and dragged the toe of his boot through the dirt. "Well."

Min waited a moment, until it became apparent Kaz had nothing more to offer the conversation after leading it onto this interesting path. He dug around between his shirt and his tunic and pulled out a bread roll. "Hungry?"

Kaz took it, his fingertips brushing Min's palm. "Thank you."

Min tried not to look too hard at his ass as they continued walking.

"WE ARE neither of us woodsmen," Min decided that evening, squinting in the fading light at the rudimentary shelter they'd built. It was a lean-to of branches that would probably serve as no decent respite from the wind at all, and a paltry mound of leaves and bracken.

"No," Kaz agreed, picking a leaf from his hair. "But it will be warmer than the bare ground."

Min broke a bread roll in half and shared it with Kaz.

"I wish we had some real food," Kaz said as they huddled in their shelter. "A nice, hot stargazy pie."

"I prefer my food not to stare back at me," Min muttered.

Kaz huffed out a breath of laughter and ate the rest of his bread.

It was no hardship to curl up next to Kaz. It was no mild torture either. Min was more than capable of keeping his hands to himself. Sleeping with Kaz was no different than sharing a bed with Harry, except Min was less likely to get cracked in the face with a flying elbow, which made for a pleasant change.

He listened to the soft sounds of Kaz breathing, the leaves rustling under him as he shifted, and worried about Harry. He hoped Harry had gotten away from the fae. And he hoped Robert Sabadine understood that Min hadn't spirited Kaz away out of his family's grasp. He hoped he understood that Min would get Kaz to Amberwich in time to have Harry's curse lifted or die trying.

A terrible, twisting thought dug into Min's mind. What if Harry wasn't in Amberwich when Min got back? What if he hadn't survived the fae? Well then, Min supposed, all his ugliness would be free to manifest, wouldn't it? He wondered if Kaz would help him seek his revenge, in return for removing the collar. And so what if it destroyed the world and Min along with it? If he had failed Harry, what did he care if he died? And what did he care for anyone else who got in the way at all? Other men, Min supposed, might have consciences that spoke in soft but stern voices at this point, but Min had only ever heard silence, a void inside him that had nothing to do with being impervious to magic.

Well, perhaps not a void. Perhaps there was something there. But Min was a pragmatist, and he'd gone to sleep most nights on a full belly because of it. He would allow the voice inside him to call Kaz a regret, but he would not allow him to become a call to action. Not when Harry's life hung in the balance. And that, Min thought, was as fair as he could be.

The canopy of leaves above them sighed, and shifted in the breeze like the surface of the ocean. It parted here and there and allowed glimpses of starlight. It was quiet and beautiful, and a lovely boy slept at Min's side.

And that, Min thought, was as far as he could let that go.

"I am not a good man," he told the sleeping Kaz. "But I'm not bad enough to choose you over Harry."

The moonlight slanted over Kaz's face, illuminating his cheekbones, his snub nose, and the bow of his lips. He looked delicate, ethereal, beautiful in a way that reminded Min of the fae, without tipping over the edge into something alien, something cold and terrifying. Whatever else he was, Kaz was too human for that.

Min dozed at length, and slept, and the whispers of the night around him—alive with insects and the soft footfalls of small animals— filtered into his mind and gave him strange dreams of feathers and fae and a small gray cat that curled up in a warm lump on his stomach and purred.

When he woke up, Kaz was gone.

CHAPTER 12

IF THERE had been anything in Min's stomach, he was sure he would have vomited it all over his boots as he paced the small clearing where they'd built their shelter. He felt nauseated, almost feverish, his scant grip on this entire situation unraveling faster than a ball of yarn in the clutches of a cat. Kaz was *gone*. Kaz was gone, and Min was in a fucking forest, and Harry was as good as dead, if he wasn't already *actually* dead.

Min stopped and dragged his fingers through his hair. Forced himself to take a breath.

Stupid.

He should have known Kaz would run. To where, it didn't matter. It didn't even matter that it would probably just deliver him faster into the claws of the fae. How often had Min thought of Kaz as an animal caught between two traps? And of course Kaz was driven by fear. Of course he would run. Any little animal would.

Min sucked in another deep breath and stared around the clearing in the early morning light. Dew glistened on the ground and dripped off the ends of leaves. A spider's web glittered between two naked branches. The light filtered down through the leaves, not bright enough to make the damp woods gleam or to entirely lift the chill. Tiny hollows held puddles of mist still, and the air smelled of petrichor.

There were no footprints Min could see in the damp earth. No flattened patches of grass. No helpfully snapped twigs on the bushes that might indicate which direction Kaz had taken. Of course not. He was a human being, not a deer, and Min was no huntsman in any case. Not in this environment, at least. Give him a tortuous maze of dark alleys and rain-slick cobbles and he was in his element, but here? Min had no fucking idea.

Min could do nothing except choose a direction and follow it.

He thought he was walking the same direction as yesterday, but that was only a guess.

He was lost. He *had* lost. The knowledge of it sat in his guts as heavy as lead. Min had always hated to lose, but this was like no loss he'd faced before. This wasn't about his pride or about money. This wasn't about having a few lean weeks where he avoided his landlord and lived on porridge at the Footbridge Tavern. This wasn't about having to abase his dignity and ask his mother for coins, like some beggar pleading for alms. This time, losing meant losing Harry, and Min had no idea how to even accept a loss like that, let alone recover from it.

Harry was a fool. A stupid little fool with all the common sense of a dog in heat, but he was *Min's* fool, and Min couldn't envision a life without him.

Min's eyes stung as he stumbled down a slope that was steeper than it looked, dirt and grit slipping under the soles of his boots, and caught himself on a branch to prevent himself from falling. He turned and looked back at the slope and saw that his were not the only boots that had left gouges in the earth. His heart tumbled over its newfound hope. Was it possible he was inadvertently following Kaz's footsteps? He had taken the most likely looking path—probably not an actual thoroughfare so much as the path of least resistance through the tangled undergrowth of the woods—so perhaps Kaz had done the same?

Min refused to hold on to that hope for now. It would only be more bitter in the end if he nurtured it now. Min was a pragmatist.

And yet….

He followed the path cautiously. Sunlight flared up ahead, and Min stepped out of the shadows of the trees and found himself on the bank of a stream. Not the same one as yesterday. Where that had been a narrow, murky sliver cutting through the mud, this was wider, deeper, and the water ran clean and clear. It was wide enough that the sunlight hit it and it shone.

There was a bundle of clothing on the bank: boots, a cloak, an undershirt, and a grimy green kirtle and a belt.

And on the bank of the stream knelt Kaz, scooping up handfuls of water and splashing them on his face and torso. If the sunlight shone on the surface of the water, then it gleamed on Kaz's pale skin, painting him with a brilliant sheen. Min wouldn't have been surprised to discover he was as iridescent as mother-of-pearl.

Relief hit Min, hard and fast. He feared his legs suddenly didn't have the strength to hold him, so he clung to a tree for support and tried to remember how to breathe.

Kaz hadn't run.

It took Min a long moment to come to terms with that realization. Perhaps Kaz *should* have run, but he hadn't, and if Harry was still alive after yesterday, then there was a chance Min could keep him alive. Could get the curse removed and save his idiot nephew.

Kaz could have run, but he had stayed, and Min was overwhelmed with both gratitude and pity, neither of which he was accustomed to entertaining. He swallowed, his throat dry, and watched Kaz.

Kaz was kneeling with his back to Min. His breeches hung low on his hips, covering enough of him that his modesty was more or less protected but offering teasing glimpses of the top of his thin braies when he leaned forward to scoop more water toward him. His skin wasn't unmarked: Min saw the blue-black lines of ink on the curve of his hip that disappeared into the fabric of his breeches and remembered the night in the hut outside Anhaga when he'd discovered Kaz had a tattoo. He'd thought it was on the other hip, but he must have been mistaken.

Kaz leaned forward, cupping water over his head. Bright droplets sprayed around him like rain as he straightened up again, and water sluiced down his shoulders and back as he squeezed it out of his hair. Even his iron collar gleamed with it.

Enough.

Min felt like an interloper. He lifted his hand from the rough bark of the tree and stepped forward. "Kaz?"

Kazimir twisted around, wide-eyed, his damp hair flying. "Min."

He scrambled to his feet and then stooped to collect his clothes. He hugged them to his chest, his damp hair sticking in tendrils to his neck, and Min tried not to notice the inviting angle of his collarbones and the dip in between them that he would very much like to have explored with his touch. And possibly his tongue.

"Here you are," he said dumbly.

Kaz's eyes widened even farther. "You thought I'd run?"

"It crossed my mind," Min said, the echoes of his cold fear reverberating through him even now.

Kaz creased his brow. "Where would I go?"

Min appreciated his honesty and the fact he didn't treat Min like a fool. If Kaz had stayed it was only because running might mean exchanging his terrible fate for one infinitely more horrifying. Kaz knew exactly what waited for him in Amberwich—a chain, metaphorical if he was fortunate, but possibly literal—but the fae? The fae might want to tear him into pieces and feast on his blood and bones. Min couldn't blame him for choosing to live, even if that life would likely be a miserable one. Min had thought perhaps he'd panicked like a little animal, but no, Kaz was at least as much a pragmatist as Min. A wretched, bleak pragmatist.

Min smiled at him slightly. "True."

Kaz hugged his clothes to his chest with one arm and raised his free hand to rub awkwardly at the back of his neck. "I think that—"

"What's that?" Min stepped closer, drawn to some mark on the side of Kaz's neck, just behind his ear.

"Oh." A flush rose on Kaz's throat, and he moved his hand away for a moment.

A feather. A small feather, intricately inked in delicate black lines against Kaz's skin, with the point of its vane poking out from underneath his unruly hair. Another tattoo?

Kaz reached up and touched the end of the tattoo. He drew his hand back again, and Min saw the tattoo was no longer there against his skin. Instead, sticking to the ends of Kaz's fingers, was a damp black feather.

Sons of Rus.

Min's heart beat faster as he met Kaz's gaze.

Kaz's throat bobbed as he swallowed, but his gaze was steady. "They're fae magic, I think. I've never heard of a Gift that could do it."

"Do *what*?"

Kaz drew his fingers through his hair, and this time a clawed foot appeared from his hairline, followed by the tip of a wing, and suddenly a tattooed raven was tumbling down the slope of his neck, ruffling its feathers as it came to a stop on his shoulder.

Kazimir traced the raven on his shoulder, and the ink-thin lines thickened, morphed somehow, and then the raven was a solid thing, a *real* thing, and it was perched on Kaz's shoulder. Its ink-black feathers shone in the sunlight, and it tilted its head to give Min a sharp-eyed stare.

Kaz tapped the bird's head with his finger. "This one likes to be called Knifebeak."

Min raised his eyebrows.

"His real name is Chirpy," Kaz said. The raven squawked and snapped its sharp beak at Kazimir's fingers, and Kaz's mouth quirked. "It is! Chirpy!"

This one, Kaz had said, and Min thought suddenly of the warm little cat he'd dreamed had slept on him the night before. And there had been a cat before that, hadn't there?

He put a hand on Kaz's free shoulder and turned him.

The tattoo of the cat on Kaz's hip was moving, like an illustration in a manuscript come to life, the ink twisting and turning on the vellum page that was Kaz's skin. It stalked up his spine, tail lashing, and then it too was real, dropping to its feet on the bank of the stream and prowling forward to twine around Min's ankles.

A little gray tortoiseshell cat, just like the one Min had seen in Pran.

"This one is Taavi," Kaz said.

"How is such a thing possible?" Min leaned down to run his fingers down the cat's arching spine. He could feel its rumbling purr under his touch.

"I don't know," Kaz said softly. "I never knew. I never knew *anything*."

He turned away to pull his shirt on and possibly to hide the sudden shine of tears in his eyes.

And that, Min thought as Taavi the cat curled around his legs again, was just another tiny piece in the ugly mosaic that was Kazimir Stone's tragedy.

Or his duplicity.

MIN HATED the woods.

It seemed to him an endless nightmare of tree roots, rough ground, hidden holes, and paths that ended in dead ends that necessitated backtracking and trying all over again. He wouldn't have been surprised to find they'd walked for hours and barely covered a mile. He was tired, his feet ached, and there was a spider's web in his hair.

He was also worried Kaz was still leading them in the wrong direction. Min was suspicious both by birth and by profession, and the fact he couldn't understand the nature of Kaz's Gift was troublesome. The iron collar should have prevented him from using his human Gift, and weren't the fae supposed to sicken with the touch of iron? Iron had burned Kaz two days ago, and yet now he barely seemed to notice it at all.

Kaz could still follow leylines—perhaps not so unusual, and his explanation had seemed plausible. But he also had a cat and a raven that defied the iron collar he wore. Shouldn't they have become as lifeless as Kallick's dusty bones when Min had put the collar on him?

It was troubling.

It bothered Min that Kaz was either a naïf or that he was lying.

It bothered him even more that he even entertained the idea it was possible Kaz was a complete innocent. He was pretty, but Min had known plenty of pretty people. He'd never before second-guessed his own suspicious nature simply because he wanted to put his dick inside someone.

If Harry were here, he'd raise his eyebrows and make some comment about Min finally finding his conscience, perhaps. But Harry wasn't here, and the last thing Min needed was to discover he had a conscience.

A few paces ahead, Kaz stopped suddenly. Min came up beside him.

They were standing on the edge of a small clearing, almost perfectly circular. There was a pool inside of it, and Min's dry mouth tried its hardest to water at the sight of what appeared to be clean, deep water.

And yet something held him back.

It was the perfection of the clearing, he thought, and the fact he could no longer hear any birdsong. The sunlight gleamed on the surface of the pool, and Min felt an overwhelming urge to step forward and to fall to his knees and drink. It was a need that ran deeper than his thirst. The moment it came over him he knew he should fear it, and also that he would not be able to resist it for much longer.

Min felt a chill, his skin prickled, and he remembered suddenly the words of an old song one of his mother's girls used to sing as she darned her stockings by the kitchen fire:

Light down, light down. We are come to the place where ye are to die.

He was so tired, though, and the water looked so fresh and cool. What would it matter if they stopped here for a while? He was so tired.

Kaz's fingers curled around his wrist, as tight as iron. "We will not drink here."

"No." Min shook his head to clear it, his heart beating fast, and they made their way around the clearing instead of through it.

Whatever had been waiting for them in that clearing—the woods holding their breath in anticipation—Min hoped they had escaped it. Every flash of light through the canopy of leaves, every shadow slipping through the trees…. Min couldn't shake the fae, could he? Whether they were really there or not.

He traipsed through the woods with Kaz, ignoring his dry throat and hoping they were still heading for Amberwich.

"Tell me about Harry," Kaz said sometime later as they shared the last of Min's stale bread rolls.

Min shrugged. "What's to tell?"

"You show yourself to the world as a man who thinks only of himself, but you're risking your life for Harry."

Min didn't like the way Kaz's gaze seemed to bore straight through him.

"You read too many tales of heroes and villains," he said curtly. He rubbed a piece of bread between his thumb and forefinger until it was a ball and popped it into his mouth. "Harry likes those sorts of stories too. But it's a mistake to believe that a man can't be entirely selfish if he thinks of others too. Harry is important to me. He's my eyes and ears in Amberwich. He's good company, and he knows more filthy jokes than my mother. I don't want him to die because I would miss him but also because it would make my life more difficult in a multitude of practical ways. Make no mistake, it's that selfishness that drove me all the way to Anhaga."

"You think it's selfish to love someone?"

"Yes," Min said. "And before you counter that, don't forget that I saw your old master's skull land in a pile of dust. You were selfish too, sweeting. You didn't even allow Kallick's bones to rest when he died."

Kaz's dark eyes gleamed, and he blinked quickly. "He didn't need his bones anymore."

"You defiled his corpse. Some people might even say you defiled his memory."

"I'm the only one who remembers him!" Kaz's voice cracked.

"Selfish," Min said. He resisted the urge to reach out and trace his fingers along the trembling line of Kaz's jaw. "A selfish little child."

"You mock me!"

"No. I'm a selfish little child as well, at heart. And so is every man, though few will admit it."

Kaz huffed. "You think you're so clever! You think it takes some special talent to see into the true hearts of men. It doesn't! You're just shallow and bitter, and you think the whole world is too!"

It was more words than they'd ever exchanged, probably, and Min was unsurprised it had led them to this moment. He'd goaded Kaz, because he was exactly the person he said he was: a selfish child. And in this moment he was a selfish child who was scared for Harry, scared for the inexorable arrival of the full moon, and scared for the moment the blood curse would activate. So he prodded and pricked because it was better to feel anger than despair, wasn't it? It was better to feel like he had a purpose and wasn't just wandering around lost in the fucking woods. And some might say—his own mother chief amongst them—that most everyone who met Min ended up hating him, so why waste time getting to the foregone conclusion?

Min curled his mouth into a mocking smile. "And you are either a fool, Kazimir—"

"I am *not*!"

"Or you are playing me for one," Min finished. "You're to be bound in iron your whole life, kept under the thumb of your grandfather, *married* to your own uncle, and you really believe there is anything in the hearts of men but greed and cruelty?"

Kaz swallowed, his throat bobbing. He lifted his chin. "I believe that not all men are like them."

"Then I fear you will be disappointed," Min said. "Over and over again."

"Fuck you," Kaz said. He clenched his jaw tight for a moment, the muscles in his cheeks trembling. Then he opened his mouth again: "Fuck you."

And he turned and stalked away.

Min followed him, because what the hell else was he to do?

THE AFTERNOON shadows deepened in the hollows on the ground. Min's feet hurt, and his throat was as dry as a gravel pit. Kaz hadn't spoken to him in hours, and Min wished he could say the silence was a blessing. It felt more like a burden, though, as if someone had thrown a heavy blanket over Min and blocked out the light. Kaz's silence felt as oppressive as an overcast day, or one where a thick haze of smoke lay in the air. Min was used to people who used words as weapons, not silence. But then, Min had been raised in a brothel, surrounded by women with tongues as sharp as their wits. Kaz had grown up with a corpse for company.

Even a corpse might be more talkative than Kaz right now.

At the top of a slight rise where the trees thinned a little and the dry leaves were thick underfoot, Kaz stopped. He bowed his head and rolled his shoulders, then unfastened his cloak and dropped it to the ground. He was wearing his shirt pulled through the iron collar again, like a ruff. His kirtle was unlaced. He raised a hand to the back of his neck and tapped his fingers on his nape. Then paused and did it again.

"What are you doing?" Min asked.

"Come on," Kaz murmured. "Come out, Chirpy."

He tapped his fingers against his pale skin a third time, and a sharply inked beak followed the path of them, snapping. Kaz curled his long fingers and was suddenly holding a handful of squawking raven. A tiny black feather spiraled to the ground.

Kaz brought the bird around to his front and raised it so he could look it in the eye. "Find water."

The raven glared at him.

"Knifebeak," Kaz said, his voice cajoling, his eyes wide. "Find water, please."

He tossed the raven into the air, smiling as it took wing and cleared the trees.

Impossible, that he should have had the magic to conjure life into the bird with the iron collar around his neck. But the cat and the bird were different from Kallick, weren't they? Kallick had been a puppet. The cat and the bird did not seem to be controlled by Kaz's will at all. They simply *were*, and they were as confounding as their keeper.

Kaz's blood, part fae and part human, seemed to not follow the rules of either.

Kaz peered up at the sky, squinting into the light.

Taavi the cat slipped out from underneath Kaz's kirtle, dropping softly to the ground and sitting on his boot. Kaz dropped a hand to his side, and the cat stood on her hind legs to butt her head against his fingers.

"Are you talking to me yet?" Min asked.

Kaz looked away, but Taavi strutted over to him and curled around his ankles.

"At least one of you is, hmm?" Min scratched the cat's head.

"I am not sure what we have to talk about," Kaz said, still looking away. "Words cannot change the path we are on. Maybe I am a fool, though, because I didn't realize you hated me."

"I don't hate you, Kaz," Min said. His throat ached from more than his thirst. "But I can't be your friend."

Kaz turned his head to meet his gaze. He looked suddenly, achingly *young*. "Why not?"

"Because...." Min shook his head helplessly. "Sons of Rus, Kaz! Because it would be fucking *heartbreaking*!"

In the sudden silence, a bird chattered from somewhere nearby, and Min felt he had revealed way too much of himself to Kaz's wide gaze. He felt almost naked, stripped bare.

"Oh," said Kaz quietly at last. He crossed his arms over his chest and hugged himself. "Oh. I'm sorry. I didn't—I didn't understand."

"I don't hate you," Min said. "But I can't be your friend."

Kaz nodded, his gaze dropping.

Min looked up as he heard the piercing cry of a raven overhead, and moments later Chirpy dove down, alighting on Kaz's shoulder and chattering in his ear. He ruffled his feathers and nipped at Kaz's earlobe.

"Good boy," Kaz murmured. "Clever bird."

Chirpy preened.

"Did he find water?" Min asked hopefully.

"Better," Kaz said. He pointed. "He says the road's just over the next rise, and there's a carter coming this way now."

Min stooped to pick up Kaz's cloak. "Then let's move. My feet are killing me."

Kaz flashed a wavering smile and fell into step beside him.

CHAPTER 13

JODERMAN THE goose farmer was not a talkative man, bless him, but his one good eye lit up when Min produced three shiny quadrans from his purse and asked for a ride to Amberwich. The back of Joderman's cart was filled with crates of geese he was transporting to market in Amberwich, and Min had never been happier to be hissed at and abused. He and Kaz sat in the back, their aching feet hanging down, and drank Joderman's watered-down beer and ate the corned mutton and bread his wife had packed him for the journey. Joderman had apparently weighted Min's three quadrans against the cost of an empty belly and discovered he liked the result.

Min had managed to ascertain from the brief words he'd exchanged with the man that they were no longer on the road from Pran. They must have cut through the woods instead of doubling back to the road they'd fled. Joderman came from a village called Halford. Min had never heard of it and didn't particularly regret the gap in his knowledge. The important thing was they would be in Amberwich by nightfall. Joderman, like many of the farmers who came from miles around to sell at the markets every nine days, would camp outside the city walls overnight, only taking his cart inside the city just before dawn to set up. Min and Kaz, unencumbered by a cart, a horse, and over thirty angry geese, would part company with him at the gate and continue on to—

Min's heart tumbled over a missed beat, and his stomach clenched.

They would continue on to deliver Kaz to Edward Sabadine, that venomous snake, and Min would never see him again. He would be kept collared—no doubt about it now that Robert knew he was a necromancer—and treated as a prisoner in the cold bosom of his family. Min wished he could believe Kaz would at least be given a gilded cage, but he'd felt the ice in Edward Sabadine's stare. There wasn't an ounce of compassion in the old man's body. He was cold-blooded.

But Harry would live.

Harry would live, and Min had to believe that was worth it. He couldn't afford to falter now, to stumble on the final steps of this loathsome endeavor.

The day drew on, and Min was rocked into a doze by the sway of the wagon, back and forth, back and forth as it juddered over the road. They passed fields of crops and of goats and sheep and cows. They passed cottages and shrines and once, a group of barefoot children carrying fishing poles. Once or twice riders on horseback appeared in the distance behind them, growing closer and closer until they drew alongside the cart and then overtook it. The road became a little wider and a little busier with each slow-passing hour.

Kaz sat in silence, twisting pieces of straw into shapes and then straightening them out again and starting over.

Min drew his legs up and shuffled around so he was facing the front of the cart. In the distance, the walls of Amberwich glowed in the afternoon sunlight, a smoky haze hanging above them, and Min had never seen a more beautiful sight. They were still too far away for Min to make out any landmark except the Iron Tower, which rose above all the other buildings in the city, strong and forbidding. The king himself dwelt there, where the iron not only protected the city from the Hidden Lord, but also protected the king from the Gifted. The history of Amberwich had been a bloody one at times, and no king, Min supposed, slept entirely soundly.

The sun was setting by the time Joderman drove the cart off the side of the road into a field already full of carts and carters, horses and livestock, crates and bales. Min slid down from the back of the cart, landing in something soft that he hoped was mud rather than the alternative. He held his arms up for Kaz, helping him down to the ground.

"Thank you for the ride, sir," he said, and Joderman nodded in acknowledgment and made a noise that sounded something like "yarp."

Min and Kaz continued toward the city walls and the old portcullis gate. This wasn't Stanes Street, but Market Street. Market Street cut through the western quarter of Amberwich. Their route to Sabadine's house from here would take them within spitting distance of the Iron Tower on the King's Hill. Strange that the Iron Tower was so visible from outside the city; from within, under the eaves and the awnings and the overhangs of houses and shops and inns and taverns, a man might never even catch a glimpse of it.

Min didn't know the western quarter as well as he knew the eastern. He could find his way, but not well enough to risk any shortcuts down narrow alleys. Getting lost wasn't Min's only concern. In the eastern quarter, Min knew exactly where the cutpurses and rogues gathered— he gathered with them on most occasions—but he had no desire to run into any who didn't either count him as a friend or had at least agreed not to stab him out of professional courtesy. Once they passed under the portcullis and entered the city proper, Min and Kaz kept to the main road.

Min sucked in lungfuls of smoky air that tasted like home.

Beside him, Kaz's footsteps faltered. "Min…."

Min turned to look at him.

In the growing darkness, his face was pale, and tears shone on his cheeks. "Min, I don't want to go."

And here it was, Kaz's breakdown, a lot later than Min had expected it if he was honest with himself. Which he rarely was. But the burden had been bound to crush the boy sooner or later. This was the moment Min had been dreading, where all his previous cruelty would feel so very small.

Kaz scrubbed at his cheeks with his sleeves. "I don't want my grandfather to lock me up. I don't want to marry my uncle." His bottom lip trembled. "I hate them. I *hate* them."

They had stopped in the street between an inn and a taproom. The inn was quiet, but there was light and noise spilling out of the open door and shutters of the taproom. A woman shrieked with laughter—a strident, drunken sound that seemed to mock Kaz's misery.

"I don't want to go," Kaz repeated. "I have to, and I will, but I don't *want* to."

And that was the crux of it, wasn't it? That was the unfixable rot at the heart of the matter.

"There is still a sennight until the full moon," Kaz said. "I know you can't be my friend, but can you pretend, just for tonight?"

Min felt a rush of some sharp emotion he couldn't name pass over him. "What are you asking me?"

Kaz wiped his face again. "I don't want my uncle to be the first man who has me. I want you to be the one to do it, so that at least there will be once in my life that it's not...." He shrugged.

Rape, Min thought. *So that it's not rape.*

"That's a terrible idea, Kaz."

"I know," Kaz said with a wavering smile. "But you're handsome, and I don't hate you, and I don't think you hate me either, and I just want something for *me*, Min, just once. I am selfish, like you said. And why shouldn't I be?"

Well, why indeed?

And Min was selfish too.

He stepped forward into Kaz's space, tucked his hand under Kaz's chin, tilted his jaw, and leaned in to take the kiss he'd wanted for days. Kaz let out a hot huff of surprised breath, but then his mouth was pressing back firmly against Min's, his lips closed, and Min thought he had probably never had a kiss that was so *innocent*. Kaz wanted to fuck, and he didn't even know how to kiss. Had Min been a better man, that might have given him pause. But Min was not a better man.

He broke the kiss, keeping his mouth pressed against Kaz's cheek and nuzzling his face to prevent him from shying away. He caught Kaz's right wrist softly and moved his hand to his shoulder. When he released it, Kaz kept his hand in place. Min lifted his right hand and curled his fingers gently around Kaz's throat, just above where the iron collar rested. He could feel Kaz's frantic pulse hammering in his jugular. Min lifted the boy's chin again and brought their mouths together once more.

Kaz's breath was hot against his lips.

Min used his tongue to coax the seam of Kaz's mouth open. Kaz tasted like Joderman's beer, and Min chased the bitter taste with his tongue, slipping it over Kaz's teeth and against the roof of his mouth before he withdrew and sucked for a moment on Kaz's lower lip.

Kaz made a small surprised noise and dug his fingers into Min's shoulder. Min's other hand found Kaz's head, and he slid his trembling fingers through his hair.

Min deepened the kiss again, this time darting his tongue against Kaz's and then pulling back to encourage Kaz's tongue to follow.

Kaz moaned and shivered.

Min sucked at his lower lip again for a moment and then, regretfully, pulled away.

Kaz's dark eyes were wide, his pupils large. His wet mouth hung open, and his jaw worked for a moment before any words spilled out: "You… you will give me tonight, then?"

Against all his better judgment, probably, but a lifetime of making terrible decisions had lead Min down a lot of enjoyable paths.

"Yes," he said. "Just tonight."

Kaz nodded, and then another burst of raucous laughter from the nearby taproom ushered them deeper into Amberwich.

THE FOOTBRIDGE Tavern was a light in the cesspool that was this particular neighborhood in the eastern quarter. Like any light, it attracted insects. There was a group of them in the street outside as Min and Kaz approached: sons from noble Houses who were trying too hard to look like they weren't at all intimidated. They were full of swagger and braying laughter as though they wouldn't all scream and run at the first sight of actual danger.

"Keep your cloak on," Min said to Kaz. The last thing he wanted to do was explain Kaz's collar to anyone. "We'll get some food, maybe some beer, and go to my place."

Kaz nodded.

Min eyed the nervous noblemen closely as he held the door of the Footbridge open for Kaz. He had barely followed him inside when burly-armed Freya grabbed him by the forearm.

"Step out the back door and you'll have eyes on you," she growled.

Min swore under his breath.

"Two of them," Freya said. "Hanging around like flies on shit. Aulus spotted them yesterday."

Men from the Sabadines' household, Min wondered, or were some of his older debts catching him up at last? Whatever the case, it did rather put a crimp in his plans for spending the night with Kaz.

Unless….

Well, desperate times and all that.

He dug into his purse to thank Freya for the warning and turned and steered Kaz out the way they'd come.

"Where are we going?" Kaz asked.

"The one place that anybody who knows me would never think to look."

THE MAN on the door recognized Min and let them in.

The place was busy, as always, and smelled of alcohol and perfume. Min took Kaz's hand and drew him toward the back of the house, past doors that opened onto opulent parlors, and up the stairs. The rooms were just as opulent here, but the doors were closed.

There was another set of stairs at the back of the house, dark and narrow, but Min knew his way.

Min was surprised to find the attic room above his mother's brothel in good repair. The bedding smelled a little musty, but the room was free of dust and cobwebs. He moved forward to throw the shutters open and allow some fresh air in, while Kaz looked around curiously.

Min's psaltery lay on a stool beside the low wardrobe. His mother had hired a man to teach him to play the instrument in the hopes Min could entertain her customers with some hitherto undiscovered musical talent, but Min had been terrible at it. He poked at it spitefully, plucking an untuned string that twanged mournfully in response. Even now Min felt the urge to set fire to the thing.

The little carved box that Min had collected his treasures in since he was a child was still sitting on the wardrobe. Min opened it curiously: three copper coins, several ivory betting chips he'd never cashed in, and a silver cloak pin that had been gifted to Min when he'd been fifteen by a nobleman customer of his mother's who'd tried desperately for months to get into Min's pants. Min was surprised his mother hadn't sold it. He was also surprised she allowed him even a few moments to reacquaint himself with his childhood room before she stalked up the steps to tell him what a waste of space he was.

Kaz jumped when the sharp rapping sounded at the door, but Min only rolled his eyes and pulled the door open.

"Good evening, Mother."

Mairead Decourcey had the fixed, narrow stare of a hawk that had spied a particularly fat rabbit. She was a striking woman, Min supposed. He probably owed her his good looks, although he would never admit it. She was almost fifty now—although she would never admit *that*—but she carried her age well. She was more beautiful than many women half her age.

"Well," she said, crossing the floor to light the lamp on the table by his bed. "You're not dead. How surprising."

Min smiled. "I flatter myself that I'm full of surprises."

"You flatter yourself because nobody else will." Mairead's gaze shifted to Kaz. "Who's this?"

"None of your business."

Mairead raised an eyebrow. "Where's Henriette?"

Min bridled at that, as he always did. "His name is Harry."

Mairead pressed her mouth into a thin line. "Finally got sick of you, did she?"

"*He,*" Min said pointedly, "is fine." He hoped it wasn't a lie. "For some reason he doesn't have fond memories of this place or of you. I can't imagine why."

Mairead *hmmph*ed. "I suppose you're in some sort of trouble, aren't you, if you're here?"

"Not the sort that will bring the guard to your door," Min said. "Beyond that, it's no business of yours."

Mairead raised her eyes to the ceiling, as though she was petitioning a particularly vengeful god to strike him down. She probably was. Then she looked at Kaz again. "You can do a lot better."

Min clenched his fists. "That's none of—"

"I was talking to the boy," Mairead said and raised her eyebrows.

Min had no reply. It was a fair call, actually.

Mairead regarded him silently for a moment, a calculating look in her eye. "Well," she said at last, "I'll have some water sent up, shall I? You look like you've been rolling around in a sewer."

Min smiled thinly. "And food too, please."

"You think I'd let you starve?"

"I shall do you the courtesy of not answering that."

She snorted, straightened the heavy necklace that rested on her bosom, and sailed out of the attic room.

Min made a rude gesture after her and then sat on the edge of the bed and peeled his boots off. Kaz sat beside him and did the same.

Mairead was back moments later, followed by a gaggle of girls in various states of undress. What they lacked in clothing they made up for in food, water, and wine. Min thought he recognized one of them, but he didn't remember her name. He thanked them and glared at his mother while she fussed around setting the serving tray down on the bed just so, as though Min were a rich customer instead of her reprobate son. He didn't fall for it for a second.

Kaz stared at the floor, his cheeks bright as the girls flittered around.

"Good night, Mother," Min said pointedly at last, and Mairead smirked at him and ushered the girls from the room.

Min closed and bolted the door behind them.

The basin on the low wardrobe was full of hot rose-scented water now, with a clean sea sponge floating on the cloudy surface. Min submerged it and then squeezed the water out of it. He gestured Kaz closer.

"Can I wash you?"

Kaz's flush deepened, but then he nodded and lifted his shaking hands to his throat. He dropped his cloak to the floor and reached for the laces of his kirtle. He loosened them and tugged his kirtle over his head. His shirt came next, revealing the pale planes of his torso to Min's hungry gaze. Then he loosened the ties on his breeches and pushed them down, revealing a pair of thin linen braies that hung loosely from his hips. He raised his gaze to meet Min's and then dropped the braies as well.

Beautiful.

Kaz was lean and pale, although his flush extended down to his chest and painted him a pinkish hue. There was a slenderness to him that Min liked; he was no manual laborer with bulging muscles—though Min quite liked those in a man as well. Kaz's cock was a good size, inclined more to length than to girth, and the moment they were both clean, Min fully intended to discover if it tasted as nice as it looked.

Min dropped the sponge back into the basin and stripped his own clothes off.

He was not shy. Never had been, thanks to growing up under this roof. He knew he was good-looking; he had heard it too many times to doubt it and had preened in front of the mirror as often as the vainest girls downstairs. He'd once been as slender and pretty as Kaz, but that had been at least a decade ago. Min wasn't counting, though, because his vanity didn't need to suffer that blow. He was still young, thank you, however much Harry laughed at him and told him he wasn't. Besides,

Min had matured like fine wine, or perhaps cheese. He hadn't gone stale and moldy. He had *sharpened*.

Kaz's gaze was certainly appreciative.

"Come here, sweeting." Min took the sponge again and delighted in the way Kaz shivered when he swept it down his chest. Kaz's nipples hardened in the wake of the sponge, and Taavi, curled up on his hip, opened her eyes and flicked her ears as a droplet of water slid down Kaz's skin.

Kaz's cock was already half-hard, but Min teased him by paying it no mind. Instead, he washed his chest, his sides, and under his arms, and crouched down to reach his legs. Then he turned him around and washed his back and his perfect ass. Min's mouth watered at the sight of it and at the thought of sinking deep inside and making Kaz cry out in pleasure. He swept the sponge over the globes of Kaz's ass and then down into the cleft. Kaz jerked in surprise, his breath rushing out of him. The touch of the sponge on his hole drove him up onto his toes for a moment.

Min laughed and turned Kaz again. He dipped the sponge in the water again and this time rubbed it over Kaz's abdomen, following the sparse trail of dark hair down from his navel to his cock and balls.

Kaz jerked again as Min ran the sponge over his cock, his breath shuddering out of him. "Min!"

"Shah, sweeting," Min murmured, pressing harder. "So beautiful."

Kaz squeezed his eyes shut as his cock twitched under Min's attention.

"Done," Min said and tossed the sponge back in the basin. He waited until Kaz blinked his eyes open and then leaned in and kissed him gently. "Go wait on the bed and tell me if my mother's cook is still a miracle worker."

Kaz trailed over to the bed, sitting down and picking at the tray of food as Min washed himself. It felt good to clean away the dust from the road. It felt better to have Kaz watch him as he did.

"It is good?" he asked with a smirk.

Kaz looked guiltily at the half-eaten sweetmeat in his hand. "Yes."

Min finished up and prowled over to the bed. He shoved the pillow up against the headboard and sat down, stretching his legs out. "Come lean against me, Kaz."

Kaz obeyed, angling his body awkwardly away as though Min hadn't had his hand on his dick mere moments ago.

"Do you need to put a shirt on?" Min asked him.

Kaz looked surprised for a moment and then reached up and touched the iron collar. "No. No, it doesn't seem to burn like it did."

Min pushed away his disquiet at that admission. If the iron had hurt when he first put it on, then it should have still been hurting now, but Kaz seemed to have developed a tolerance for it, like the old gulchcups at the Footbridge Tavern who needed to swallow down twice as much beer as other men to feel half as drunk. Kaz's Gift, perhaps because of the addition of his strange blood, was unlike any other he had known, though Kaz didn't seem to fully realize it.

"Good," he said instead, and reached out for the tray. He inspected the dishes and also the small vial of oil he knew had nothing to do with food at all. He selected a dish of sweetbread pieces, baked in crumbs. He picked one out and held it up to Kaz's face. "Open."

Kaz opened, and Min popped the sweetbread inside his mouth. He dragged his fingers against Kaz's lower lip as he withdrew them, and Kaz shivered at the touch. His cheeks burned red, but he opened his mouth again when Min fed him the next piece. By the time they had moved on to the honey-mustard egg halves and cheese, Kaz had relaxed and was lying curled against Min's side, one hand splayed against Min's chest, rubbing his fingertips over the hair there. Kaz's cock was hard and hot against Min's thigh.

Min kissed him between bites, soft, lazy kisses that tasted of the finest dishes from his mother's kitchen.

He set the empty tray aside. "Ready for more, sweeting?"

He wasn't talking about food.

"Yes," Kaz whispered, raising his chin for another kiss. "Yes, please, Min."

CHAPTER 14

THEY TOOK it slowly.

Kaz was nervous, his inexperience evident in his wrinkled nose, his bitten lip, and the awkward way he responded at first to Min's touches, as though he was embarrassed by his body's reaction or by Min's scrutiny of it. Min, for his part, couldn't even remember the last time he bedded a virgin, but it was no matter to him. And besides, Kaz was a hot-blooded young man. It only took until Min had Kaz's cock in his mouth for Kaz's eager enthusiasm to overcome his apprehension.

Kaz was a feast of delights.

He came so hard that even Min was surprised and struggled to swallow him down. Then, afterward, they drank a little wine, and Min played Kaz's body better than he ever played the damn psaltery. His fingers stroked Kaz's skin, plucked at his nipples, and danced up the strings of his ribs. Kaz, in his turn, made sounds that were sweeter than any music.

Min left a trail of kisses over Kaz's chest, laughing softly against his skin as Taavi, affronted, leapt off Kaz's hip and landed, a proper cat, on the mattress. She dropped down onto the floor and vanished under the bed.

Chirpy, for his part, stayed hidden in Kaz's hair. Min never even glimpsed a feather or a claw.

Bright moonlight streamed in the window. It bathed Kaz's body in silver light and made him seem almost otherworldly, as ethereal as the fae, but Kaz's features weren't as sharp as theirs. Min didn't fear fangs when they kissed.

Min set a slow pace, but it was inexorable. They both wanted this, they both demanded this from a world that was unfair, and there was no way either of them was going to waste the only opportunity they had to be selfish in this way and be together for as long as the night lasted.

They didn't speak, but Kaz curled his fingers through Min's, and whenever Min raised his head to look at him, he found that Kaz was looking back. This, Min thought, was both their first real meeting as well as their slow farewell.

Min kissed him again. Kaz's mouth was hot and wet, and he shivered as Min licked inside it. Kaz made a tiny sound of disappointment as Min leaned away from him and reached for the small vial of oil. Min opened it and drizzled the oil on his fingers.

Kaz watched wide-eyed.

Min leaned down and kissed him again, settling himself close enough beside him to press kisses to his mouth even while his hand dipped down between his legs. Kaz shifted nervously, the muscles in his thighs tightening. His breath was hot against Min's mouth as Min pressed his index finger gently inside him.

The movement pushed a noise of surprise from him.

"Beautiful," Min murmured, and Kaz exhaled shakily and relaxed again.

Min twisted his finger, reveling in the tremor that ran through Kaz. He withdrew his finger and then pressed two inside him. He would love to be doing this in the daylight. Love to use each touch, each kiss, to strip away another veil of Kaz's anxiety. Love to see him *shameless*.

Min kissed him on the jaw and scissored his fingers.

He was beautiful. So beautiful.

Kaz melted slowly under Min's attention, his legs falling farther apart and his hips starting to lift with each gentle thrust of Min's fingers. Min opened him slowly, until he had three fingers inside him and Kaz was moaning softly for more, tossing his head from side to side.

"Please, Min. Please."

Min shifted, positioning himself in the cradle of Kaz's thighs. He lifted Kaz's legs, tilting his hips up. Then he took his aching cock in his hand and moved so the tip of it kissed Kaz's hole. He pushed in slowly.

Kaz's face was a symphony of emotion: anxiety, desire, discomfort as Min breached him, and, finally, surprise as Min seated himself fully.

"Breathe through it, sweeting."

Kaz squirmed. The muscles in his thighs trembled. "Oh!"

"You are beautiful," Min said, encouraging Kaz into a gentle, undulating rhythm.

Kaz's cock was hard. Each careful thrust from Min caused it to leak more and more. He arched his back, eager for more, and Min obliged him, thrusting harder, deeper. Kaz dug one hand into the mattress. He curled the other one around his cock, stroking himself in time with Min's thrusts. His body gleamed with sweat. His kiss-bitten lips shone, and the moonlight glittered in his dark eyes.

Min wanted this moment to last forever, but it was too ephemeral to grasp.

Kaz cried out as he came, his muscles tightening and releasing as he tumbled over the edge of the abyss, and Min, hips stuttering, followed him down and replied to his sated smile with a series of sweet, gentle kisses.

MIN LEFT Kaz dozing and went downstairs for clean water. He was barefoot, wearing only his breeches, and naturally his mother cornered him in the kitchen. She had always impressed on him the need to dress impeccably and to be both witty and gracious. Mairead Decourcey didn't run a cheap establishment.

She looked him up and down, and Min waited for a rebuke. Instead, she said, "Still hungry?"

"No. I just want some more hot water."

"I'll have one of the girls bring some up." Mairead's expression softened, and Min didn't know how to read it. "Do you know what you're doing, Aramin?"

Min felt his mouth twist into a bitter smile. His mother had always been perceptive. It was why they butted heads so often, probably. He'd never been able to get a lie past her. "Hardly ever."

Mairead pursed her lips for a moment, as though she was biting back words, and then she nodded. "Go back upstairs. I'll send the water up."

Min nodded and escaped.

When he arrived back in the attic room, Kaz turned to him and smiled, and they both pretended the dampness on the boy's face didn't mean he had been crying.

DAWN HAD barely softened the darkness when Min and Kaz left the house. Streaks of pale pink and orange lay against the dark blanket of the sky, heralding the approach of the sun. The streets were still dark, though; the faint light hadn't filtered down to the cobblestones yet. It was market day, so there were already a few people in the streets, walking briskly to keep ahead of the slight chill. Soon the dribs and drabs would become a bustle as more and more people climbed out of bed to hurry to the marketplace. Market days were always busy in Amberwich, surpassed only by the festival days that came around once every few months.

Min and Kaz walked in silence, their fingers loosely linked.

Min had told Kaz he would give him the night, and now he found that he wanted to give him what he could of this morning as well. It wasn't enough. It would never be enough.

They walked slowly, the streets widening as they passed out of the eastern quarter and by the Shrine of the Sacred Spring, where the leaves on the trees danced in the breeze. The torches around the temple proper were still lit, burning down slowly as the dawn settled over the city. Min thought briefly of Aiode Nettle.

He and Kaz climbed the slope of the hill out of the valley, to where the workshops and storefronts gave way to the garden walls and porticos of the private houses of Amberwich's richest men. It felt as though no time at all had passed before they were standing in front of the wide portico of the Sabadines' house.

"I don't remember it," Kaz said softly. "I don't remember it at all."

Min wondered if that was because it had been years since he'd been here or if he'd been as much a prisoner inside those walls as a child as they intended to make him now.

"I'll come for you," he said suddenly. "When Harry's safe again, I'll come for you."

"Don't. Don't say that." Kaz blinked and tears slid down his cheeks. He tightened his grip on Min's hand. "Don't make promises you can't keep. You're cleverer than that."

Was he? Min wondered. He didn't feel clever today. He felt as though there was some grotesque creature burrowed into his rib cage, and it was squeezing his heart in its thick, ugly hands. He felt as though he could hardly breathe.

Min had always known life wasn't fair, but this was the first time since he'd been a child that he wanted to scream and beat his fists about it.

"You gave me all I asked for," Kaz said softly. He lifted Min's hand and pressed his mouth to his knuckles. "Thank you. I won't forget you."

Like a happy memory, Min thought, *or an aching scar?*

Kaz dropped Min's hand and squared his shoulders. He held Min's gaze and nodded.

Min knocked at the door and, moments later, a narrow-eyed servant opened it.

"What is your business?"

"Aramin Decourcey," Min said. "I'm here to see Edward Sabadine."

"The master is still abed." The servant sniffed. "As any *decent* gentleman is."

"Then wake him," Min said firmly. "And tell him I have brought his grandson home."

The servant looked from Min to Kaz and back again, jaw dropping, and opened the door wider to let them inside.

Min felt the same creeping sense of dread he had the first time in this house. There was an oppressive weight that seemed to hang over the place, and Min was sure it was all to do with the evil old snake who lived here.

The servant showed them to the room remembered from his first visit, the walls painted in pastoral scenes of livestock and harvests. Min didn't sit and neither did Kaz. They weren't waiting long before Min heard footsteps in the hall outside, and a moment later Robert Sabadine appeared in the doorway.

"I thought you were dead," he said.

Min gave a half bow. "Sorry to disappoint."

Robert shook his head slightly.

"Is Harry here?"

Robert's jaw tightened, which gave Min the answer he needed before he opened his mouth to confirm it. "Yes."

"I don't like you," Min said, "but I trust that you are a man of your word."

"He's unharmed," Robert said. "He will be safely returned to you and the curse lifted, I swear."

Coming from Robert, Min actually believed the assurance. He wouldn't have, though, from the man who now stepped around Robert to enter the room. Edward Sabadine. He was wearing soft shoes and an embroidered purple bed robe, and his white hair was mussed with sleep, but he still managed to exude an air of cold menace.

"Well," he said, his dark eyes glinting. "You actually did it. Come here, boy, and let me look at you."

Kaz, his head down, stepped forward.

Edward looked him up and down and then reached up to flick his curls away from a pointed ear. Kaz flinched away, and Edward gripped a handful of hair to restrain him. "Stand still, you mutt!"

Min clenched his fists at his sides, fighting the urge to intervene, and caught Robert's unreadable gaze.

Edward resumed his inspection. "Do you remember how to address me?"

Kaz's shaking voice was hardly louder than a whisper. "Yes, my lord."

"Good." Edward released his hair. "You belong to this House now, do you understand?"

"Yes, my lord."

"To whom do you bow?" Edward demanded.

"T-to you, my lord," Kaz whispered.

Min's chest tightened. "Sir," he said, drawing the old man's attention back to him and away from Kaz, for all the good it would do in the long run. "May I remind you that I am owed my payment?"

Edward's piercing gaze found him, and his thin mouth curled into a smile. "A boy for a boy, wasn't it?"

"Yes, sir."

Edward clicked his fingers, and the servant who had been lurking by the door scuttled forward like a cockroach. "Go and fetch the Decourcey brat. Have Abelard remove the curse."

"Yes, my lord." The servant scuttled away again.

"You must tell us, Decourcey, how you escaped the fae." Edward stepped away from Kaz, clasping his hands behind his back. "Robert tells me he thought you had both been killed."

"Even the fae have their weaknesses," Min said, which was an answer that would strengthen his reputation better than the truth: it was dumb fucking chance that had saved his miserable hide. Dumb chance and Kaz.

Edward let out a bark of laughter and said, approvingly, "You are no coward, are you?"

Actually he was an inveterate coward, but Min only smirked and inclined his head.

"And Kallick gave you no trouble getting the mutt away?"

Min met Kaz's gaze. "No, sir. No trouble."

The lie would serve no purpose, probably. Robert must have told Edward already that Kaz was a necromancer. Yet it was one thing to know in theory what Kaz's actual Gift was and another to know he'd practiced it to animate his master's corpse for over a decade. Min couldn't be sure that Edward would treat Kaz any better if he didn't know about Kallick, but the lie still came easily enough.

Kaz looked achingly grateful.

Min told himself there were a hundred things he wanted to say to Kaz, a *thousand*, but that was another lie, wasn't it? They'd barely spoken on their walk from the eastern quarter, because of all those things Min wanted to say, there wasn't a single one that wouldn't have cut like a knife.

Tomorrow.

Tomorrow this would all be behind him. Tomorrow he would take his usual table in the Footbridge Tavern, Harry at his side, and wait for someone to approach him with an offer of a job. Someone who had heard of Aramin Decourcey's reputation for walking through locked doors and passing beneath the notice of the Gifted and all their wards and spells, and who had enough coin in his purse to pay handsomely for Min's trouble. A sordid, grubby transaction made in a sordid, grubby tavern, but compared to all this, it would feel as clean and clear as a draught of water from a mountain spring.

Min just had to make it through today first.

"Ha!" Edward laughed. "I knew that old fool of a hedgewitch was all bark and no bite!"

Min was saved from having to respond by the slap of footsteps from the hall, and suddenly Harry was darting into the room and flinging himself into Min's embrace.

"I thought you were dead!"

"It seems nobody had any faith in me at all," Min replied archly. He squeezed Harry tightly and then released him so he could inspect him as closely as Edward had inspected Kaz, though with a world more care. There was a faint red flush on Harry's cheek, as though he'd slept on it, but the sigil that had marked his curse was gone.

Min was almost overwhelmed with relief, but he didn't dare show it here. To show a man like Edward Sabadine that he had a heart was like showing his throat to a wolf. A heart was a weakness to a man like that, just another place to sink his fangs.

"I believe this concludes our business," he said.

"I believe it does," Edward agreed. "If the boy ever shows his face here again, mind, I'll cut him up and feed his remains to my hounds."

"Understood, sir," Min said, gripping Harry's shoulder tightly. He looked to Robert, who nodded at him shortly, and then to Kaz. Kaz did not meet his gaze, and Min didn't blame him. Min wasn't the only one who knew not to show Edward Sabadine how to wound him. It was better they parted as strangers, and not the friends they had been last night.

Friends.

The word was insufficient. There had been more between them than friendship. There had been a different emotion altogether compressed into the places where there shouldn't have been any room for anything at all: between their mouths as they kissed, between their clasped palms, between all of the places their bodies touched.

The tightness in Min's chest was almost painful, and his throat ached. "Good day, then."

And he steered Harry out of the room, toward the front door, and then through it into the daylight.

MIN STILL had enough of Robert Sabadine's money in his purse to get rollingly drunk, and he did it with relish. He sat at his customary table in the Footbridge Tavern with a jug of Swann's foulest and strongest ale at his elbow and a cup in his hand. The ale churned in his guts in a way that promised it'd be fighting its way back out any moment now, but Min didn't care.

Harry sat with him, shoveling porridge down his throat like he hadn't been fed in days. Maybe he hadn't. The Sabadines were probably not the most generous of hosts.

"Kept in a storeroom since we got back to the city," Harry said around his porridge when Min slurred the question out. "Wasn't even any food in there. Just linens. I pissed on a board-cloth, then folded it up and put it back in the middle of the pile."

Min snorted. "That's my boy."

"How did you escape?" Harry asked, his forehead wrinkling. "On the road, with the fae?"

"No fucking idea," Min said, and took another swallow of ale. "Just grabbed Kaz and ran into the woods." He closed his eyes for a moment, remembering the way he'd pressed his hand against Kaz's mouth and how warm his breath had been on his palm.

"You just ran?" Harry prompted, and Min wondered if he'd stopped talking for too long. He was drunk enough that his brain was having difficulties with the concept of time.

"He saved me, though, I think. There was this clearing, with a spring in it. Made my head muzzy just looking at it. I would have drunk from it if Kaz hadn't stopped me." He set his mug down, glaring at it when ale sloshed over the sides. "How did *you* escape?"

"Rode like hell and didn't look back."

Min dragged his finger through the puddle of ale on the scarred tabletop. "Good strategy."

Harry quirked his mouth. "I learned from the best."

Min was the best? Funny, because at the moment he felt like the fucking *worst*, and it wasn't even the ale that was to blame, though it certainly wasn't helping. His guts churned again, and Min took another swallow of ale to remind them who was in charge.

The Footbridge Tavern was mostly empty at this early hour. There was a girl sweeping last night's straw out the door and into the street and a man leaning against the bar and staring into the middle distance as he sipped from a large mug. Min vaguely recognized him as the baker from the next street, who routinely escaped his harridan of a mother to get quietly drunk at the Footbridge. Min had always felt a sense of warm camaraderie with the fellow.

A man and a woman were slumped together at the table in the opposite corner. They were both snoring, and the woman was drooling a little. A skinny dog, whip-thin tail lashing, wandered up to them hopefully and sat at the man's feet like he was waiting for a treat. Swann stomped through the taproom, heading for the kitchens, and the dog reevaluated its chances and followed him instead.

"Did you fuck him?" Harry asked suddenly.

Min frowned. "Who? Swann?"

"No! Kaz!"

"Oh. Yes." Min picked up the jug, held his cup, and more or less managed to get some ale from one to the other without pouring too much over the table. "Yes, I did. Last night."

"Do you love him?"

"*Pfft*. He's a necromancer who is half fae and… and half *Sabadine*. I don't know which is more dangerous." Min laughed, although he wasn't sure what was funny. His own stupidity, perhaps. "A man would be a fool to fall in love with someone like that."

Harry shrugged his skinny shoulders. "Plenty of fools in the world, Min."

Well, wasn't that the pathetic truth?

"I abducted him," Min mumbled into his ale. "I delivered him into the hands of his poisonous family. I am the architect of his misery."

Harry snatched his cup away from him. "You're a drunken fool, and you're no architect of anyone's misery. You're not as important as you imagine yourself. An architect? You're nothing but a *tool*."

Min took a moment to think through that. "I don't know if you are consoling me or insulting me."

"Why can't it be both?"

"That's fair."

Harry gestured Freya over to the table. "May we have some water, please, Freya? Before Min drowns in his cups."

Freya grunted in acknowledgment.

Min sighed. "I told him…." He was briefly distracted by Harry's fluffy dandelion hair and reached out to try and pet it.

Harry ducked away. "You told him what?"

"I told him that I'd come back for him. Once you were safe." He attempted a smile and couldn't be sure how successful it was. "And do you know what he told me?"

"What?"

"He told me not to make promises I couldn't keep."

"That's good advice, Min," Harry said, raising his eyebrows. "But how do you know if you can keep your promises or not, unless you actually get off your ass and try?"

Min blinked at the water that Freya set down in front of him.

Harry made a good point, actually.

CHAPTER 15

MIN WOKE with a throbbing head and an urgent need to piss. The afternoon light flooded across the grimy floorboards of the garret room in a haze of gold. Min rolled out of bed and shuffled over to the pot in the corner to relieve himself. He was fairly sure he pissed straight beer. Swann could have bottled and resold it, and nobody would be able to tell the difference.

Harry was seated at a stool by the window, a book open on his skinny knees. "Eel?" he asked around a mouthful, holding the jar out to Min. "Saved you the brine too."

Min's stomach churned, but he accepted the pottery jar. He ignored the eels and swallowed down a mouthful of the salty brine they were pickled in instead. It was disgusting, but Min had never discovered a hangover cure as reliable. It was cheaper than visiting a hedgewitch too. The brine burned on the way down his throat, but Min kept it down.

"Ugh." He passed the jar back to Harry. "Almost makes me miss the fresh snipe eels in Anhaga."

"Straight from the nets," Harry said, his cheek dimpling as he quirked a corner of his mouth. He dug around in the jar and pulled out a piece of pickled eel. "The beer was good in Anhaga too. The mind-numbing terror of the fae, though? Not so much."

"Not so much," Min agreed wryly, dragging his fingers through his sleep-tousled hair. "How long did I sleep?"

"A few hours." Harry jammed the lid back on the jar. "Are you sober now?"

Min shrugged. "Sober enough."

"Good." Harry set the jar on the table, then stood up and crossed over to the bed. He crouched down in front of it and reached under the sagging frame to haul out the wooden box that contained the tools of their trade.

Min sat down on the second stool, and Harry unrolled a scarred piece of vellum over the table.

Ah. It was a list of members of the Ansgot House and a reminder of Min's last big job. One of the scions of the House had helped themselves to his inheritance prematurely, in the form of an amber reliquary worth more than most houses in Min's neighborhood. The elder Ansgot had rallied from his deathbed, fueled entirely by spite, and had shown both the decency not to order the innocent servants immediately flogged and the good sense to bring in Min to retrieve the reliquary so his family's dirty laundry wasn't aired out all over the city. Min and Harry had taken a fortnight to track down the culprit and another three days to steal the reliquary back. Last Min had heard, the third Ansgot son had mysteriously been sent to the countryside due to his heretofore unknown health problems. Min wouldn't have been surprised to learn those health problems included multiple stab wounds and that the young man was actually buried out in the countryside, but that was really none of his business.

He and Harry had eaten well for weeks thanks to the Ansgots.

Min reached for the jar of eels and risked another mouthful of the bitter brine as Harry scraped the vellum clean.

Harry always looked attentive in moments like these. His brow was creased in concentration, and he used his thumbnail to pick at the little spots of ink that refused to lift under the blade of the knife. He was careful when he worked with vellum—though this stuff was old and had been cheaply bought to begin with—and Min had often thought that with his love not just of books but of all the parts of their creation, from the smell of the ink to the intricacy of their stitching, that if Harry had been born to a better station, he would have made someone a brilliant scribe.

Harry selected a pen from the scant collection in the box and a small pot of ink. He uncorked the ink, dipped the pen inside, and closed his eyes for a moment as though recalling details to his memory. Then he began to draw, and Min watched as a map of the Sabadines' house appeared in thin lines on the vellum.

Harry had a good eye for detail, but he couldn't have seen that much from his few days locked in a room or his furtive nocturnal visits to Talys that had started this whole mess.

Harry looked up and smirked, as though he knew exactly what Min was thinking. "I rode beside Talys once we lost you and Kaz. Robert was so beside himself he hardly spared us a glance. We had hours to make sure I got it right."

Clever boy. And clever girl too.

"And Talys knows exactly which room the servants were preparing for Kaz." Harry tapped on the map. "It's in the middle of the house. No windows, of course."

"Of course. And what sort of wards do the Sabadines have?"

"I don't know. I never came across any, but Talys says her grandfather's rooms and his treasury are warded."

"But not her room?"

Harry shrugged. "I guess he cares more about his purse than her safety."

Min wasn't entirely surprised. What was Talys but another chattel? And Edward Sabadine probably preferred possessions that couldn't talk back.

"I only saw the one sorcerer when I was there." Harry touched his cheek and shuddered. "It would be strange if they had more than one in their employ."

"Hmm." In Min's experience, the sort of people who relied on powerful wards relied on them a little too much, making it easier for Min to slip past them. One sorcerer or an army of them, it made no difference to Min's ability to get into the house. Of course, getting in was never going to be the problem. Min wondered if Harry, for all his planning, had considered *why* Min had asked about the wards. He let it pass for the moment. "The Sabadines have household soldiers too."

"At least a dozen are quartered in the house," Harry agreed.

"A dozen? How rich is the old snake?"

"Rich enough to be very paranoid." Harry continued to work on his map. "He is a powerful man, and he has the king's ear. He has a lot of enemies."

"All well-deserved, I'm sure."

Harry's mouth quirked in a quick grin. "No doubt. So, a dozen soldiers and about the same in servants. Plus Robert, who is the only son still living there."

"The others managed to cut their leading strings, did they?"

"Oh, there's a story there," Harry said. "Robert married without his father's permission, didn't he? He went away on some business of the king when he was a young man and came back home a widower with a brown daughter. Edward wanted him to say Talys was illegitimate, because he was supposed to have been promised to some woman from a noble House the whole time, but he refused to do it and the woman's father broke the engagement off because of the slight. Talys says that Edward has been punishing him for it ever since."

It was hard to imagine Robert Sabadine as a rebellious youth and even harder to imagine him as ever standing up to his father. But it was all too easy to imagine him bending to his father's will to guarantee his daughter's legitimacy. Edward Sabadine didn't inspire loyalty; he forced it by taking hostages. Min knew that all too well.

He looked back to Harry's map. "So a dozen soldiers?"

Harry nodded and chewed his lip worriedly.

"Hmm." Min leaned over to inspect the map. "I've been in houses with about as many before. It's not impossible." He jabbed at a room on the map. "Talys's room?"

Harry nodded. "She'll open her window when it's time. And this is the room where Kaz is being kept."

The room was closer to the heart of the house. Windowless, as Harry had said, and Min would have to pass through most of the main rooms to get to it. He wondered if he could be lucky enough not to meet anyone coming the other way.

Min chewed on his thumbnail for a moment. "And how will Talys know when it's time?"

"Her bedroom window overlooks the street. Neither of us can be seen in the street, of course, but all we need to do is pay that brat Aulus to wear a red scarf around his neck and go and stand there for a while. When Talys puts a white shawl out of her window, we'll know she's received the signal that it's happening that night."

Min was silent for a moment, then he shook his head. "You two really have put a lot of thought into this, haven't you?"

"We have," Harry said. "The hardest part is still yours, of course. I can't go into the house, or at least into the part where Kaz is kept, without running into the wards, but—"

"No," Min said. "I don't want you anywhere near that house again, Harry."

He'd half expected Harry to argue, but the boy only nodded. "Fine. I can show you how to get in, though, and how to get to where Kaz is being held."

"And then what?" Min asked quietly, his stomach sinking.

"What?"

"I'm a void," Min said. "I can get in and out without tripping a single ward. But Kaz can't."

Harry looked down at the map and then back up at Min again. "No, I thought about that too. He's not a void, but he's a necromancer."

Shit. Min knew where this was going. "Harry...."

"No, listen. Necromancers are more powerful than sorcerers. You'll just have to take his collar off!"

"He's a *necromancer*!"

"Yes," Harry said. "That's my *point*, Min."

"It's mine too," Min shot back. "You want me to uncollar a necromancer? Have you any conception of what he could *do*?"

Harry's brow creased. "But we're *rescuing* him. The collar would have to come off some time anyway, wouldn't it? Min? Wouldn't it?"

Min closed his eyes for a moment. All those fantasies of Kaz burning the world? Sons of Rus, but they'd felt *good* when Min had thought Harry's life still hung in the balance. Now, though? Now Harry was safe, and Min had selfishly remembered that, though the world was imperfect and cruel, it was the only one he had to live in.

"No!" Harry slammed the pen down. "You love him!"

"Harry." Min looked down at the ink-splattered map and the pen that was still spinning on the vellum. "I barely know him."

"But you want him to be free, don't you? Don't you?" Harry's face was red with anger. "Because if you take him out of that house but keep him in a collar, you're no better than his grandfather! Free means free, Min! It doesn't mean just chained up in a different place!"

"He could destroy the city. He could probably destroy the world if he put his mind to it."

"He could, but that doesn't mean he will." Harry jutted his chin out. "He could have raised an army of the dead in Anhaga—hundreds of them or thousands—but he never did, did he? He just hid in that house and made poultices for fishermen."

Min sighed and closed his eyes again. Harry was right. Of course he was. Kaz was a necromancer, but he was no monster. He was a boy, shy and sweet in the darkness but with a spine of steel when it mattered. He was a boy who had protected himself from both the fae and the Sabadines before Min had come along and—Kallick's dry old bones aside—hadn't harmed another person to do it.

So there was that.

There was fear too, though, dark and nebulous like some shadow rising from the deep, and Min couldn't quite shake it.

But Harry was right.

Harry was right.

Min studied the map again, following the path he'd need to take from Talys's room to Kaz's. Removing Kaz's collar wasn't even an option, after all, if Min couldn't get to him.

One step at a time.

Those dozen soldiers were worrisome.

What Min needed was a distraction. And for that he needed just the right hedgewitch.

THE EVENING service was just finishing at the Shrine of the Sacred Spring when Min and Harry arrived. The torches along the wide tree-lined avenue leading off the street and to the temple entrance had been lit and glowed more strongly as the dusk softened into night. The air smelled faintly of smoke and damp earth.

Min and Harry bypassed the temple and headed for one of the side buildings. The door was open, and so they entered and hurried up the stairs to Aiode Nettle's room. Min rapped sharply at her door and plastered on his most charming smile as she wrenched it open.

"Well, fuck me sideways," Aiode said, ignoring Min's smile completely and instead reaching out to grip Harry's chin and turn his unblemished cheek toward the light. Her freckled face lit up with astonishment. "You actually did it."

"One reprobate prentice successfully returned to the Sabadines," Min said dryly. "Right from under the eye of the Hidden Lord."

Aiode released Harry and regarded Min curiously. "There's more to this story, isn't there?"

"Oh, much more," Min said. "Buy me a drink sometime and I'll repay you with all the lurid details. In the meantime, I need a favor."

Aiode arched her brows. "A favor? I'm not sure you understand the nature of our relationship, Aramin. As in, we don't have one."

Min knew he liked Aiode for a reason. He had always been unreasonably attracted to snark.

"Not a favor, then," he said, putting his foot in the door before she could close it in his face. "An opportunity."

She looked dubious. "An opportunity for what?"

"When I first told you about all of this, you called Edward Sabadine a poisonous old toad. It seems there's no love lost there."

"I've actually never met the man," Aiode said, "but I know his reputation. And I find him detestable, yes."

"Then how would you like the chance to help me get my revenge on him for what he did to Harry?"

Aiode was silent for a moment, and then she smiled slightly. "What is it that you need?"

"Saltpeter," Min said. "As much saltpeter as you can get me."

"Saltpeter?" she asked. "Well then, I think your story just got even more interesting."

Min smirked and gave her a slight bow.

Later that night, two temple servants, looking nervous as kittens that had tumbled into a dog pit, turned up at the Footbridge Tavern with a small sack of saltpeter each. Min thanked them, pressed a coin into each of their palms for their troubles, and hauled the sacks back to the garret room where Harry was waiting with the pots.

THERE WAS a shaded corner a block down from the Sabadines' house. Min took up residence there the next day and occasionally glanced down the street to where Aulus, the tiny scoundrel, was walking back and forth in full view of Talys Sabadine's bedroom window, wearing a bright red scarf.

Talys's window remained closed all day.

It remained closed the next day too, and the next.

The full moon Min had been dreading for so long came and went, and still Talys's window stayed closed.

Finally, seven days after Min had delivered Kaz back to the Sabadines, a white shawl lay discarded on Talys's windowsill, the edges fluttering in the breeze.

MIN AND Harry didn't usually work with anyone else, but Aiode Nettle wasn't like anyone else. Since she had supplied the saltpeter, she said, she was going to see how they used it. And it's not like she and Harry would actually be inside the house at all, and Min could hardly stop her from loitering on a public street in the middle of the night, could he? And she'd given him such a sharp look when she asked that he'd admitted he could not.

Their plan would draw a hell of a crowd anyway, once it was underway, so it wasn't as though she would stand out.

Min parted with them at the corner of the block. He turned down the side street, making his way to the back of the house, where Harry promised the wall was easy enough to climb, and Talys's window overlooked the back garden. Harry and Aiode would be busy at the front of the house, leaving Min to hopefully get in and out undisturbed.

The wall, as Harry had said, was no challenge. Min climbed over it and dropped soundlessly into the garden below. The night was bright. Min could see easily enough and would have to take care not to be seen in turn. He kept to the shadows of the hedges and shrubs as he treaded quietly toward the back of the house.

Talys's window was still open, and the shawl was still hanging out of it.

A handy tree, its boughs broad and strong, gave Min the boost he needed to reach the windowsill, and from there it was a simple enough matter to climb inside. He swung a leg through the window, shifting his weight, and then the toe of his boot found the floor and he was in, standing in the darkness and waiting for his eyes to adjust from the comparative brightness of the moonlight outside.

He didn't have to wait, as it happened.

A lamp flared suddenly, and Min lifted a hand to shade his eyes even as he squinted toward the figure seated on the bed. "Talys?"

"Is there a Decourcey yet who hasn't climbed through that window looking for my daughter?"

Not Talys, then. Min lowered his hand, staring warily at Robert Sabadine and wondering just how much damage he'd do to himself if he leapt straight out the window again.

"Well, she's probably safe from my mother," he said.

Robert's answering snort didn't convince Min that he'd quite developed a sense of humor over the situation yet. Robert rose to his feet, and Min was very glad to see that he didn't appear to be armed. Of course, he was a Sabadine. He probably had six different knives strapped to six different places Min couldn't see. He probably slept with them.

"I knew Talys and your brat were planning something," Robert said. "Clever."

"Oh, the cleverness is all your daughter's, sir," Min said, his heart beating fast. "You should be very proud."

Now that drew a thin, bitter smile from the man.

"She told you, then, about the plan." Min tried not to feel the sting of betrayal. He'd been a fool to put his trust in Talys in the first place.

Robert's jaw clenched. "I caught her trying to put hellebore root in the soldiers' beer supply."

Sons of Rus! The soldiers would have been vomiting for hours had she succeeded. She definitely was clever. Ruthless too.

Robert held Min's gaze. "Your plan failed."

"Poison was never part of my plan," Min said. Only because he hadn't thought of it, but why muddy those waters? "I prefer distraction."

"I swore to Talys that I wouldn't hurt you," Robert said. "Or your nephew. But if you ever attempt to return here again, you won't be leaving. Kazimir is beyond your grasp. You never would have reached him anyway."

"Possibly," Min said. "Have you never done a hopeless thing just because you knew that if you didn't, it would eat at you for as long as you lived?"

Robert's shoulders stiffened. "No."

"Well, this was the first time for me as well, so it may happen for you yet."

Robert glared at him. "You're a fool."

"No doubt." Min inclined his head and swallowed around the ache in his throat. "I have no right to ask anything of you, sir, but, as you say, I am a fool, so I will proceed. Kazimir isn't your enemy. He's just a boy who has done nothing to earn your hatred except to be born, and that was no fault of his. His blood, his Gift, they are hateful things, but he did not ask for them, and he doesn't deserve to be punished for them."

Robert clenched his fingers into fists.

"I do not believe you are a cruel man," Min said honestly. "Just… be kind to him, please. He has known very little kindness, I think."

He could not read Robert's silence.

"Please," he said again softly, his chest aching.

"It is out of my control," Robert said at last. His voice rasped a little as he spoke, as though the words were difficult to force out. "My father is sending him to the Iron Tower at dawn, where he will be placed into the custody of the king."

Min's stomach clenched. "And treated as a *fae*? The enemy? Just so your father can curry the favor of the king?"

"It is out of my control," Robert repeated, a muscle in his cheek twitching.

"The king's favor," Min said, "and all for the cheap price of your own sister's child. Or do you think of him as your husband now? How *was* the wedding, sir? Was there dancing? Cake?"

Robert stepped toward him, his face a mask of rage. "Get out. Get out of this house now, you insolent fucking dog!"

For a moment Min thought Robert would strike him, but suddenly, from the direction of the front of the house, there was a dull boom. And then another, and another, like the rapid barrage of thunder cracking overhead. Doors slammed throughout the house, boots tramped, and voices yelled back and forth. Min smelled smoke.

"What the fuck is that?" Robert exclaimed.

"That," Min said, forcing a smile even as his throat ached, "is the distraction."

The noise and smoke should have drawn the soldiers guarding Kaz's door to the front of the house. It should have been the work of moments to break the lock and free Kaz while the soldiers and the servants ran about in panic as the pots of saltpeter, burning rags shoved in them, smashed against the portico and exploded into flames. It should have been the both of them climbing out the window and both of them slithering down the tree and into the garden while the focus was on the front of the house.

It should have been two of them fleeing into the night.

But Min was alone when he climbed back over the wall and dropped down into the street.

He was alone as he slunk off into the night.

And Kaz, wherever he remained, was alone too.

THE COLD night air stank of smoke. Trails of it floated through the air like wisps of cloud before dissipating into nothing. As Min slunk away from the Sabadines' house, he could hear shouting in the street. The harsh voices carried farther than they would have during the day when the other noises from the city would have swallowed them up. At night, all noises seemed louder.

The street dipped gently toward the valley, and Min followed it down. He walked for several blocks until the streets around him narrowed. There was a tavern nearby that marked the boundary between the quarters, and while it was certainly too close to the mansions of the nobility to be anywhere in Min's budget, it wasn't exclusive enough that he looked out of place lurking outside. Anyone passing would think he was a patron who had come outside to catch some fresh air or to piss in the street.

Min leaned up against a wall and waited for Harry and Aiode to catch him up.

His chest ached, and it had nothing to do with climbing into windows and jumping over walls. His eyes stung as well, and he knew better than to blame it on the cold or the smoke.

Min was not a man unaccustomed to failure, but the weight of this one wasn't only his to bear, but Kaz's as well. What was that old saying about a burden shared? No. No, because thinking of Kaz, who must have heard the explosions and wondered if they meant rescue, only made the weight of his failure press more heavily on Min's shoulders. To have offered him that glimpse of hope, only to have it crushed slowly as nobody came....

Min curled his mouth into a bitter smile. Yes, because what this already miserable night needed was for him to imagine a thousand different scenarios of Kaz's suffering, all of which were designed to cut more deeply than the last. What would his perverse self-hating brain conjure up to torture him with next?

And thinking brought it immediately into being: Kaz's face, pale in the moonlight, his eyes shining. *"I don't want my uncle to be the first man who has me. I want you to be the one to do it, so that at least there will be once in my life that it's not...."*

So that it wasn't what had already happened when he and his uncle had been married.

Be kind to him, please.

Min had petitioned gods in the past who were easier to move than Robert Sabadine, but he'd tried.

He closed his eyes and leaned against the rough wall.

It counted for nothing in the end, but he'd tried.

He opened his eyes as he heard footsteps—thin boot soles skidding over grit—and a moment later Harry rounded the corner with Aiode following.

"Min!" Harry exclaimed, his gaze going past him and then coming back again. He pulled up short, his brow creased in confusion. "Min, where's Kaz?"

Min didn't trust himself to speak. He shook his head in answer and then turned and headed for home.

CHAPTER 16

MIN SWALLOWED painfully as he followed Harry and Aiode up the steps to the garret room.

Harry pushed the door open. "We have wine somewhere. Want some?"

"I want the whole bottle, I think," Aiode said mildly. There was none of her usual sharpness in her tone. She put a hand on Min's shoulder as he moved past her, and squeezed lightly. "I'm so sorry, Aramin."

There was nothing in her tone except sincerity, and Min figured he must have looked bereft indeed to have inspired a cessation of their barbed banter. Her pitying gaze told him that Aiode knew now this had never been about revenge against Edward Sabadine. She'd very probably known it from the start.

Min nodded and crossed the floor to the bed. He sat and stared at his boots for a moment, and at the bright moonlight spilling across the dusty floor, and then closed his stinging eyes. He was tired. He wanted to crawl under the blankets and never come out. Instead he listened as Harry and Aiode moved around the room, speaking briefly and in hushed tones as though Min was some fragile thing and even a sound might shatter him.

The sagging mattress dipped further as weight settled on it beside Min.

He blinked his eyes open.

Aiode held a cup of wine out for him.

Min took it. "Cure for a heartache, hedgewitch?"

Aiode tipped her head back and drained her cup. "This is the only one I've ever found that works, to be honest."

Min snorted and threw his wine back as well.

Harry refilled their cups and sat on Min's other side.

"I've never met a void before," Aiode said at last.

Min drank again. "How long have you known?"

"Well, a man would have to be courting death to attempt what you did tonight," she said, "unless he was either at least a sorcerer equal to Sabadine's or a void. And you are no sorcerer, Aramin."

"And far too craven to be courting death," he murmured.

"I'll drink to that too." Aiode knocked their cups together.

"Strange," Min said. "The entire thing was doomed to failure, but I put no thought at all into how it would feel or what I would do when it did fail. And yet here I am."

Harry scrubbed his hand over his eyes.

"Ah, well." Min set his cup down on the floor. "What happens in all those stories you read, Harry, when the heroes are defeated?"

Harry shook his head. His throat clicked when he swallowed. "They never are."

"Must be nice." Min rubbed a hand over his tight chest. Kaz was gone, but the ache remained. Min didn't begrudge it. It was all he had left. He reached down for his cup again and raised it to his mouth. The wine was thin and bitter. He took a mouthful and then spat it out again as something wet and stringy snagged against his lips. He picked whatever it was from his lips and held it up toward the candlelight to inspect it.

A twig of some sort?

No.

A thin feather, the vane stuck to the shaft with wine.

Min's heart skipped a beat as he looked toward the open window.

A raven perched there, huddled over as though enfolded in misery. Min blinked his vision in an attempt to clear it, but the raven remained.

Min set his cup down on the floor. He rose to his feet and walked slowly toward the window.

"Chirpy?" he asked in a voice hardly louder than a breath. If this was a spell—and how could it be anything else?—then Min wanted to sink into it, not to shatter it.

The raven let out a small, sad noise and tilted its head to look at Min.

Min held out his hand, and the bird fluttered and flapped toward him, ungainly and almost comical. He landed on Min's wrist and tapped his beak against his thumb. The bird was a solid weight, claws digging into the skin of Min's wrist. The last time Min had seen the bird, he had been traced in ink on Kaz's pale skin. The tip of a feather, the curve of a claw, or the sharp end of a beak appearing out of Kaz's dark curls, the literal bird's nest of his unruly hair. But tonight the bird was real, a solid weight shifting on Min's wrist.

Min's chest tightened. "Chirpy, where's Kaz?"

Chirpy made that same mournful sound, and Min watched, his heart clenching, as a glistening tear formed in the bird's eye and slid down his glossy black feathers.

"Chirpy?" Min asked, and the raven tapped his thumb again, feathers fluttering. "Don't cry, Kaz. Don't cry."

Because Min had no doubt in that moment the tear that dropped onto his wrist, that burned as hot as a coal, was Kaz's. That the raven was some unknowable part of Kaz, some facet of him that was as impossible to grasp as his shadow or his spirit but just as fundamentally *him*.

Ravens couldn't weep, but Kaz could.

"Kazimir," Min whispered. He raised his free hand and stroked his fingers down Chirpy's glossy feathers. He could feel the bird's heart beating rapidly through the gentle touch. "Oh, my sweeting."

Chirpy sidestepped up Min's arm, shuffling onto his shoulder. He tapped his beak against Min's cheek, scraping it over his stubble, and then tapped it against the shell of his ear. For a moment Min was lulled by the raven's sorrow and the gentleness of the gesture. But only for a moment.

From outside in the moonlight, bells began to toll.

Min's blood ran cold as he stepped toward the window.

The alley outside was still; unusually so, given it ran past the back door of the Footbridge Tavern. Min watched the shadows that the moonlight made and listened to the bells as the sound rolled over Amberwich like a wave, rippling out from the Iron Tower where they must have sounded first, and picked up by each shrine and temple throughout the city.

Min had heard the bells of the Iron Tower rung before in celebration of some event worth remembrance, and those that hung by the city walls tolled at night to signal the ending of the day and then, hours later, the dawn. He had heard bells before when fires broke out in parts of the city, but he had never heard them all ringing at once, each one a voice that became a chorus of alarm.

"Sweet Mother of the Sacred Spring," Aiode whispered. "What can it be?"

Nothing good. It could be nothing good.

Chirpy squawked and dug his claws into Min's shoulder.

"What are you—*fuck*!" Min reared back as Chirpy bit his earlobe. He slapped at the raven, but Chirpy dodged him and fluttered to his other shoulder. "Sons of Rus, Chirpy!"

Chirpy squawked and tugged at Min's hair.

"Knifebeak! Stop!"

But apparently it wasn't Min's choice of name that had the raven so worked up. He fluttered around Min's head like an angry black storm cloud, feathers slicing through the air, darting in and out of Min's flailing arms to peck at him.

"Min!" Harry shouted. "He wants you to go with him!"

"What?" Min dropped his arms and glared at the raven. The raven, taking a break and perching in the nest of Harry's fluffy hair, glared back.

"He wants you to follow him," Harry said. He stepped toward the door, and the raven let out an approving sound not unlike a pigeon's low trill. "See?"

"Is that it?" Min asked. "You want me to go with you?"

Chirpy ruffled his feathers and squawked.

"To what end?" Min wondered aloud, and Harry and Aiode stared back at him helplessly.

To the bitter end, probably, but Min reached for his cloak anyway.

THE STREETS were no longer empty, and those people not clustering in them, Min guessed, were awake behind their doors and shutters, fearful to know what the tolling of the bells throughout Amberwich meant. The city felt like a living thing tonight, and not any majestic beast at all, but some sort of growling skittish stray. It was a fearful half-wild dog cornered with hackles up, as likely to lunge and draw blood as it was to turn tail and run. And Min, along with every other soul in the city, was nothing but a flea caught on its back, hoping to avoid its snapping jaws.

Min kept his wits around him and his knife close to hand as he hurried through the moonlit streets with Harry and Aiode. Chirpy flitted ahead and back, ahead and back, as though he was drawing Min along on a lure. There was an association there—strings and puppets and a dead hedgewitch's hollow *"Who are you?"*—that Min didn't want to dwell on. If he was in Kaz's thrall, after all, it had nothing to do with his Gift.

The cool breeze tugged at the edges of Min's cloak as he followed Chirpy. Fingers of colder air prickled his skin. He was half-surprised that Chirpy appeared to be leading them away from the center of the city and the Iron Tower, but it wasn't until they were on Stanes Street that he realized Chirpy was leading them out of Amberwich altogether.

The torches burning on the portcullis over Stanes Street threw sharp dancing shadows over the worn-down cobblestones and the walls of the surrounding houses. A company of men, all wearing the livery of the King's Guard, stood in serried lines in the massive shadow of the gate, weapons at hand, and it seemed suddenly absurd to Min. Thirty men here, and probably the same amount at every other gate in the city, and Min could only think of one reason the city bells were tolling out their warning. What the hell could these thirty men do but cower and flee if the fae walked up to the city walls? It was the Iron Tower that protected Amberwich from the fae, not any gate or guard or weapon.

A gray-robed mage stood amongst the soldiers. He was thin and narrow, a praying mantis, and he had a pinched, anxious look to him that wouldn't have been out of place on a nervous whippet. He clearly wasn't confident his Gift could repel the fae if they approached Amberwich. Neither was Min.

He wondered how close the fae could come before their magic was weakened by the Iron Tower. Min and every occupant of Amberwich had been told their entire lives that the fae could not tolerate iron, but Min didn't know if he could believe it. Kaz was part fae, and the iron collar had subdued his Gift of necromancy, but his fae magic? Taavi and Chirpy should have been frozen on his skin, shouldn't they? And he'd still been able to follow the leylines in the woods.

The iron collar had burned when Min had put it on Kaz in Anhaga. Then, days later, Kaz had been closing his hand around the chains in the manor house in Pran, and he had told Min they felt like stinging nettles. If Kaz's body had learned to tolerate the iron, was it possible it would one day stop working entirely? And if it was true for Kaz, then why not for the rest of the fae?

Would the Iron Tower protect Amberwich forever?

Did it even protect them *now*?

Min wasn't prone to flights of fancy, and he wasn't the sort of man who got drunk in cheap taverns and muttered about how the king and the Gifted were nothing but liars and tyrants building palaces on the broken backs of working men, but he couldn't help but wonder if the gray-robed mage's fear was that of a man who knew he was about to watch a house of cards come tumbling down.

The thought of it made the hair on the back of Min's neck rise and his skin prickle.

From farther down the street, he saw a trail of people hurrying toward the city. It took him a moment to understand what was occurring: the people whose homes were outside the ancient walls of Amberwich were seeking refuge inside. Some were lugging possessions. Some were carrying children. And all of them, pulled from their beds by the frantic ringing of bells, looked afraid.

Chirpy fluttered to the top of the portcullis and perched there, peering down at Min.

A burly bearded man stepped in front of Min, one beefy palm held up. "The gate is being closed by order of the king. If you've people out there to fetch, you might not make it back in time."

"Understood," Min said.

Min had made a lot of stupid decisions before in his life. He was known for them. (Ask his mother. Min suspected she kept a detailed list.) And the one he was about to make now, well, that was probably the stupidest of all of them. And yet... yet Kaz had sent Chirpy to him, and that *meant* something. Min didn't know what the fuck it meant, but he was sure it meant something. Even knowing what was waiting on the outside of the city walls—and he knew in his bones exactly what was out there—Min couldn't ignore that.

He trusted Kaz.

Strange how that had happened, but here he was.

Kaz had never run from him. Kaz had stopped him from drinking from the pool in the woods. Kaz had found their way back to Amberwich, when it had meant a life of captivity. He could have fought Min, but he never had. He could have run and let Harry die, but he hadn't. Kaz had never led Min wrong, when he so easily could have, and perhaps he should have. And Kaz had given himself to Min that night in his old room. And maybe that was because Min was the pick of a bad bunch, but Min thought maybe it was more than that too. It was for Min, at least. Not the bright, burning inferno of love Harry thought it was, like smashed pots exploding into flames against a door, but it was an ember, maybe, with a small and steady glow. Min could feel its warmth.

It didn't matter what it was anyway. It only mattered that Kaz deserved better than his fate, and that if there was any hope at all, Min couldn't desert him now. And perhaps it wasn't hope that waited outside the city walls, but it was something. And something had to be better than nothing.

Min squared his shoulders and glanced back at Harry and Aiode. "Wait here for me."

He walked under the portcullis, through the darkness, and back out into the moonlight. When he turned to check, Harry and Aiode were still with him, and Chirpy swooped down to alight on his shoulder.

They walked on.

The houses stood farther apart now. The cobblestones turned to dirt. The city slowly dropped away.

They walked in silence, Chirpy swooping ahead in long arcs and then circling back again, and the bells of Amberwich growing quieter as the three of them paced out their distance from the city walls. Out here, without the dark buildings crowding in, the night seemed even brighter. The world was awash in silver light, and Min felt as though he had fallen into a dreamscape where nothing was quite real, or perhaps passed beyond the veil into a different world entirely. His breath was as loud as an ocean and muffled all other sounds. Only the sharp crunch of his boots on the dirt kept him anchored as each step forward revealed another shape taking form out of the strange light: low stone walls and hedgerows, crofts and cottages, posts and pathways, and trees that shifted and shivered like anemones in the breeze.

The bells in Amberwich tolled in faint warning in the distance, and up ahead Min heard a clear high ringing in answer. The moonlight shifted like mist, and through it a pale horse appeared at the top of a rise in the road. The horse breathed steam from its nostrils into the cold night air.

The rider turned its head and looked directly at Min.

Min had heard it said that great men like kings and heroes could read their fortunes in the heavens, in the fiery comets and intricate constellations that lit up the night sky. Min wasn't proud enough to think he had ever done anything in his life to earn himself a fixed mark in the heavens that sailors could plot safe passage by, but he'd sometimes pondered the hazy spread of stars, indistinguishable from one another, and wondered if one of those more modest beacons belonged to him. Even under a humbling field of infinite stars in a never-ending sky, Min had never felt so small as he did now, because what was the rider except the moon himself? Bright and blazing, the light of him swallowing up all the stars.

Min watched, his heart in his throat, as Chirpy fluttered toward the rider.

The fae held out his hand, pale in the moonlight, and Chirpy landed there and stilled.

For a moment nothing happened, and then, in a burst of movement, a flock of ravens burst from around the fae in a cloud, wheeling higher and higher into the sky, spiraling upward in a whirlwind of flurrying feathers and harsh cries. And then they were gone, vanished into the night as though stolen on a breath.

The fae flicked his wrist, and Chirpy fluttered from his arm onto the head of the horse, and perched there on the beast's silver forelock.

The fae alighted from his horse, his robes rippling like the surface of a lake before they settled again. Chirpy darted back to the fae's shoulder.

"His magic comes to me," the fae said, and Min didn't understand how he heard the words so clearly when there was still some distance between them. The fae's voice was strangely accented, the cadence more like music than speech, but if it was like music, then it was like none Min had ever heard before. It was music no man could make. It was the music of the wind whispering in hollow places, or the hum of cicadas in the distance on a summer's afternoon, or shallow water skipping over stones. "It calls to me."

The fae's features were sharp, beautiful, cold, and cruel. A fraction too exaggerated, too much like an eerie doll carved to look uncannily like a human. What had Min thought back in Anhaga? Like a dream, the moment before it became a nightmare.

"I am Llefelys," the fae said. "You know me as the Hidden Lord."

Min hadn't known it was possible to be even more afraid, but his blood turned to ice in his veins. A lifetime of bluster and bullshit had trained him never to show fear—but this was fear greater than any he had ever known or could even properly conceptualize. He was an insect to the Hidden Lord. He was a gnat, and the Hidden Lord was a tempest.

Min inclined his head. "I am Aramin Decourcey."

The fae stepped toward him, his boots soundless on the dirt road. "You are the one who took him from Anhaga."

"I am," Min said and waited for the heavens to fall.

"Where is he?" the Hidden Lord asked. His expression shifted, but Min couldn't read it. He couldn't tell if it was anger or anguish or an attempted mimicry of something else. He wasn't aware the fae could feel any emotion at all. They were heartless, weren't they? They were cold and unfeeling and took amusement in pointless cruelty, like children pulling the wings off flies. But there was *something* in the Hidden Lord's face as he spoke again, and the music of his voice hit a straining note: "Where is my son?"

Min reeled back. He heard Harry gasp from somewhere behind him.

Well, *fuck*.

"They have poisoned him against me," the Hidden Lord said. "They taught him to fear me, to use the very blood that I gave him to keep me from him. And now they have enslaved him in iron. His magic comes to me, and it weeps."

Chirpy made a mournful sound.

Min blinked and felt as though his entire understanding of the world had shifted.

Anhaga, he thought wildly. He'd been there and seen it but never even questioned what it was he'd witnessed. The Hidden Lord hadn't crossed the borders and slaughtered the inhabitants of Anhaga, though he was a creature from a nightmare. The fishermen in Anhaga still put their boats out every day. The women still sold their goods in the marketplace. The children still played in the dusty streets. The Hidden Lord had only come to Anhaga after Kazimir was sent there. And he had knocked on the peeling green paint of Kallick's front door each night, only to be repelled by Kaz's Gift and his fae magic.

Min had seen it with his own eyes, but somehow he hadn't realized.

The Hidden Lord wasn't at war with the king. He never had been. He'd only ever tried to reach Kaz.

Min lifted his chin. "Sir, what do you want with Kazimir?"

"Kazimir," the Hidden Lord echoed, and there was something like wonder in his tone. "She called him Kazimir. She said she liked the sound of that name."

Another blink.

Another shift.

Because no. Unless this was some trickery, Min could not imagine any woman discussing baby names with the creature who raped her.

Sorrow and pity welled up in him, and not for the terrifying creature that stood in front of him, but for the boy who had been told from the moment he was born that he was an abomination, a mongrel, a violent and bloody stain on the memory of his mother. That lonely brokenhearted boy who had only known hate from the people who should have cared for him.

From his perch on the Hidden Lord's shoulder, Chirpy squawked and fluttered his feathers.

"Avice was my heart." The Hidden Lord stroked a long finger down Chirpy's back. "She was my heart."

Min could barely breathe.

The Hidden Lord lifted Chirpy in front of his face. "You are a storm, my son. You are the lightning on the ocean. You call my magic to yours, and you are stronger than iron. When you break, no man will be able to contain you. You will leave destruction in your wake."

Min repressed a shudder.

The Hidden Lord raised his hand, and Chirpy wheeled into the air with a piercing cry.

Min looked up as black feathers rained down, a thick heavy blanket of them that blocked out the moonlight. Min raised a hand to cover his mouth as the feathers swirled down, afraid he would choke, but the feathers turned to dust before they hit the ground and vanished into nothing.

When Min looked at the place where the Hidden Lord had stood, he was gone and the jingling of the bells on his horse's trappings was already fading in the distance. And, at the edges of the world, the dawn was creeping in.

Min shook his head and blinked, and it felt as though he was coming up from sleep. A moment later Chirpy reappeared, fluttering madly, and landed with a thump on Min's shoulder. Min's fear caught him at last. His heart beat faster, and he worried his shaky legs wouldn't hold his weight for much longer. He turned, staring wildly at Harry and Aiode.

"All of that just happened, yes?"

Harry nodded, slack-jawed.

"Your Kazimir is no mere hedgewitch," Aiode said, her voice hitching.

"No," Min agreed. His gaze slid over her shoulder and landed on the distant walls of Amberwich. From this distance he could only make out the city walls, faint in the glow of the dawn, and the Iron Tower atop the King's Hill.

Kaz.

Robert had said Kaz was being sent to the Iron Tower, and so that was where Min had to go. He had no fucking idea what to do once he got there, but that was where he had to go, because the Hidden Lord said that Kaz's storm was building, and Min didn't think they had very long at all until it broke.

CHAPTER 17

ALL OF this, Min thought wildly as he and Aiode and Harry hurried along Stanes Street. All of this because Harry had climbed in Talys Sabadine's bedroom window and under her skirts. How fast it had all spiraled out of control and left Min on a larger stage than any he had ever wanted to walk on. Min much preferred to slip under the notice of powerful men, and tonight he had spoken to the Hidden Lord himself— and even lived to tell the tale—and now he was on his way to the Iron Tower. Fate was a twisted bitch indeed when somehow Min ended up in the middle of all this bullshit.

The bells of Amberwich had fallen silent sometime in the early morning, and now an uneasy calm had settled like a shifting mist over the city. Min didn't trust it for a moment.

The portcullis gate was still open, and the stream of pedestrian traffic that last night had been rushing to get inside the city was this morning replaced by restless crowds demanding answers that the King's Guard could not give. The fae were at the walls of Amberwich, and there was nowhere to run.

An orange-robed wizard had joined the pinch-faced mage at the portcullis at Stanes Street, and Min wondered if the city's other gates were as poorly defended. A wizard was barely a step up from a hedgewitch. Wizards were alchemists. What was he going to do to defend Amberwich from the Hidden Lord? Transmute some lead in his direction? Where were the sorcerers, the highest ranked of the king's Gifted, who might actually stand a chance against the fae?

Unless....

Min's heart clenched as the vicious thought caught him.

Unless all the king's sorcerers were busy dealing with the fae already inside the city walls. Kaz must have been at the Iron Tower already. If so, what secrets did the king's sorcerers think Kaz could teach them about his father's strange people? And how did they intend to learn them?

Chirpy, huddled on Min's shoulder, burrowed in close to his throat, and snapped his beak anxiously against the shell of Min's ear.

A ripple of unrest ran through the crowd gathered along Stanes Street, and Min caught Aiode by the elbow and pulled her closer as a man almost barreled into her. She stumbled a little but caught her footing again and thanked Min with a nod. Even Harry, who was usually as slippery as a greased weasel, was struggling to pick a path through the crowds. Min met his worried gaze and knew they were both thinking it: How long until these brief flares of panic descended into violence? Crowds made a dangerous beast, unpredictable and volatile. Min much preferred to watch them from a safe distance.

They pushed on, heading for the Iron Tower, skirting around the dip of the valley in the center of the city to reach the King's Hill.

A wall ran around the base of the King's Hill, broken up here and there by gates large enough to drive wagons and horses through. Nobody entered the king's land without permission of the Guard. Even Min would never have dared attempt it. He was an excellent thief, but not a total idiot. He balked when he saw the closed gate on Guildhall Street, but Aiode strode forward. Her red hair was a mess, and her shoes and the bottom few inches of her green kirtle were covered in dust. She looked every inch the sort of hedgewitch who'd been digging around in weeds and brambles, but she was still Gifted and still outranked any common soldiers.

Outranked them by a mile, it so happened. She rapped on the door set in the gate and waited, her chin lifted imperiously, as the slot on the door opened and a soldier peered out at her.

"Lady Anarawd!" the man exclaimed. The slot slammed shut again, and Min heard bolts being shifted behind the heavy door.

Min exchanged a look with Harry.

"Anarawd!" Harry whispered, his eyebrows vanishing under his scruffy fringe. "Min, that's the king's family name!"

Well then. Apparently Min's habit of falling for people entirely out of his league was not without precedent. Aiode Nettle, his magnificent ass. Tricky hedgewitches and their tricky false names. If Min had known Aiode was an Anarawd, he might have attempted to acquit himself better between the sheets. Or at least apologized respectfully for his failure.

Aiode threw him a knowing look. "I did have a life before I tumbled into your disappointing bed, Aramin."

"And here was I thinking you'd been born a grubby little mudlark," Min said.

"If we survive this," Aiode said, "I shall have to remember to resent you for that."

Min gave her a short bow. "Noted."

The door in the gate creaked open.

Min and Harry followed Aiode along the wide path that curved up the side of the King's Hill, cutting through the parklands. If Min hadn't been so sure he was walking into yet another disaster, he might have taken time to appreciate the beauty of his surroundings, dotted here and there with fountains and sculptures and flowering bushes that hid the stench of the city with sweet perfumes. But probably not. Min didn't really give a fuck about gardens, and he had a lot more on his mind this morning. Like how to save a half-fae necromancer who was trapped between two very powerful men and could combust at any moment. Not literally, Min hoped, but what did he know about Kaz's powers? What did anyone know about them?

Whatever Kaz was, it was new.

"Min, look!" Harry pointed toward the Iron Tower.

A spiral of ravens swirled around the roof. There must have been between ten and a dozen of them—an innocuous enough number, and possibly even an innocuous enough sight, but Min felt a chill run through him all the same. Was this where the Hidden Lord's ravens had vanished to? If Kaz's magic, via Chirpy, had been drawn to the Hidden Lord, then was the Hidden Lord's magic drawn back to his son's? Stronger than iron, the Hidden Lord had said, and now the Hidden Lord's ravens circled the Iron Tower. Were they there simply because Kaz had willed it? The implications of that were terrifying.

Min was certain Kaz was inside the Iron Tower now. When it came to Kaz and his fae magic, he didn't believe in coincidences.

There was a formation of guards gathered at the base of the Iron Tower, armed with pikes and sarissas. There were about twenty or thirty men in total—the rest of the King's Guard must have been positioned at the gates along the city walls instead. Their barracks, Min knew, were

somewhere in these parklands, along with the Sorcerers' Guildhall, the
Treasury, and the various other chancelleries it took to run a kingdom.
The mechanics of government were a mystery to Min. The affairs of
the king and the noble Houses had always seemed to him to be a nasty
business, poisoned by the machinations of ambitious men, which made
it one of the few things Min could actually look down on. It was rare that
Min could take the moral high ground on anything, and he did enjoy the
opportunity when he could.

Min half expected the soldiers to challenge them as they approached
the Iron Tower, but Aiode's green kirtle—or, more likely, her birth
name—allowed them to pass unimpeded.

Min had never been this close to the Iron Tower, but he didn't have
time to take much in as they approached. Because right at that moment,
a sound like the crack of thunder tore through the air, a flood of panicked
courtiers and servants burst out of the Tower and fled, and, above them
all, the roof of the Iron Tower shifted, seemed to shimmer for a moment
in the early morning light, and then shattered apart like delicate glass and
crashed to the ground.

MIN HAD never been inside the Iron Tower before, but he imagined
it was usually nicer than this. Dust and smoke filled the air, obscuring
Min's sight, and all around him he heard the panicked cries of men and
women still trying to find their way to the exits and the creak and moan
of metal as though the Iron Tower was trying to tear itself apart. The
walls shuddered. Sconces shifted, windowpanes cracked, great fissures
appeared in the plaster walls, and the chandeliers swung and shuddered
like the Iron Tower was a ship rolling on a storm-tossed sea.

Chirpy shrieked and fluttered away.

Min's courage, such as it was, might have failed him except that
Aiode strode forward and Harry, the reckless little fool, darted after her.
Min tugged his shirt up over his mouth and followed them.

Aiode clearly knew her way through the rooms and galleries of
the Iron Tower. She led them to a set of curving stairs that shuddered
alarmingly and, placing one hand on the wall to steady herself, began to
climb them.

Harry called out a hoarse warning too late.

A portly man, shrouded in dust except for his red gaping mouth, shoved his way down the stairs, sending Aiode stumbling backward.

Min caught her before she fell past him, holding her against the wall.

"Fucker!" Harry yelled at the dusty courtier, but the man was already gone.

Min took the lead, Aiode and Harry falling in behind him.

On the third floor, they came to a set of doors and a man shoving at them relentlessly. He was tall, well built, and covered in so much dust and plaster that Min didn't even recognize him for a moment.

And then he did.

"Decourcey," Robert Sabadine snarled. "What are you doing here?"

"Enjoying a platonic relationship with my nephew," Min shot back. "You?"

Robert straightened up, panting for breath. "You joke at a time like this?"

A chunk of plaster smashed on the floor beside Min's boots. "You mistake me, sir. That was no joke."

"Min," Harry snapped.

Min held up his palms. "Fine. What's happening in there?"

"I have no idea," Robert said. "My father... he brought Kazimir to the king."

"As a prisoner?"

"As a hostage!" Robert snapped. "The Hidden Lord is at the gates!"

"And why the fuck do you think that is?" Min demanded. "Coincidence? The Hidden Lord is at the gates because you've imprisoned Kazimir!"

"*You* imprisoned Kazimir!" Robert dragged a hand over his face, wiping streaks of sweat through his mask of dust. "Where are the guards? I need to get this door open! The king is inside, and I fear his sorcerers cannot subdue Kazimir!"

"And you think you can?" Min almost laughed.

"The king is inside," Robert repeated.

Right. Duty and honor and suchlike. Robert Sabadine seemed like the sort of man who would fling himself willingly into death for the sort of abstract concepts that had never troubled Min in his life. Noble of him. Stupid, but noble.

Metal screeched against metal, and the Iron Tower shuddered.

"Go," Min said to Harry. "Get out of here."

Harry shook his head and jutted his chin out. "We're a team, Min."

Min had a sudden flash of memory of a terrified eleven-year-old, long hair worn in ribbons and bare feet sticking out from underneath the ratty hem of a dress that had been handed down too many times.

"Do you want to get out of here, kid?"

They'd been a team since that moment.

"Harry," he said now, helplessly, because he didn't know what was waiting for them behind the door, and Harry wasn't a void, and if he didn't walk away from this, then everything would have been for nothing, and Min couldn't lose him. Not after everything.

But Harry shook his head again.

The bones of the Iron Tower screamed, and another shower of dust and plaster choked the air. Min heard shouting from nearby and the sound of boots thumping on the stairs, and then a knot of soldiers joined them at the door.

"Get it open!" Robert shouted at them. "Your king is inside!"

The soldiers struggled with the door, and at last, with a crack, it gave, sending the men spilling into the gallery beyond it.

Smoke, Min thought at first, but no. Feathers. The air was full of feathers. They hung in the air like dust motes or like seaweed swaying underwater, buoyed by invisible currents. Min stepped forward, sweeping a path clear with his hand.

A man lay sprawled on his back on the parquet floor, his blue robes twisted around him. A sorcerer. His eyes were open and rolling in his skull. He was clawing at his own arms, his fingernails digging bloody furrows in the flesh.

"Get it off!" he screeched. "Get it off me!"

An illusion, Min thought, stepping over the man, and a hell of a powerful one to get past a sorcerer's defenses. To do such a thing was almost unthinkable. To do it inside the Iron Tower should have been impossible. Pride—Kaz was *magnificent*—battled with fear inside him.

Because Kaz was *terrifying*.

At the end of the gallery, Min saw them: four more sorcerers encircling a figure standing hunched over on the floor. There were other men nearby, pressing up against the trembling walls as though they would offer them any protection. Courtiers, probably. Dust blanketed their fancy hats and fur-lined collars. And one must have been the king, though he wore a shroud of dust—and his fear—the same as any other man. A philosopher might make a point of that.

And there was Edward Sabadine, too, eyes bulging as though he was being strangled to death by his own intestines. The old man looked fucking petrified as a feather drifted down past his face.

As Min watched, one of the blue-robed sorcerers staggered back, shrieking.

Another shudder ripped through the Iron Tower.

Kaz lifted his gaze. His fingers were wrapped around the iron collar Min had fastened on him. His face was pale, and his eyes... his eyes were white like a blind man's. Min could see the veins under his skin as though they had been drawn there in ink. The black lines lay on his skin like spiders' webs or the cracks in enamel. The veins in his cheeks, his throat, and his forearms were all black. He had never looked less human to Min's eyes than in this moment.

Kaz opened his mouth, and the sound that came out was the piercing, chilling cry of a raven. The tower shook again, every feather hanging in the air shuddered, and Min watched in horrified amazement as Kaz wrenched his arms and the iron collar fell onto the floor in pieces. The chunks of it crumbled away like charcoal.

One of the courtiers screamed, and all the windows in the gallery shattered as one.

Are you doing this? Min wanted to yell at Kaz, but the words wouldn't form. They weren't the right words in any case. Of course Kaz was doing it. What Min really wanted to know was whether he was controlling it. Whether he could stop it. Whether he *wanted* to. The Hidden Lord had said that no man could contain the storm once it broke, and the cold knot of fear inside Min's gut worried it was true.

"Stop him!" one of the courtiers cried out, his hands over his ears like a toddler in the midst of a tantrum. "Stop him!"

"We are surrounded by *iron!*" a sorcerer shouted back.

Their magic was weak in this place. Kaz's... Kaz's was not.

Kaz climbed slowly to his feet, his chest heaving under his sweat-slicked shirt.

The storm, Min thought wildly. *The storm is about to break.*

One of the soldiers—a braver man than Min—rushed at Kaz. Kaz lifted a hand without even looking at him, and a flash of blue light sent the man flying back. He landed in a crumpled heap on the floor.

One of the sorcerers—a man exactly as brave as Min—tried to flee. Kaz flicked his wrist, and some invisible string tugged the man back toward him, screaming and struggling. Kaz flicked his wrist again and flung the man against the wall. He hit it with a resounding crack and slumped to the ground.

The air smelled of feathers, of plaster dust, and of the sky before a storm.

The three remaining sorcerers, two women and a man, circled Kaz warily. One of them reached out toward him, flinching back as her hand struck some unseen barrier between them and blue light flared brightly.

Robert Sabadine stepped forward.

Min caught him by the arm. "Don't be a fool."

He glanced behind him. Harry stood with Aiode. They were clutching hands tightly.

"Leave," he mouthed.

Harry shook his head stubbornly.

If they survived this, Min would tan his hide.

Min drew a breath and crossed the parquet floor. He approached the sorcerers surrounding Kaz and stood where he thought the unseen barrier was. Then, because he couldn't resist what might be his last chance to be a cocky asshole, he winked at Edward Sabadine and stepped through the barrier to where Kaz stood.

"Hello, sweeting," he said softly.

Kaz's blind gaze fixed on him. "Min?" he asked tremulously.

Min felt a rush of relief that Kaz still knew him. That he hadn't passed beyond Min's reach. That despite what he looked like at the moment and despite the carnage he was raining down on the Iron Tower, that he was still Kaz. "Yes, Kaz, it's me."

"Min!" Kaz darted out a hand and gripped his wrist tightly. "Min, it hurts! It *hurts*!"

And then his legs gave out and he crashed to his knees on the floor.

Min followed him down. "Kaz?" He put a hand on Kaz's cheek. His skin was burning. "Kaz?"

"Min." Kaz raised himself up, holding Min's shoulders. His breath was hot against Min's throat. "Min, I want to go *home*. Why won't they let me go home?"

The whole world seemed to hold its breath in that moment. The feathers shivered in the air. Min held Kaz and rocked him gently back and forth, shushing him like he might have a child, if he'd had a paternal bone in his body. But Kaz was scared and hurt, and angry too, and Min didn't know of any other way to offer him comfort, and so they knelt there, surrounded by people who had harmed Kaz, who had been cruel to him just because of the strange blood that ran in his veins.

His chest felt tight and his throat ached. He hated himself for the part he had played in this. He wanted to lift Kaz up in his arms and carry him out of here. Carry him all the way back to Anhaga, if that was what he wanted, where he could live in his messy little bedroom in Kallick's house and mix potions and poultices all day and watch people's unremarkable little lives play out in the square below. If Min had never wanted to be caught up in all of this mess, then neither had Kaz.

If he walked away, what would happen? The Iron Tower was shuddering and shaking around them like a leaf caught in a gust of wind, but it still stood. And while it did, it subdued the Gifts of the three sorcerers who still remained on their feet. If Min carried Kaz out of here, would they follow? Would they be able to harm Kaz once they were free of the Iron Tower? Min had heard that sorcerers could perform curses that tore the flesh from a man's bones just by speaking the right words. What would happen to Kaz if these sorcerers had full command of their Gifts again? Were three sorcerers a match for the strange combination of Kaz's Gift and his fae magic?

Min didn't know. He couldn't know. Every damn thing about Kaz was unknowable. What had Min thought that night he'd captured him in Anhaga?

This impossible boy.

This strange, inexplicable, beautiful, and impossible boy, and Min wanted him like he'd never wanted anything else in his life. Wanted him, but more than that he wanted him to be free, and to be happy, and to be *safe*. He wanted it so much he felt as though his chest might burst from the aching need of it.

Min had always prided himself on his quick thinking, but there was too much happening here, too many variables to guess at how every one might play out. He couldn't see past Kaz and how he was hurting and the way his breath hitched as he sobbed silently against Min's shoulder.

"Sweeting," he murmured, running a hand through Kaz's unruly hair. "Oh, my love."

It seemed as good a time as any, he supposed, to let the word slip out of him while the Iron Tower collapsed around them.

Kaz shivered and trembled in his embrace and gave no indication he'd heard.

He was an injured little animal, Min thought, ready to lash out and hurt those who had hurt him. Which left Min here holding the wolf by the ears, too afraid to let go.

"Min," Kaz whispered. "Min, I got so angry."

"I know you did, sweeting," Min whispered back. "You blew the roof off the Iron Tower."

Kaz didn't seem to hear him. "I got so angry I think I woke them up."

"Woke who up?" Min asked.

And in the sudden silence, in the distance, Min heard screaming.

Kaz leaned back slightly to look at him. His eyes were still white, and his veins still black as lines of ink across his pale skin. He laughed suddenly, and the sound of it, sharp as the ringing of a broken vessel, sent a chill down Min's spine. *"Everyone."*

Min had no idea what was happening, but the sorcerers had eyes that he did not. One of the women gasped and clutched her throat.

"The dead!" she cried out, lifting her gaze to stare out a shattered window toward the city. "The dead are waking! The boy is a necromancer!"

Kaz's laughter echoed all around.

CHAPTER 18

IN THE center of the storm, it was calm.

Min knelt there with his arms around Kaz, Kaz's unearthly laughter muffled for now against his shoulder, and looked around the room. Black feathers hung in the air as though they were floating underwater, or perhaps hanging from a thousand invisible strings attached to the shuddering ceiling of the gallery. The three sorcerers still encircled them, just a few steps back from whatever magical wall Kaz had placed around himself. Against the closest wall, Min saw Edward Sabadine and a group of four other men. One of the men was elderly. The three others were perhaps around Min's age. Their fancy clothes were covered in plaster dust. One of them had reddish hair underneath his wig of dust, and Min wondered, on that passing resemblance to Aiode alone, if he was the king. He looked like an ordinary man. He looked afraid.

Back toward the door of the gallery, Aiode and Harry stood with Robert Sabadine and the soldiers. The mage who had been thrashing on the floor like a landed eel was silent now. He lay there limply, and Min had no idea if he was alive or dead and no particular care to find out either way. The soldier Kaz had flung against the wall was crawling back toward his fellows.

"Kaz," he whispered. "Kaz, come back to me."

Kaz continued to laugh.

"Kaz, you need to stop this." Min dragged the fingers of one hand through Kaz's curls. He gripped the back of his neck, fingers digging in a little, unsure now if it was an embrace or if it was censure. "You need to stop whatever you've done."

Kaz reared back suddenly, pushing away from Min and landing on his ass on the floor in an ungainly sprawl of limbs. His white eyes shone. "They have to pay, Min! They have to *pay*!"

"Far be it for me to get in the way of your revenge, sweeting," Min said, his heart thumping wildly even as he struggled to keep his voice steady, "but Harry's here too. And Aiode. You haven't met her, but she's a good person. Better than I deserve as a friend in any case. Revenge should be exacting, Kaz, not indiscriminate."

Kaz's blind gaze slid around the room.

"And what about the people in the city?" Min asked. "What about the people you know? That girl in Anhaga and her fishermen brothers. You remember you told me about them?"

Kaz blinked slowly. There was a bluish cast to his pale black-veined skin now, as though he was very cold. Min could feel the heat radiating from him, though. Kneeling in front of him was like sitting too close to a fire.

"And what about Joderman and his geese?" Min asked, forcing a smile and wondering if Kaz even heard the words. "And his wife who packed him mutton for lunch that we ended up eating instead? What about those strangers we passed in the street the night we reached the city? Do any of them deserve to pay? And what about my mother, hmm?" He reached out and caught one of Kaz's hands. Made an exaggerated grimace. "Well, *maybe* my mother."

Kaz's mouth quirked at that.

Min's heart tumbled over a beat. Kaz was still in there, and Min was reaching him.

And then Edward Sabadine, the vile old fuck, ruined everything.

"What are you doing??" he bellowed suddenly, stalking forward with more courage than Min would have thought he had in him. "Why do you not act? Kill him, you fool! Kill him!"

And there was a certain logic in that, of course, and Min would indeed be a fool not to consider it. He was a void and the only man in the Iron Tower who could reach Kaz without being blasted back across the room by his magic. But also, he wasn't the one who'd brought a half-fae necromancer into the Iron Tower to begin with, and fuck Edward Sabadine for thinking Min had any obligation at all to clean this mess up. And fuck him twice for assuming that murder was the only option. And fuck him a third time, hopefully snapping his brittle geriatric bones in the process, for shouting something like that aloud.

Kaz flailed back again, his mouth open in a soundless cry as though he thought it was *true*. As though he thought Min would actually kill him.

"Kaz," Min said, reaching out for him. "Sweeting. I would never—"

Kaz pushed away from him, his face contorted by terror, and raised his shaking hands.

The feathers in the air shivered and shifted. A soundless wave burst through the gallery, and the Iron Tower began to collapse.

Min heard the scream of tearing metal and looked up at the ceiling just in time to see it crumbling down toward him.

He didn't even have time to raise his arms to shield his head.

Dust.

Choking dust.

Min blinked in a vain attempt to clear his vision. Was he dead? And if not, then why not? Was he mortally hurt? He couldn't feel it yet, but he didn't trust it either. He probably was dead, because the ceiling—and the three stories above it—had just landed on his skull.

Definitely dead.

He blinked again.

Light too. Sunlight. It dazzled him.

And a woman's voice, raised in a song as soft and sweet as a lullaby.

Min lifted his head, shaking dust from his hair, and looked around. Feathers still hung in the air, drifting in slanted columns of dust, and— Min's breath caught in his throat—so did the ceiling, like a child's puzzle broken apart in a tantrum, thrown into the air but somehow not yet landed. The sunlight blazed through the places where the ceiling and the walls had broken apart. When Min looked up, he could see three stories worth of rubble hanging in the air above him—cracked tiles and shattered boards, chunks of plaster and masonry, iron bones snapped like twigs—and glimpses of the sky beyond.

The Iron Tower hadn't collapsed, he realized. It was still in the middle of collapsing, except that somehow it had frozen at the moment of disaster.

Rubble and dust and feathers shifted for the woman who walked toward them, parting like the waters of a bow wave. The woman wore no cloak or hood, just a plain white gown. Her dark hair spilled down her back. Her feet were bare. This must have been what she looked liked when they buried her.

"Avice!" Robert's voice cracked on the name.

The shade walked on, still singing softly. She passed Robert, passed the courtiers cowering against the wall, passed the blue-robed sorcerers, and then passed through the invisible barrier that separated Kaz and Min from the rest of the gallery.

And then she stopped and fell silent.

Min was half-afraid to look at her. He dropped his gaze to her feet and saw that they were covered in dust. It took a moment for the strangeness of that to make itself known to him. In Pran she'd remained dry despite the rain, but here she was dusty? Min lifted his gaze.

She was as young as her son. As beautiful too. Min could drown in her dark eyes as easily as he'd drowned in Kaz's.

"Kazimir," she whispered, and his name sounded like a prayer on her lips, hopeful and fearful in equal measure.

Kaz looked up. His mouth moved, but no words came.

"Kazimir," she whispered again, and held out her pale hand toward him.

Kaz reached up, his trembling fingers touching hers.

She was not a shade at all. Whatever she was, she was real. She was here. Kaz had woken the dead, and Avice Sabadine was here.

Kaz stumbled to his feet, as ungainly as a newborn colt, and stood there, white eyes blinking, as Avice caught his face between her palms. They were a mirror image. Dark-haired and pale-skinned. They might have been twins.

"Oh," she said softly. She combed her fingers through his hair, tucking his curls behind his pointed ears. She ran her thumb over his cheekbone, brushing away the tears that shone there. The bluish tinge to Kaz's skin vanished under her touch. The black lines faded. "But you're so tall!"

Avice was shorter than her son by half a head, but Kaz still seemed somehow smaller. A child, Min thought. A frightened, lonely child, afraid that his mother hated him.

"I'm sorry," Kaz whispered. He closed his eyes. "I'm so sorry."

Avice leaned up and pressed a gentle kiss to one eyelid and then the other. Kaz flinched at the first kiss, stood frozen for the second, and when he opened his eyes again they were the eyes of the boy Min knew: dark and clever and shy and human.

Taavi the cat tumbled out of Kaz's untucked shirt, leaping down onto the floor. She batted a paw at the hem of Avice's gown and then skittered back.

"You have your father's magic," Avice said. "I hoped you might." Her smile was beautiful. "He made flowers bloom in the winter, just for me."

"No," Kaz said softly. "No, he *hurt* you."

"He did not," Avice said, catching Kaz's hands in her own. "He could not. I went into the woods at Pran when the servants all told me not to. I followed the sound of bells, and there he was. Llefelys, your father. I should have been afraid, I think, but I wasn't. He held out his hand and I went to him, and the woods played such music for us!" She closed her eyes for a moment as though the memory of it had overwhelmed her. When she opened them again, she was smiling. "I would have danced with him even if a thousand years might have passed in one night. But the dawn was just the next day after all, and I had a path of flowers through the snow to follow back home. And from then, every time I went into the woods, he was waiting for me and it was like summer."

"No. No, that's not what...." Kaz shook his head helplessly. "H-he hurt you and I *killed* you!"

"I loved him," Avice said. "And I loved you, even when you were just a flutter in my belly. I wanted nothing more than to hold you when you were born and to sing you all the lullabies my mother once sang to me, but it is not your fault I couldn't. If want was enough, I would never have left you, my Kazimir."

Min's chest ached, and his was not the only one.

From the other end of the gallery, Robert let out an anguished sound.

Avice turned her head to look at her brother. "I loved him," she repeated. "And he loved me."

Robert stumbled forward, knocking chunks of floating plaster and pieces of brick to the floor. "Avice!"

"Hold!" Edward bellowed suddenly. "That is not your sister! It is a trick, or—or a demon! It lies!"

Avice tightened her grip on Kaz's hands, her face still turned toward Robert. "He locked me in a room in the manor house and bolted the door and windows. He nailed rowan to every wall and laid iron across every threshold. And all because I told him that I loved a fae! He would not let me speak to you or any of our brothers. He stopped Llefelys from coming for me, and he would not let me *leave*!"

"Lies," Edward said, his voice dust-ragged and reed thin. "All lies!"

Robert's face, drawn and grim, said he knew exactly who the liar was here. "You told me she was raped. You told me the creature that did it was a monster."

"He is a monster!" Edward cried. "And the boy is an abomination! Look at him! Look! He is a *necromancer*!"

Robert stared at his father. Something imperceptible passed across his face. Min might have mistaken it for smugness, if he'd believed Robert could ever lower himself to be so petty. "I knew that already."

Edward's jaw dropped. "You *knew*?"

"You dragged him back from Ânhaga to make him a hostage for the king," Robert said. "You thought his Gift was worthless because he was a hedgewitch. Only a fool would have told you his true Gift. With a necromancer at your command, your ambition would be unbridled. You would have used him to attack your enemies. No House would have been safe from you, not even the House of Anarawd."

Min was grudgingly impressed at Robert's unexpected show of honor. Edward was not.

"You faithless dog!" the old man exclaimed, reaching for the knife in his belt. "You traitor to your own blood!" With more speed than Min would have credited him with, he darted toward his son. He struck.

Robert twisted away from him but let out a grunt of pain. "Are you *mad*?"

Which, in all honesty, Min felt was a question that had been thoroughly answered already. He'd known it the moment he'd set eyes on the old man. Yes, Edward Sabadine was mad, drunk on his own ambition, and as foul and fetid a creature as might have crawled out of the open sewers in the eastern quarter.

"Tell her!" Edward taunted. "Tell your sister what you did to her mongrel of a son! Tell her how you wed him!"

Robert pressed a hand to his side where Edward's knife had glanced off him. He kept his gaze fixed on his father. "To get him out of your clutches, since you wouldn't let him go until it was done. Which of us were you truly punishing? The boy or me?" His mouth twisted into a bitter smile. "It was me, wasn't it? It took you twenty years, but at last you found just the right indignity to force on me."

Edward showed his yellowing teeth in a vile grimace. "Tell her how you fucked her son!"

"I didn't touch him! How could I? He looks exactly like her!" Robert turned to face his sister, his desperate plea written on his face. "Avice, believe me, I would never—"

"Look out!" Min shouted.

Robert spun back to face his father, just in time to dodge what might have been a fatal blow. He caught his father's arm, and they wrestled for control of the knife.

"Sweeting," Min said. "Remember how I said that revenge should be exacting?"

Kaz nodded, his dark eyes wide.

"Now might be a good time."

Min remembered again that it was said sorcerers could tear the flesh from a man's bones with just an uttered incantation. Apparently Kaz didn't even need words. He lifted a hand toward his grandfather, there was a sharp cracking sound, a strangled scream from the old viper, and then no sound at all except that of wet pieces of flesh and bone hitting the floor.

Ew.

Min decided not to look too closely at the remains. Nausea battled with delight, and while Min was confident delight would win out in the end, he didn't want to spoil its chances.

His stomach twisted as a tremor ran through the Iron Tower.

Robert Sabadine blinked dumbly, reaching up to wipe a spray of blood from his face. "I—I—" He gulped in a breath and tried again. "I—"

"I think you broke him, sweeting." Min climbed cautiously to his feet at last. "Do we survive this, Kaz? In all of Harry's books, the evil dragon is killed and the hero survives. We're lacking a hero, I suspect, but I'm quite partial to the idea of survival. But here we are in the middle of a collapsing tower, and the dead are risen, and I don't know how it plays out from here."

"I...." Kaz looked to Avice.

She smiled at him sadly and pressed her palm to his cheek. Some silent conversation passed between them. Tears sprung in Kaz's eyes, and he shook his head emphatically.

"Yes," Avice said softly. "Yes, you can, and you must. It's too much. You can't hold it for much longer."

"I only just met you!"

The air shuddered, and the Iron Tower shifted and swayed underneath them. A lump of brick hit the tiles next to Min's boots.

"You must," she repeated. "Your will brought me here, Kazimir, but this is... this is not what the dead look like. You know that. The dead are not kind, my child, and this is not where we belong."

"No," he whispered. "Please."

"I love you," Avice said. "We will meet again one day, but for now you must let me go."

Kaz blinked, and tears slid down his face.

"I love you," she repeated, and leaned in to kiss his cheek. "Now, go." She turned to Robert. "All of you, go."

Min heard the courtiers scuttling like cockroaches for the door. He hoped Harry and Aiode were already ahead of them.

"No," Kaz said. His jaw trembled.

The Iron Tower shuddered again, and the floor pitched. A wall cracked open and sunlight blazed through the feathers and the dust.

Avice looked to Min, beseeching him.

Well then. Just another thing Kaz would hate him for. He gripped Kaz by the arm and pulled him away.

"No!" Kaz screamed. "No!"

Min managed to drag him a few feet away. Kaz struggled, as mad as a wet cat, pushing and kicking and yowling, but he hadn't been raised in the eastern quarter, had he? Min had been fighting dirty since the time he could walk. And once he had pulled Kaz through whatever invisible barrier had protected him from the sorcerers, Robert grabbed Kaz's other arm.

They ran for the door.

Min saw flashes of color through the dust and the feathers: the blue robes of the sorcerers, a green kirtle that might have been Aiode's, and the russet of a courtier's tunic.

"Min! Please!" Kaz screamed, pulling back.

Min and Robert wrestled him through the door. Min caught a glimpse of Avice Sabadine standing in the gallery in her white gown. She raised her hand, and Min saw that she was holding a bright yellow blossom that hadn't been there before. She raised it to her face, closing her eyes and smiling as she smelled it. The Iron Tower screamed again, one of the walls tumbled inward, and then she was gone.

Choking dust blinded Min, and he stumbled down the stairs still clutching Kaz's arm, Robert on the other side. Another gallery, this one lined with the busts of kings and queens going back hundreds of years or more. Stern marble faces pitched forward and broke into pieces as the Iron Tower fell.

Stairs again, and then, finally, blessed sunlight, and Min was still running, dragged along by Robert with Kaz as their tether.

It was a hedge that caught them finally. Somebody tripped into it, and then all three of them were on the ground in a tangle of limbs. Min rolled out from underneath and stared back at the Iron Tower just in time to see it shudder one last time, like some old starving workhorse letting out a final breath, before collapsing into a pile of bones.

A wave of dust blocked out the sun, and for a long moment Min was aware of nothing except the body on top of his and the sound of quiet sobbing in his ear.

Min twisted his neck. Dust and rubble lay as thick as snow on the grassy parklands of the King's Hill. He glimpsed Harry and Aiode, the courtiers, the soldiers…. And standing there like grotesque parodies of the statues that dotted the place, three figures wearing what might have been fine silk once upon a time but which now hung from them in clumped threads like lichen. The dead men had no faces that Min could discern, only rotting flesh and cavernous spaces where their eyes had been. One of them wore a tarnished crown. There must have been a sepulcher somewhere close by, Min realized, where the remains of kings were supposed to lie undisturbed, except that Kaz had woken them.

And this, Min thought, this was why necromancers were fuel for nightmares.

He thought of every crowded little graveyard in the city, every tomb, every charnel house. Were rotting hands digging through dirt even now, seeking the daylight? The city of Amberwich had been built on countless generations of the dead. There might have been millions of them, mouthless, putrid, pushing their way through cobblestones and cellar walls, through floors and foundations. A wave of the rotting dead, rising up through the city. Amberwich would drown in corpses.

"Kaz," he said, his voice rasping. He reached up and held the back of Kaz's neck. His palm slid against his gritty skin. He turned his head. Pressed his mouth to Kaz's cheek, and tasted dust. "End it. End it, please."

Kaz let out a juddering breath and then a whimper and lay still.

The dead men crumpled.

In the city, the bells continued to ring out for a long time.

CHAPTER 19

A CLOUD of dust hung over the King's Hill like fog.

Min wrenched his aching body off the ground at last and climbed to his feet. He tugged his shirt out of the neckline of his tunic, breathing through the sweat-damp cloth in a vain effort not to choke. He leaned down to help Kaz up and then Robert. They were both as dusty as an old maid's dowry chest, and Robert had a dark patch of blood on his side that was slowly growing larger.

Min blinked dumbly at the massive pile of rubble that had once been the Iron Tower and then blinked again as a dust-covered cat appeared somewhere near the top of it and then picked a dainty path toward the ground. Taavi. Chirpy swooped down to follow her.

"Sabadine." It was possibly the redheaded man who spoke from underneath a mask of dusk. "Your fae has destroyed my tower!"

"Half fae," Robert said stonily. "Sire."

Definitely the king, then.

"And with the rest of them at our gates!"

Min snorted, his shirt puffing out from his nose.

The king stared at him. "Who the fuck are you even?"

"Aramin Decourcey," Min said, giving a short bow and a bonus flourish of his hand. "At your service, sire. And it does strike me that, yes, while you no longer possess a tower, all of the iron is still here, so it's probably very likely that the Hidden Lord is still unable to enter the city. The properties of the iron remain, after all, even if their configuration is somewhat... scattered."

The king opened his mouth, closed it, and opened it again. He pointed a dirty finger at Robert. "You knowingly brought a necromancer into the Iron Tower."

"Yes, sire," Robert said. "Into the Iron Tower, whilst wearing an iron collar, both of which should have prevented him from using his Gift. Forgive me for not predicting an entirely unprecedented event."

Min wondered if Robert's open wound had made him susceptible to infection by Min's virulent strain of sarcasm or if the death of his father had led him to rediscover his balls. Either way, Min liked him a lot more today than he had last night. He might even be tempted to drink a beer with the man if they managed to walk away from this and not end up swinging from a gibbet instead. So long as Robert paid the tab.

"Sire," Min said in what he hoped was a conciliatory tone. "Of course you are angry. This morning you had a tower, and now you do not. I am not a man who has ever possessed a tower, but I imagine that if I were, then the loss of one would be very upsetting. But you are alive, and isn't that what really matters?"

The king stared at him, and then at Robert. "Who *is* this fool?"

"Aramin Decourcey," Min repeated. "Fool, void, and the reason that you and your sorcerers aren't currently painting the walls of your former tower with your own guts."

The king darted his gaze uneasily to Kaz.

"What we have here, sire," Min said, pressing his advantage, "is an impasse. You have your sorcerers, and I have this necromancer. And I think you would be a braver man than me to bet your Gifted against mine."

"Are you threatening me?" the king demanded.

"No, sire," Min said. "I am only making sure we are both in possession of the same facts."

Min had dealt with powerful men before. He'd talked his way out of dark alleys with a knife pressed to his throat. He'd built his entire career on his ability to navigate the shifting sands of alliances amongst the most dangerous men in the eastern quarter. He'd even won arguments with his mother, not that she'd ever admit it. And he'd done all of that without a necromancer by his side. A king was only a man. A man who commanded an army, but the point still stood, right? Min hoped so.

"Sire," he said, "you cannot keep Kazimir in chains. You may have the right, but you do not have the ability. If today has proved anything at all, then it is that. Your sorcerers couldn't contain him when he wore iron. Your tower couldn't contain him."

"A necromancer could destroy this entire city. He almost did!"

"But he stopped," Min said, aware of Kaz, wound as tightly as the strings of a psaltery, shifting anxiously from foot to foot beside him. "Sire, this conversation is pointless. What must we do with Kazimir? How can we chain him to our will? And the answer is, we cannot. What can be done? Nothing, unless Kazimir allows it to happen."

Min was under no misapprehension that he could control Kaz. He'd stopped him, but only by giving him a moment to come back to himself. And that, honestly, was the only power Min wished to have over Kaz, necromancer or not. He'd put him in a collar once, and he would hate himself forever for having done it.

The king stared at Min a moment longer, and Min couldn't read the look in his eyes. He looked back, keeping his shoulders straight and his face impassive. He was balanced on a knife's edge here and didn't dare blink.

"Sire," he said. "I'm the one who put the iron collar on Kazimir. Despite that, there were many times he could have run from me. There were times when he could have betrayed me to the fae, and he did not. I know my word is worthless to you. Kazimir's may be as well. But if you let him go, I swear he will not strike at you."

He couldn't bring himself to look at Kaz. The boy who'd only ever wanted to make potions and poultices and be left alone.

The king pressed his mouth into a thin line.

And then Aiode appeared at his elbow, wreathed in dust and impatience. "Oh, sons of Rus, Brenin! I have dirt in all my crevices. Just let him go!"

"And have him fall to the Hidden Lord?" the king asked, but there was nothing combative in his tone, and Min felt cautious hope stir in his chest.

"Kazimir," Aiode said. "Would you swear your fealty to the king if he asked?"

Min glanced at Kaz in time to see him nod, a halo of dust bursting from his hair.

"There," Aiode said, as though that settled matters. "He will swear it."

A king's pride was a strange thing, Min thought. The man knew he had no power here at all and that any oath of Kaz's might easily be a lie, and yet a gesture like this was necessary. Kaz could destroy Amberwich with a single word—something that would undoubtedly give the king nightmares for the rest of his days—but if Kaz knelt and swore his loyalty, then the charade was maintained.

The king regarded Kaz and then nodded sharply. "Then kneel, Kazimir Sabadine."

Kaz knelt.

"Do you swear your fealty to your king?" the king asked.

"Yes, sire," Kaz said, his voice rasping. "I swear it."

The king stared down at him unhappily for a moment and then waved his hand. "Stand. You are banished from Amberwich, Kazimir Sabadine, but your oath to me is not forgotten. You remain my subject and not the Hidden Lord's. I will allow you a day to leave the city walls, after which you will never darken them again."

Kaz nodded cautiously. "Yes, sire."

"And you, Robert," the king said. "You're banished too."

"Sire!" Robert exclaimed.

The king's stately poise vanished in a heartbeat as he rounded on him, gesturing wildly at the massive pile of rubble. "That was my fucking *house*, Robert! I lived in that! Fuck off and go and raise goats in Pran!" The king jabbed a finger in Min's direction. "And you. I'm not entirely sure who you are—"

"A fool," Aiode said helpfully. "But a harmless one."

The king grimaced through his mask of dust. "Whoever you are, you'd better get out of my sight before you're banished as well."

Min knew exactly when to beat a strategic retreat. He bowed and then grabbed Kaz by the hand and got the fuck out of there.

AN HOUR later, Min was luxuriating in a hot bath with a damp cloth laid over his closed eyes.

"He just exploded!" he heard Harry exclaim from outside the door. "Like, have you ever dropped a rotten peach on the street?" He made the accompanying grotesque noise.

Talys's laugh was full of both disgust and delight.

Even in his own house, nobody was wasting any time mourning Edward Sabadine.

Robert Sabadine hadn't invited Min and Harry back to his house, but Min and Harry had come anyway, because Robert's house had amenities that Min and Harry's garret room did not, and he was clearly too shocked by the morning's events to refuse them. His blood loss probably had something to do with that. The wound was not too deep, but it had bled freely. Aiode had cleaned it, slathered a poultice on it, and bandaged it. Min suspected Aiode was still poking around somewhere in the house too. He'd last seen her heading for Edward's private rooms, where he was sure she intended to rifle through all his correspondence and report the depth of his perfidy back to the king.

Robert hadn't bothered accompanying her. He was busy packing.

Min heard the door creak open. "If that's you, Harry, you'd better have brought me a drink."

"It's not Harry."

Min dragged the wet cloth from his eyes.

Kaz was clean. He was dressed in neat clothes that didn't quite fit his frame, and his hair was more or less tamed. The points of his ears peeked out from his curls.

"Are you finished packing?" Min asked him.

Kaz's mouth quirked. "Nothing to pack."

Of course not.

Kaz closed the door behind him and leaned against it. "There are some books I might take, if my uncle allows it."

"Another bookworm," Min said. He rolled his eyes, knowing his smile belied it. "You're as bad as Harry."

"I think you read more books than you pretend," Kaz said. "You certainly know how a story should end. You said in the Iron Tower that it's over when the dragon is killed. But are you really not the hero, Min?"

"No, I don't think so." Min shrugged, and water splashed against the sides of the tub. "I didn't even win the hand of the beautiful princess in marriage, did I? Well, the prince."

Kaz raised his eyebrows. "I never would have taken you for the sort of man who cares for the bonds of marriage."

Min laughed. "Well, that's also true. I suspect I won something better than your hand. And before you do me the dishonor of assuming I'm talking about your lovely ass, I'll have you know I mean your heart."

"You think you've won my heart?" Kaz's expression was unreadable.

Within the space of a day, Min had faced the Hidden Lord, the king, and the specter of the rising dead. He wasn't going to be intimidated by this.

"Well," he said, dabbling his fingers across the surface of the water. "It only seems fair, don't you think? Since you stole mine."

Kaz ducked his head, but not before Min saw the small, satisfied quirk of his lips.

"Ridiculous thing to steal," Min continued. "Ugly, impractical, and totally worthless."

"Maybe so." Kaz let out a huff of breath that was almost as good as a laugh and lifted his gaze again. "But I like it well enough."

Min's chest tightened as Kaz crossed the room and knelt beside the tub. He showed Min a crooked smile and fished the cloth out of the water. He wrung it out, fat droplets of water splashing into the tub, and then reached for Min's hand.

"Your knuckles are grazed."

Min shivered as Kaz rubbed the cloth over his hand.

"So they are." Min couldn't remember that happening, but his knuckles weren't his only small injury. He had scrapes and scratches all over, a series of tender spots on his left hip that would be a patina of bruises in a day, and every muscle ached. He'd complain about all of that later, probably, when his wonder at actually having survived had faded a little.

Kaz kept his gaze fixed on Min's knuckles as he drew the cloth gently over them again. "I was... I was so scared today, Min. I've never been that angry. It was like a door opened in my mind and I stepped through it, except there was nothing on the other side and I was just falling and I couldn't stop." His breath hitched. "I couldn't stop. I would have killed them all if you hadn't been there. I *wanted* to kill them all."

Min drew his hand back and shifted awkwardly in the tub so that he could twist his body toward Kaz. He cupped Kaz's face with his wet hands and angled it up so that Kaz was looking at him. "But you didn't."

"But I *wanted*—"

"But you didn't." Min ignored the twinge in his back. "You stopped yourself."

Kaz's eyes were wide. "*You* stopped me."

"Sweeting, no power in the world could have stopped you unless you wanted to stop." Min shook his head slightly. "You listened to me, but you're the one who stopped yourself. This power in you, this mix of your Gift and your fae magic, it's extraordinary, Kaz. Nobody has ever seen anything like it before. It's big, and it's scary. It's a storm to the little insects in the air like me, but you reined it back in. You stopped it."

Kaz wore a worried frown.

"I was twelve or thirteen when I discovered I was a void," Min said. "There was a man, a mage in the employ of some important House, who used to come to my mother's brothel with his master. He wasn't interested in the girls, but he was quite interested in me, the dirty old goat. I remember one night he promised me a gold coin in exchange for certain acts. I, being every inch my mother's son, asked to see the money upfront, intending the whole time to take the coin, kick him in the balls, and escape out the back window."

Kaz snorted.

"A flawless plan." Min smirked. "And so he gave me a coin, and all the girls gasped and cooed and burned with jealousy to see a shiny gold coin in my grubby fingers. But do you know what I saw?"

Kaz shook his head.

"Copper." Min snorted. "He'd put an illusion on a copper coin and tried to cheat me with it."

"What did you do?" Kaz asked.

"I demurred," Min said. "I pretended I thought it was gold, and I gave it back to him and stammered that I was very honored by his attention, but my mother would tan my hide if she found out her dear sweet boy was selling himself. And then I fled. It took me all of a week to realize that being a void was a sort of a magic of its own, as powerful as any Gift. Do you know how many rich men have flimsy locks on their doors because they think their household mages can protect their treasures?"

Kaz wrinkled his nose, and Min wondered if he was thinking of the runes and sigils and wards Min had strolled past in Kallick's house.

"I grew dizzy with the possibilities," Min said. "Drunk with them! For months I was reckless. I stole more coins and jewels than I could even carry half the time and threw around my money like a spoilt little lordling. I thought I was untouchable."

"But you weren't?" Kaz asked.

Min shifted, water sloshing, and lifted his right leg out of the water so Kaz could see the scars on the back of his calf. "Voids, it turns out, are impervious to the Gifted, but not at all to guard dogs."

Kaz winced.

"You got bitten today, sweeting," Min said. "Most of us do, at some point, and we learn to be more cautious going forward."

Kaz chewed his bottom lip, and Min idly enjoyed the distraction for a moment.

"You got bitten," he repeated at last, "but you're still running."

Kaz closed his eyes. "I'm tired of running, though."

"I know," Min said, wiping his thumb along Kaz's cheekbone. "But you're almost home."

They were both still and silent for a long while, until the cooling water of the bath was no longer as pleasant as it had been, and Kaz's knees must have been aching. When Min rose from the tub, water sluicing over the edges, Kaz averted his gaze. Min stepped out, dripping water on the floor as he reached for a linen towel. He wiped himself down quickly and knotted the linen around his waist. His filthy clothes were still on a pile on the floor where he'd stripped them off earlier. Harry's lay with them, because Min had been kind enough to give him the first bath. Robert and Kaz had bathed elsewhere, which seemed very luxurious. Min didn't even own a single tub—or any servants to fill them—let alone two.

Min dropped the linen towel on the floor, risking a quick glance behind him to see if Kaz was watching. Kaz flushed and looked away, and Min preened inwardly before turning around again.

"I wonder if I can prevail on the servants to get something to eat," he said, changing the subject to distract Kaz from his embarrassment.

"I doubt it," Kaz offered up. "The house is in an uproar, and the servants are running around like headless chickens. But they probably wouldn't notice if we took food from the kitchens."

Min snorted. "Kaz, you're a Sabadine. You have every right to take whatever you like from the kitchens. This is your house, until tomorrow at least."

"You're saying I should demand cake?" Kaz asked, the hesitant smile apparent in his tone.

Min laughed. "Cake. And sweetmeats. And honeyed figs. And a pig stuffed with a goose stuffed with a hen stuffed with a quail."

"Stuffed with a dormouse?" Kaz teased.

"Of course!" There was a change of clothes folded on a stool by the stack of linens, and Min shook out a pair of breeches and stepped into them. They fitted well enough. He hoped they belonged to Robert or one of the servants, and not Edward. Min had no moral objections at all to wearing a dead man's clothes; he just hated Edward so much that he didn't want his dick touching anything Edward's once had. "And the dormouse can be stuffed with a baby shrew. It'll be a tight fit, but I'm sure your cook is up for the challenge."

Kaz's laughter was quiet and warm.

Min tugged a shirt on and then a tunic in a pleasant shade of blue that undoubtedly brought out his eyes. The tunic was a little tight across the shoulders, but Min liked the color enough that he was sure he'd forget to return it. The stockings he found were well worn and darned in a few places but still thick enough that he didn't feel the grit in his boots when he pulled them on. Then, straightening up, he combed his fingers through his hair to tame it a little and decided that this was as presentable as he was likely to get without a razor.

He turned to face Kaz, expecting him to be wearing a smile after their ridiculous talk of food, but Kaz's expression was grave once more.

"What is it?" Min asked.

"Min, what will happen when I leave Amberwich?" Kaz asked. "The fae... they're still out there."

Min reached for Kaz's hand and held it. He raised it to his mouth and pressed his lips to Kaz's knuckles. "And you fear them, just as you fear that part of yourself that comes from them. You were lied to, Kaz, and it might take you a long time to unlearn that lie. Your father loved your mother, and she loved him. I cannot pretend to fathom the way the fae are, but I do not believe your father wants to harm you. I think he wants to *know* you."

Kaz held his gaze. "I've been afraid of them my whole life. I want to be brave, like my mother, but I don't know how."

"I don't know either," Min said. He closed his eyes and rested his forehead against Kaz's. Breathed in the scent of him, the closeness, the warmth. "But you're already the bravest person I know."

"Liar," Kaz whispered, and pressed his mouth to Min's in a soft kiss.

"Usually, yes," Min said, opening his eyes again. "But with you, sweeting? Never. How could you not be brave? You are the son of Avice Sabadine, who reached out and took the hand of the Hidden Lord. She was fearless."

Kaz hummed and then pulled back abruptly. His eyes were as big as an owl's. "Wait? The Hidden Lord? My father is the Hidden Lord?"

"He is. Did I forget to mention that? Because I might not be the hero of this story, but it turns out you're actually the prince." He grinned at Kaz's shocked expression. "Now close your mouth, sweeting, before you give me all sorts of ideas."

Kaz snapped his jaw shut, blinking rapidly.

"Because first we need food," Min said, tugging him toward the door. "After that we can see what else we can fit in our mouths, hmm?"

IT WAS quite a procession when Robert and Kazimir Sabadine were banished from Amberwich. A group of the king's blue-robed sorcerers followed the cart the next morning, along with a dozen soldiers. The parade picked up gawkers and gossips along the route from the western quarter all the way down Stanes Street. Robert was stony-faced, ignoring the jeers of the people in the street who didn't know the full story but were quite right in assuming he had something to do with yesterday's horror. It wasn't every day that someone from a House as powerful as the Sabadines' was banished, but it wasn't every day that the Iron Tower fell and the dead rose either, so the crowd was smaller than it might have been. Min suspected that many residents were still locked inside their houses, trembling. It would take a long time for fear to release its grip on Amberwich.

Min, sharing a beer with Aiode outside a shithole of a taproom just inside the portcullis on Stanes Street, watched the cart approaching and set his beer down.

"It's been a pleasure," he said and held out his hand.

She shook it with a wry smile. "It's been *something*."

Min flashed her his most charming grin and then stepped out of the shade of the tavern's awning onto the street, where Harry was shifting from foot to foot in anticipation.

The cart creaked down the street.

Robert sat up the front with the driver. In the back, Talys and Kaz perched on trunks. Kaz wore a hood pulled up over his ears, but Talys's head was bare. She was scanning the crowd, ignoring the jeers with an imperiousness she had clearly inherited from her father. When she saw Min and Harry waiting at the side of the road, she smiled brightly.

The cart stopped.

Harry and Min threw their bags into the back. Harry climbed up first and held a hand down for Min.

"Room for two more?" Min asked, watching to see if Robert's rigid spine would actually snap.

Talys's smile grew, and Kaz ducked his head to hide his grin.

Min hauled himself up into the cart and they set off, passing under the portcullis and leaving Amberwich behind.

CHAPTER 20

Four months later

THE BELLS at the ugly little shrine in the market square of Anhaga rang out at least a dozen times a day, and not at any evenly spaced intervals either. No, they were unprotected from the weather, and any decent blast of wind from the ocean, or any stupid seagulls that decided to perch on them, could set them ringing. The residents of Anhaga had long since stopped paying any attention to them at all, which very much diminished the point of them, Min felt, but who was he to complain?

Well, he was Aramin Decourcey, and he had so far complained to the keeper of the shrine, to Heron the innkeeper, to the Guild of Fishermen—who admittedly had nothing to do with the bells but seemed to be the most important group of men in Anhaga, so Min had felt it was worth a try—and to Kaz, who, like all the others, had just laughed in his face.

Today, though, as the bells rang out, the townspeople did not ignore them. Instead a number of them gathered around and cheered the happy couple as they left the shrine after proclaiming their vows in front of Anhaga's local deity, which, unsurprisingly, was some sort of fish creature.

Min, leaning against the exterior wall of the Three Fishes, folded his arms over his chest and smirked as Harry and Talys stepped back out into the sunlight. Harry's dandelion hair was flyaway in the breeze, and Talys's veil fluttered as well.

Harry looked over toward him, grinning broadly.

Brat.

Cocky little brat.

Grubby little no-name guttersnipe, and here he was married to Talys Sabadine, a girl way above his station. Well, her father's banishment had fixed that little problem, hadn't it? Talys Sabadine was beneath the consideration of any nobleman now, and most of the merchant class, and she'd never looked happier. Neither had Harry. His grin looked about ready to split his face.

Edward Sabadine, if they'd found enough of him to bury, must have been spinning in his grave.

Min couldn't have been prouder.

He nodded at Harry and let the townsfolk usher the newly married couple toward the trestle tables that had been set up in the market square. Strings of cheerful decorations fluttered wildly in the breeze, and the air smelled of fresh bread, pies, and pastries. It wasn't the wedding feast Robert Sabadine had ever intended to supply for his daughter, probably, but Min bet it was a damn sight cheaper.

A pair of musicians, one with a tin whistle and one with a drum, began to play a lively tune, and a group of shrieking children ran around the square in delight. Harry and Talys took their place at the main table. Robert, who looked like he was thawing slightly since he'd arrived from Pran yesterday morning, sat at Talys's side.

Min straightened up as the door of the Three Fishes swung open and Heron appeared with several massive pitchers of beer balanced precariously on a tray. Min helped steady him as he stepped down onto the street.

"Thank you, sir!" Heron called cheerfully as he headed for the wedding table.

Heron still used the honorific, although Min had told him not to bother. He suspected Heron still labored under the misapprehension that Min was a reeve.

Min looked across the street, to the peeling paint on the green door. The door opened as he watched, and Kaz appeared. He was wearing the green kirtle of a hedgewitch, because nobody here needed to know the truth. Kaz could fulfill all the duties of a hedgewitch in any case, so what did it matter if he could also do a lot more? That was nobody's business at all.

Min stepped forward into the street to meet him.

"They haven't brought out the stargazy pies yet, have they?" Kaz asked, craning his neck to see the tables.

"Not yet," Min assured him and leaned in to steal a kiss. Then he reached up and ran his palm over Kaz's shorn hair. He missed Kaz's unruly curls somewhat, but he loved the way Kaz was unashamed of his pointed ears showing. The fearful boy that Min had dragged away to Amberwich had returned standing taller.

Things had felt fraught at first, but no longer. It hadn't taken more than a few weeks for Kaz to establish himself in Anhaga again—this time as a hedgewitch who actually left the house. It helped that each morning he trekked down the street to the harbor to bless the boats and to ask the ocean for a good bounty. There wasn't a single fisherman in Anhaga who couldn't fill his nets each day and not a single one who cared more about their hedgewitch's blood than their ability to fill their children's bellies. They were practical men.

Min tangled his fingers with Kaz's and drew him toward the center of the square. A flurry of seagulls, drawn by the wedding feast, scuttled and flapped and squawked out of their way indignantly.

Min took his seat beside Harry, and Kaz sat on his other side.

The afternoon wore on, with food and dancing and laughter. Even Robert was eventually coaxed from his seat, and into a smile, by a woman who asked him for a dance. Min held Kaz's hand for most of the afternoon, making faces at him as he devoured his stargazy pie with relish and trying to watch that Harry didn't drink so much beer he spent his wedding night expelling it again.

Min spoke to a few of the men from the Guild of Fishermen about snipe eels. He wanted to send a barrel to his mother, now that the road between Anhaga and Amberwich was safe again after all these years. Partly to brag that he got to eat them fresh from the sea, but also to ensure she got the word out that snipe eels from Anhaga were available again. At a price. And Min, if he was the first to seize the opportunity to transport the eels to Amberwich, could set that price. Kaz might have been banished from the city, but Min and Harry weren't, and they needed to look into new work. There were no rich men in Anhaga at all and nothing worth stealing.

Also, Min sort of liked it here.

Apart from those fucking bells.

The shadows lengthened and grew, and the light softened, and people began to trail away to their houses. There was no rush at dusk like Min remembered from his first visit here. The last bright tendrils of sunlight slipped away slowly and so did the people.

The dusk painted the sky in brilliant shades of pink and purple and slid slowly into darkness.

KAZ BRIGHTENED with the darkening night, humming softly to himself as he swept the floor of the front room. Min leaned on the counter and watched him. The rest of the house was a mess, mostly, but they kept the front room clean now that Kaz had opened it to customers again. He was at his happiest listening to the townspeople regale him with their stories of fevers and sprains and mysterious rashes, for some reason. Min usually beat a swift retreat when he saw them coming. The less he knew about the troubles old Dai Fisker had with passing water, the better. But Kaz was happy and that, it turned out, made Min happy too.

The house was quiet.

Harry and Talys had retired to bed already, and Robert was reading in front of the fire in the back room and being quietly tormented by Chirpy, who liked to try to turn the pages too early. This was only Robert's second visit since his banishment to Pran; he'd come once to accompany Talys—though really he'd caught up with her on the road halfway to Anhaga, since she'd made the decision to relocate without asking permission—and again now for the wedding. Living at Pran hadn't softened him exactly, but Min doubted anything would. If he was happier living in exile in Pran, and Min thought that he was, then he was too proud to admit it. Min would never like him, he supposed, but he found that he could respect him. Especially after he'd taken Kaz aside during that first visit and told him stories of growing up with Avice.

Kaz dragged the broom across the floor, and Min finally recognized the tune he was humming. His memory filled in the words: *Light down, light down. We are come to the place where ye are to die.*

"Cheerful," he commented, rearranging a few of the jars on the countertop in order of size.

"Don't do that," Kaz chided, crossing the floor to put the jars back in place. "Anyway, it's a nice tune."

"It is," Min said, swiping the broom from him and leaning it against the wall. "Apart from the fact it's about a fae luring an innocent maiden to her death."

Kaz snorted out a laugh and leaned against him. "Apart from that, yes."

"Do you think they will come tonight?" Min asked.

Kaz hummed again and listened for something Min could not hear. "Yes," he said at last. "I think so."

Min put his arms around Kaz, and they stood there in the silence. Min loved quiet moments like these. He had lived with Harry in the bustle of the eastern quarter of Amberwich for so long that a part of him had feared he would find Anhaga boring. But they'd been busy at first putting the house in order—cleaning out the wards and runes, and Kallick's dusty remains, and restocking Kaz's supply of herbs and plants—and Min had even enjoyed scrubbing the walls and sweeping the cobwebs out of every corner in the house. And afterward, when he'd worried he'd have time to miss Amberwich, he'd discovered that he liked the quiet little life they were building together. Perhaps there had been a few moments when he'd gone stirring up trouble just for trouble's sake—his crusade against the bells of the shrine being one—but by and large he liked Anhaga and the gentle pace of the lives of the people who lived in it.

He liked sharing a bed with Kaz and waking up slowly every morning. He liked wandering around the town, learning all he could about snipe eels with Harry, and then coming back to share a meal in the middle of the day with Kaz. He liked afternoons when he didn't have anything to do at all, so he and Kaz went down to the docks and watched for the returning boats. And he liked quiet nights like these most of all, when he got to hold Kaz and reflect on just how lucky he was.

Min closed his eyes and pressed his mouth to Kaz's temple. "Love you, sweeting."

"Love you," Kaz whispered back.

And right here, Min thought, was an ending he had never deserved. In one of Harry's books, a man like Min would never win the prince. It was unthinkable, *impossible*, but then, that's how the world tended to work around Kazimir Stone. And this was no ending at all, was it? No. This was a beginning.

Min opened his eyes as he heard the distant clip of hooves on the cobblestones and the faint jangle of trappings. A tiny little speck of light burst through a gap in the shutters and exploded like a firework into a swarm of wisps. They darted around the room like lightning bugs, inspecting the jars and the counter and the shelves and, annoyingly, Min's hair.

"I will swat you," Min threatened, and one of the wisps buzzed at him indignantly and darted forward. Min felt a sharp sting on his hand. "Did you just *bite* me?"

The wisp chattered and swooped around his head.

"Stop!" Kaz said, laughing. "Both of you, stop!" He waved at the wisps. "Out. Outside, now, or I'll put the wards up again!"

The wisps fluttered around him for a moment longer before vanishing out the shutters.

Kaz opened the front door and leaned in the doorjamb. Min stood behind him, his arms around his waist, looking out into the night.

The rest of the fae came more sedately, a luminous glow around them as they entered the marketplace. At a house across the street, the windows were flung open and two children learned out, waving. The wisps darted up to dance around them.

Beautiful and terrible, Min had thought once. And now, just beautiful.

Llefelys rode at the front of the procession. The moonlight painted him in silver. There was a riderless horse walking beside his, the saddle decorated in gold and silver. The procession came to a halt in front of the green front door.

Kaz turned around in Min's embrace and kissed him softly. "I'll be back by dawn."

Min had no idea where it was that Kaz went with the fae and found that it mostly defied Kaz's attempts to explain. Beyond the veil, he thought, and into the realm of the Hidden Lord. He was always tired when he came back but filled with a happiness that made his eyes shine.

Min stole another quick kiss before Kaz could untangle himself from his grasp. "I'll be here, sweeting."

Kaz darted out into the street and climbed onto the horse. Min stayed leaning in the doorway long after the fae had ridden away again and long after their light had faded.

Wherever it was Kaz went, the Hidden Lord always brought him back again.

And Min was always waiting.

LISA likes to tell stories, mostly with hot guys and happily-ever-afters.

Lisa lives in tropical North Queensland, Australia. She doesn't know why, since she hates the heat, but she suspects she's too lazy to move. She spends half her time slaving away as a government minion and the other half plotting her escape.

She attended university at sixteen, not because she was a child prodigy or anything, but because of a mix-up between international school systems early in life. She studied History and English, neither of them very thoroughly.

She shares her house with too many cats, a dog, a green tree frog that swims in the toilet, and as many possums as can break in every night. This is not how she imagined life as a grown-up.

Lisa has been published since 2012, and was a LAMBDA finalist for her quirky, awkward coming-of-age romance *Adulting 101*.

You can connect with Lisa here:

Website: lisahenryonline.com
Facebook: www.facebook.com/lisa.henry.1441
Twitter: @LisaHenryOnline
Goodreads: www.goodreads.com/author/show/5050492.Lisa_Henry
Email: lisahenryonline@gmail.com

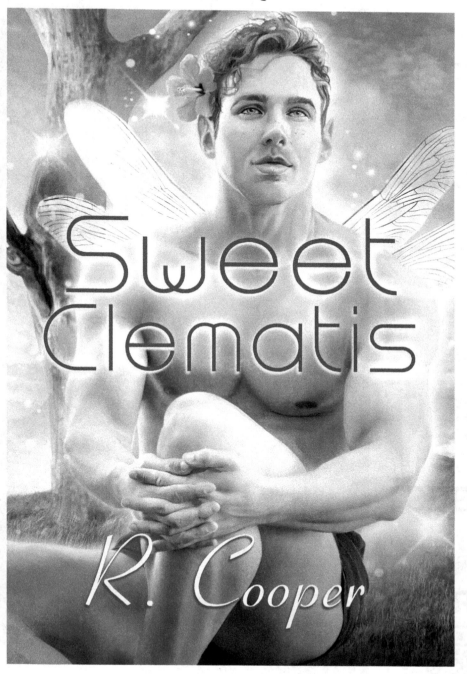

CPSIA information can be obtained
at www.ICGtesting.com
Printed in the USA
LVHW041513180719
624532LV00017B/965/P

9 781644 054659